O
M
I
M

O

M

I

M

OMIM

MICHAEL McGRUTHER

THE DARKEST PLACE IN THE UNIVERSE
IS THE GODLESS MIND.

ISBN: 978-0-578-86530-0
Library of Congress Control Number: 2021903931

www.hoselbooks.com

For Humanity

THE SAGANITES

On October 26, 2024, at precisely 12:00 p.m. Eastern Daylight Time, a powerful space signal slammed into Earth and hijacked all devices capable of playing sound—possessed by an alien frequency originating in the constellation Libra, near the boundary with Ophiuchus, straddling the celestial equator in the Milky Way galaxy. The signal broadcast a repeating garbled audio message through every device at once: "ree… ple… war… pea… omim… ree… ple… war… omim… omim."

The sonic assault lasted for three terrifying days, creating a unique global emergency that affected all nations, forcing cooperation where none existed just days before. The only recognizable word was "war" and it raised alarms in capitals and halls of power. An enemy from space was a fictionalized concept, something humankind only imagined until the signal changed the course of history on that fateful day. Fear spread before reason, and extreme measures were taken by governments "for the public's safety" in the event that the message was followed up by a surprise visit, or worse, an attack.

Governments decreed that the one uniting factor was race, after all—the human race—and demanded that the species be hidden and protected from outside interference at all costs. A whole new folklore emerged that taught of the dire consequences of contact with superior beings from other worlds. In the centuries that followed, humanity pushed its way out into moon settlements and later Martian cities, but adapted philosophically, turning inward. At the outskirts of the galaxy, Earth remained unseen in the cosmos at large. Governments restricted people from simply advocating for sending a return call, and aggressively threw radicals in jail who tried to organize politically around a first-contact platform. These radicals called themselves Saganites, named after the famed twentieth-century scientist Carl Sagan, whose speculative teachings rejected an all-powerful God/Creator and instead imagined a cosmos teeming with life to be discovered and embraced. Saganite cults, secret clubs and underground societies dreamed of escaping what had come to be known as the "Human Economic Zone," referred to as the hez. They were the children of the first Martian settlers, and popularized a culture centered around alien contact. Some of the richest eccentrics in the hez boasted about funding secret plans to break away and meet the aliens face to face. It was the underground radical movement's main objective, and over time, the movement grew to become a problem that needed to be contained by force. It was forbidden for any private human spacecraft to venture beyond the official boundaries just outside Martian space. (Only licensed asteroid mining rigs with triple-authenticated call signs accompanied by a Space Intelligence Agency escort ship that was constantly tracked and monitored, were allowed to pass the boundary.)

By the year 3024, the hez hit its breaking point. Humanity was divided between favoring mission over militia. Over time, the forbidden had become the popular desire: the majority of humans supported reaching out to the beings of the planet they named Omega and inviting them to Earth—an unheard-of sentiment just one thousand years prior.

THE BOOK OF ADAM

ADAM ADJUSTED HIS posture so he was reclining in the comfy old leather lounge chair.

His cabin in this spaceship was made to look identical to his childhood country home on Earth, using some technology that didn't exist when he was there. The scene was a realistic holographic reproduction from a picture on an old government hard drive, but as far as Adam could tell, he was sitting in his dad's armchair in front of the fireplace. The bookshelf was exactly how he remembered it, and the view outside the window to the left was the backyard he played in as a child on snowy Michigan winter days. The only out-of-place item was the small, glowing cube that sat across from him on top of the fireplace.

"Where do you want me to start?" said Adam.

"From the beginning," said a soothing voice from the glowing cube.

"One thousand years is a lot to cover."

"Tell me as much as you can remember. The more details the better. This is for the historical record of human experience in the universe."

"Is everything the same?"

"In what way?"

"Life in the hez. Is it lived how I remember it?"

"There have been improvements. After you share your story, I'll let you know what's different."

"Do people still eat organic food?"

"Of course. Are you hungry?"

"Not yet."

Adam looked at the cube in silence for a long time. Artificial intelligence was already an integral part of human life before he ended up on the other side of the galaxy, but talking to the cube felt off now that he knew what he knew—like the cube was taking in more than just audio. To Adam it felt strangely like Omimian technology, and it made him a little uncomfortable.

"What has been the biggest development that happened since I've been gone?"

"Human colonies are now present on every habitable planet in the Sol system."

"All of them? Including Pluto?"

"Pluto is humankind's most distant outpost. It is where you'll be stopping first."

"Do nations still exist?"

"Yes."

"Who governs the space colonies?"

"They're a coalition of free worlds."

"Good. Free worlds. That's good."

"Whenever you're ready."

Adam laid back with his hands behind his head, looking past the cube, into the fire, letting the dancing flames pull him deep into memories. The fire reminds him of a recent terror. He closes his eyes tight and begins.

*

It was my birthday. The last one I wanted to spend alone and miserable, so I went out for the night in Texopolis, searching for someone as lonely as me, and ended up down at Sex Club Row. I wasn't only there for the sex; I was there for the drinks and specials you get on your birthday, and I was hoping to meet someone new in a place that is not about long-term relationships. I felt sorry for the young generation who never knew what real love was. In the back of my mind I wanted to find and save one of them from a life of chemical-enhanced pleasure that made humans into empty beings. But I was no better. I did the same thing that night. Looking back, it's clear that I got my wish, but not as I could have ever imagined.

I had just turned fifty, and that meant I could retire from the SIA in six months. I partied like those six months arrived first thing in the morning. I must have had sex with a dozen different people that night, none of it fulfilling but all of it intense and crazed, fueled by an unreachable desire to feel something, anything. Deep down I was no better than the lost youth, except I did know true love, and its absence hurt, so I tried to mask it. That whole night was a huge mistake. It was the one and only time I lost control and fell prey to my basest desires. Wasted on drugs and bar potions, I finally made it home around three in the morning, smelling like a neon whorehouse. Shortly after my body hit the bed and I closed my eyes, I heard a noise in the living room. I reached into the bedside drawer and pulled out my short-range blaster. It was always fully charged, so whoever was dumb enough to break in, was about to get vaped by a madman who just wanted to sleep and forget the previous twenty-four hours of sad and lonely.

I crept into the living room with my finger on the trigger and noticed one of the windows was open. A breeze rocked the shades, making a constant flapping sound. I lowered my weapon, called out, "Dawn light," and the easy glow of soft morning light filled my apartment. I could see that it was empty, and I was being paranoid. I didn't own much, but there had been a lot of break-ins in my tower, and it had everyone on edge, including me, after a neighbor was mugged in her own kitchen by a hacked delivery bot.

Humanity, the little of it that still existed, didn't seem worth saving most of the time. I closed the window and was heading back to pass out when an emergency work call came in through the fedcom on my forearm and startled me. It's not normal to hear from headquarters at three in the morning on your day off—there are agents on duty who can handle anything at any time. I tapped the screen on my wrist-boss, freeing the holographic projection of an SIA badge with the Earth, Moon, and Mars arranged in a triangle and surrounded by a circle. The badge was glowing and hovered in the air directly above my forearm.

"Agent Adam McShane, you've been personally requested for an emergency off-world assignment, departing SIA gate 2 from space elevator south at 0500 hours" said Blue, the official AI of the central government.

"Do you know what time it is, Blue? What case is this important?" I leaned against the kitchen wall, holding back the urge to puke. Whatever was in my final birthday drink didn't want to stay down. I was a wreck.

"There is a SETI violation code six in progress. Lethal enforcement may be required. Director Tomasic will brief you when you're on the way to the SIA dock."

The fedcom gave off a tone, and the holographic badge vanished, letting me know the call was over and the orders were delivered. I had no option but to obey.

I ran into the adjoining bathroom and threw up in the sink, splashing a bit on my fedcom, which I despised wearing at this point. It was a rather clunky wrist computer that had to be worn 24/7 by all active-duty personnel in the SIA at the time. We got issued one on the very first day of enlistment, and it doesn't come off until the day you expire or retire, whichever happens first. Nobody liked wearing the fedcom, because it was more than a personal communicator; it operated like a black box that tracks and monitors every moment of your life while you serve the public. It knows your mood, mental health, racial views, and can tell if you're lying. It's on me in the shower, when I make love, and when I wipe my own behind. All SIA agents long for the day when they get cut lose from the fedcom and become free people once again.

I washed up then wobbled over to the kitchenette, set my blaster on the counter, and selected a large cup of black coffee from the in-wall dispenser. While it brewed, I realized I've only had to enforce a SETI violation code six two other times during my thirty-year career. Both were very messy, and in one incident, I lost a close friend who died way too young. SVC6 is the worst crime a human could commit in the year 3024 because it was considered an attempted murder of the entire human race. The Earth/Moon/Mars Economic Zone just celebrated the thousand-year anniversary of Signal Day (when intelligent life was confirmed to exist somewhere else in the cosmos), and Signal Day is always when the radicals start acting up too.

The signal divided humans into two warring factions, those who wanted to make contact and those who were wise enough to know better. Thankfully, those who know better had been history's winners up to that point. The peace and prosperity of the post–Signal Day era represented the longest period of time without a major conflict between nations in all of recorded human history, but that unity was slipping away faster and faster while dangerous SETI violations kept racking up too. Something was going to give, but I always assumed I'd be retired and living out in the countryside nature preserves by then.

Sipping coffee, the Cosmotic Rule all humans are taught in grade school, popped into my head, I don't know why other than it was an underlying principle to the SIA that explains in crystal clear terms what the consequences are for humanity if we're ever visited by superior beings. The code, as we call it, also applies to intergalactic civilizations and is why protecting the Earth/Moon/Mars Zone from alien discovery was the core function of the Space Intelligence Agency. I was taught the importance of keeping humanity undiscovered and believed in it. It is why I joined the SIA. Enforcing a code six means someone or some group has the ability and is actively attempting to make contact and must be stopped by any means necessary. I thought—*this is going to be a long night*—and boy was I wrong.

I showered, shaved, and got dressed in my SIA spacesuit, which hung in my bedroom closet, fresh and clean. It was the most advanced multi-world spacesuit created at the time. Wearing it made SIA agents as close to invincible as any man can be in the harsh environments of space, the caverns of the moon, and some of the most remote Martian no-go zones. Suiting up was a ritual for me, layer by layer, clip by clip.

Another perk that came with being active SIA was the private rooftop drone port. Apartment towers were required by law to have a couple of premium spots for SIA agents, and I was lucky to score a penthouse in one of the nicer parts of Texopolis that came with a private hallway that led right into my drone port. With my second coffee balanced in one hand, I felt to make sure my blaster was properly holstered with the other, then double checked that my apartment doors were all locked. All good, I turned around and exited through the opposite door and grabbed my space helmet on the way out. The vitamin-laced coffee was kicking in now, but my head still throbbed in that odd wide-awake/buzzed state of mind that was hard to shake. The good news is hangovers vanish in zero G, so I'll be fully recovered when I clock in.

The SIA drone had a hard time scanning my bloodshot eyeballs to unlock. I set my coffee on the roof and held my eyelids open with two fingers. Finally, the door unlocked and lifted up, making my coffee tumble, but I caught it just in time. While the drone began the auto-on process, I climbed in and looked up as the door came down and the dome of my parking dock opened up, revealing low clouds over my building. I could see glimpses of the Space Elevator from here, with its shimmering white line stretching from the ground into the sky and disappearing into thick cloud cover, which flashed like lightning when one of the elevator lifts passed through it. I have loved the sight of the Space Elevator since I was a little kid. When I first moved to Texopolis, I used to count the flashes from my bedroom window when I couldn't sleep at night. Now I ride it to work.

The SIA drone lifted up and out of the port, blue light-bar flashing, giving me a clear view of Texopolis, which in my time was the Earth hub of all commerce in the human economic zone. The Great Texas Space Elevator was one of a kind. No other nation on Earth could engineer one, and so Texas became Texopolis, a city the size of a state that was the size of a small country. The dash screen flashed to life and linked up with my fedcom as the drone climbed straight up then sped in the direction of the Space Elevator, about two hundred miles away.

"Agent Adam McShane verified," said the drone's AI. The screen switched to the SIA logo before a live video feed popped on with Commander Tomasic looking right at me from his office in HQ.

"You look like hell, McShane."

"Last night was my birthday. I didn't expect to get called in like this."

"Oh yeah—happy birthday. Let's hope it's not your last. This mission is deadly serious, that's why I called on you personally."

"You do know I'm retiring in six months?"

"I do. And I don't anticipate this mission taking you more than six minutes to complete once you arrive on location."

"Where to, that we have to leave so fast?"

"Mars."

"You know I'm not welcome there. It's hard to run a mission when there's a bounty on my head by two tribal gangs. The minute I pass Customs, they'll both know I'm there."

"You're not going anywhere near Valles City. Do you remember the disappearance of two Space Federation star frigates about two years back?"

"Who could forget that story?"

"Well, we found them, and one was used to modify the other and is being prepped for interstellar travel as we speak."

"Where?"

"The old Medusae Fossae mine."

"I thought that deathtrap was abandoned and sealed decades ago."

"Some rebels moved in when nobody was paying attention. They're well-funded Saganite crazies and have been working covertly to send two humans to planet Omega, and HQ suspects they have the tech to succeed."

The blood drained from my face when he said that. The senders of the signal were presumed to be superior intelligent beings, which would make them extremely dangerous to life on Earth. Little was known by the general public about who sent the signal, but the whole point of the SIA was to keep mankind from being discovered, and we did this by subverting any and all attempts at contact. This was the first time in my thirty-year career that we were being sent in to prevent an illegal spaceship from taking off. In my gut, I knew that we couldn't stay locked down away from other life in the universe forever. Someone would eventually make return contact and invite problems to this corner of the galaxy.

"Who tipped us off?"

"One of their cult members defected and got word to us. He was later found hanging inside his Valles City apartment before Martian authorities could get there to protect him."

"Animals. How many Saganites are we going to encounter?"

"That's hard to estimate."

"What's the plan of attack?"

"Blue has you going in though the launch tube to stop their illegal spaceship from taking off, and then the two cult leaders must be arrested and brought to the Lunar Interplanetary Court for arraignment."

"Who's on my jump team?"

"DeMartin and Vasquez."

"You got any intel about the Saganites' defenses?"

"Heavily armed zealots is all you need to know."

"Copy. I'll be arriving at the SIA dock shortly."

The screen went dark, and I sipped my coffee again as the drone banked right and joined the southern flow-way that arched across the state. Texopolis glittered and became a blur through the patchy fog as my speed increased. *Why does my last mission have to be the most dangerous?* is all I could think. I really didn't want to lead this enforcer team, but I had the most experience, and it needed to be done. Only now, after all that I have been through, do I feel like it was fate.

I finished the coffee just as my drone banked away from the flow-way and arched toward the docks of the Space Elevator Complex Zone. Private citizens use the ground-floor entrance, but the SIA had its own dock about one hundred stories high. Another perk I was going to miss.

As I circled in, I could see the busy operations below. People movers let off thousands at a time. Freight rigs backed their containers into bigger containers that pulled into one of the many lifts.

The view vanished when my drone pulled into the SIA dock and touched down in my designated spot. I got out just as a lift was heading up. The parking dock swayed. The sound was not easy on the ears, since I was carrying my helmet instead of wearing it. I hurried up to the door and let the eye reader perform its scan. The door opened, I walked in approached the command desk kiosk in the center with one private elevator lift entrance behind from it. Everything was automated. I placed my fedcom covered right forearm inside the reader/eye scan system and it unlocked the flight deck elevator for me. That was my final official SIA log in.

I joined Agents DeMartin and Vasquez in the changing room, where they were still suiting up because junior agents don't get to keep their space suits at home.

"Welcome back, Captain," said DeMartin, who saw me enter the room when his head popped out of his undershirt.

Vasquez looked up from locking down his boots. "Hey hey hey, it's the man himself, but you look like shit."

"Yesterday was my birthday and I was up all night, haven't slept at all."

"Well, you aged, boss," joked Vasquez.

DeMartin and Vasquez were both twenty-year-old cocksure agents like I used to be. Both were highly skilled but have never been called on a dangerous mission. They've never been in a real blaster fight, but that's probably going to end tonight. I trained them both and know they can handle whatever troubles we run into, but I do worry. First time is always unpredictable and chaotic.

"You boys ready for your first SETI violation enforcement?"

Vasquez patted the large blaster in his side holster. "I'm ready to use lethal force if we have to."

"Let's hope we don't have to. It's not fun to watch another person slowly die with a sizzling laser hole in their center."

"I understand this could be our last run with you, Cap." said DeMartin.

"I hope so. I'm getting too old for this."

"Do you know who's going to replace you in our region?"

"You'll have to wait and find out when I'm gone. I go where I'm told and do what I have to do. Blue doesn't share any more intel than that."

DeMartin and Vasquez were good kids. They looked up to me, and I knew that despite all the training, they were both nervous. We always talked about the internal politics at SIA and all agreed that being out in the field was the best part of job. It takes a certain kind of personality to join the SIA and put your life on the line against zealots who don't value the human way of life. They're willing to strap a bomb on and blow up a commercial spaceplane full of innocents, terrorize the public nonstop, and are always pushing for humans to break off into factions.

DeMartin and Vasquez closed their locker doors, and I led them out of the change room to lift pod door number one. There were less than two minutes before the next lift would pass by, so I opened the door and waved them both in.

We sat against the wall seats and strapped in. The smoky glass across from us looked pitch black while it was inside, waiting for the hitch to connect it to the lift. Once we get moving, the glass is what shields us from the extreme heat generated by the climb. I felt the first sway, meaning the next lift was just hurtled off the ground by reverse magnetic propulsion one hundred stories below. We could hear and feel it approaching, then—ker-clank, our pod became attached and lifted up with the elevator level. Moving at seven hundred miles per hour in an instant, we felt very little because of the way the pod was pressurized. Intense white light stayed on the whole way up, pulsating and flashing like a heartbeat in the sky. We rose above the clouds and then, seconds later, we could see the curvature of the Earth as the lift slowed down for docking. The lift eased itself the final few hundred feet and then clanked into position with a bounce.

SIA has its own exit that bypassed the spaceport's commercial wing, but it was visible to us though a one-way security window as we passed through to the SIA dock. The place was busy as usual. Lots of freight spaceships were awaiting their cargo, two lunar cruise liners were receiving passengers, while new arrivals exited the two lifts that just arrived from the ground. All space flights to Mars, both commercial and private, were delayed. Only DeMartin, Vasquez, and I knew why.

The SIA dock was well hidden from public view, just below the main deck. We rounded down a flight of stairs and pushed through a set of black double doors with the tri-planet logo on them. Inside the long hangar was a row of black SIA Enforcer Spacejets, all docked at an angle with their cockpit and entrance inside the hangar, while the wings and tail were dangling outside so engines could be tested preflight.

"Well, look who it is. Back so soon?" Wex said from the side of the enforcer ship he was working on. Wex was a longtime friend; we graduated from the academy together, but an accident relegated him to spaceship mechanic early on. He didn't mind. The pay was exceptional, and he never had to get shot at by an untrained loony with a fully automatic hyper-blaster.

"Something wrong with our ride?"

"HQ sent over an improved thrust booster for the engines. She's going to get you to Mars a heck of a lot faster now. Must be a pretty important mission, because this booster is one I have never seen before."

"All I care is that it works and we get back safe."

"That's why they got me installing it and not some rookie."

"I appreciate your expertise, brother."

DeMartin and Vasquez nodded to Wex as they boarded to begin their mission prep. They knew the drill and didn't need any instruction from me, so I chatted with Wex a little longer because I hadn't seen him in a while.

"You know I'm out in six months?"

"Already? We're getting old, man."

"Soon I'll be getting free." I waved my fedcom forearm in front of him.

"It's been a legendary run for you, McShane. So many stories to tell. So many Saganites brought to justice."

"I'm just glad I survived it all. What are your plans when your service ends?"

"I got two whole years to go. Might just re-up if I can't find anything better."

"Didn't we graduate in the same class?"

"Noncombat agreement is longer since I'm not going to potentially die on the job."

"Are you still going to be here when we get back?"

"I should be. You picking up some rogues?"

"We got a SETI violation code 6 and we're grabbing two Saganite fugitives to put on trial."

Wex shook his head, disgusted by of all the rogues who think the tri-planet system revolves around them. He disliked and distrusted the humanists and also kept the ancient faith like me. He was a believer.

"One of these days, someone will succeed with the alien signal breaches and then… we are all screwed."

"I agree. Something's gonna give, but hopefully not on my watch. I'll be glad when I'm done with this mission and can look for a quiet place to live, far out in the green zones."

"And I can't wait to come visit you when you do. I spend too much time up here on the dock." He finished working on the ship, put away his tools, and closed the panel.

"Knock 'em back good, brother."

"Every time."

I walked into the enforcer. It was a model X-1500 and was controlled entirely by Blue. I joined DeMartin and Vasquez in the main cabin, which was a big open space with the weapons and equipment lockers in the hull. Benches were along the sides, and the jump ramp cage was in the back. Four prisoner-restraint brackets were unlocked and waiting. The ship powered up, and I felt Wex close the engine bay and tap on the side. I took my seat opposite from DeMartin and Vasquez. We have all been on these missions before, but never to stop a ship from launching. This was new and dangerous. A 3-D mission-brief hologram began playing in the middle of the ship. Commander Tomasic walked us through it from HQ, appearing as if he was standing in the ship too.

It was a pretty clear-cut mission. Travel to the location of the rebel base, which it turns out was located in an abandoned iron-ore mine, enter through the launch tunnel (because we will be arriving with only minutes to spare, according to intelligence information), prevent the rogue spacecraft from taking off—by force if necessary—and bring the two ringleaders of the Saganite movement to justice. When the brief ended, a holographic map of the iron-ore mine remain, so we could study and walk through it before arrival. Even though AI instructed and transported us, we were on our own once on the ground.

I felt our enforcer slide out of its bay coupling, followed by that uneasy falling feeling before the engines ignited. My stomach turned, still feeling the effects of all that partying just hours ago. The ignition jolted us, and the ship banked away from the docks and started in the direction of Mars.

"Initiating hyper-drive in ten minutes. Please be seated for your safety," said Blue.

"What's our ETA to the jump point, Blue?" asked Vasquez.

"Flight time is one hour and forty-five minutes and thirty-nine seconds."

We strapped into our seats and waited, feeling the deep hum from the engines on our backs and under our feet. The tone rose higher and higher, then that telltale sound similar to an old-fashioned pistol shot from the twenty-first century (but way louder) rang out, and we were off.

"Remain seated until max velocity is reached."

I studied the holographic map still floating in the middle of the cabin, calculating in my brain what was going to take place. The chances that the rebel ship will have to be taken out as it attempts to escape from Mars was what made this mission incredibly dangerous. Both of the people we were being sent to arrest were supposed to be on the ship, and it wouldn't surprise me one bit if the timing was such that I am forced to shoot it down, to make a dramatic point that force would be used in order to warn others not to make the same deadly mistake.

"Max velocity reached. You may move about the cabin."

I stood up and used the eye reader to open the equipment and weapons locker. I grabbed two high-energy beam blasters and gave them to DeMartin and Vasquez. I grabbed BigBoy for myself, the aptly named space bazooka with a dozen different tricks up its sleeve. It turned out to be one of the best decisions I have ever made in my life. Truly.

"You look concerned, Cap," said Vasquez.

"What we're heading into is very dangerous to us all, and I want to come back from it alive and in one piece."

"I never thought I'd hear you say that."

"I've got dreams of rolling hills and farmland that I want to see in real life."

"We got this," assured DeMartin.

We stood around the holographic map, and I used my hands to swivel it around so we were looking into the launch tunnel together. It was long, rocky, and not built for launching a spaceship. The rebels managed to pour their own iron electromagnetic tracks that, when activated, would kill any of us on contact. The rebel ship was projected to break the speed of light, so if we failed to subdue their mission before takeoff, someone would have to shoot it down before it exits the tunnel. That person would die in the process. I looked at DeMartin and Vasquez, both too young for that kind of sacrifice.

"Here's the deal. I want you both to jet pack through the launch tube and try to breach their base ahead of me getting into position inside the tunnel. Intel indicates the ship is loaded above the tunnel then drops down for launch. I'm going to stay back, ready to take the ship out if you can't get inside in time."

"You'll die if that happens. Let me hold that position," said Vasquez.

"No I'll do it. You have your whole life ahead of you. I'll position myself right inside the mouth of the launch tunnel, but I'll only get one shot if you fail to capture the leaders. Their movement is too strong. HQ needs to know how they got the parts for a faster than light drive."

"Someone must be helping them on the inside," said DeMartin.

"We won't know unless we capture them alive."

"Saganites are insane," said Vasquez.

"They don't see themselves that way. They believe what they're doing is what must be done. For them it is religion."

I ordered Vasquez to prep the prisoner holding booths that were on opposite sides of the jump ramp cage, while I had DeMartin double check that our blasters were fully charged and the restraint guns were loaded. BigBoy didn't need a charge because it had a small nuclear pellet inside that gave it unlimited power. The micro-reactor gun was what it was originally called, but the minute it got into SIA agent circulation, we named it BigBoy because everyone called it that upon seeing it. And everyone learned to respect its power. The real danger for me is if I fired BigBoy while inside the launch tunnel, I was going to die an instant death. Dying while serving is heroic but not the kind of exit I was hoping for this late in the game.

When the preparations were finished, we took our seats and waited. I used the time to doze off and catch up on some lost sleep. My mind was racing about all the possible ways this could be my last day alive, but then I fell into a heavy sleep and had a vivid dream.

When I was twenty-five, I was in love with a girl named Maura, and I was planning to ask her to marry me. It was rare to meet the marrying type, since most people didn't do it anymore. We met in lower school and grew closer, always hanging out, exploring Texopolis, and just having fun being together. I loved her and wanted to make it official and join the rogue ranks of the breeders and get away from the technolust and greed of the hez. We were going to start a family and live far away from it all. She was just as committed to the old ways as I, and we both wanted to have a natural family. One day after work, I came home and found her murdered by a crazed Saganite who believed Maura was a demon that wanted to repopulate the world with demons. I know this because the killer was still in our apartment when I arrived, and he told me so. I tried to catch him, but he got away. Maura died right in my arms. Worst day of my life. Her death haunts me every single day, and I didn't know if I'd ever get over it or be able to love someone else.

The dream was jolting. I woke up bitter and ready to do my job. Blue started giving us instructions as we closed in on Martian airspace.

"We are fifteen minutes from entering Mars orbit. Activity has increased at the rebel base. Begin preparations for jump and engagement."

So far, this was all routine. We got up, pulled down our helmets, triple-checked our backup battery packs, made sure our smart suits were connected and talking. Blue came in loud and clear inside the helmets and was with me all the way up until the last second.

"Releasing jetpacks."

Three locker doors opened on the wall that had jetpacks waiting for us to back into. I stepped back until it clicked, then walked away with enough rocket power on my back to orbit Mars in pursuit of a fugitive. This was the one part of the job I looked forward to. Jetpacks are banned on Earth, pointless on the moon, but Mars… that's where a man can fly without resistance, and I loved every minute of a chase. I swung BigBoy over my shoulder and stepped into the jump ramp cage with DeMartin and Vazquez.

"Ready to knock this one out, team?"

"Yessir."

"We're here to capture the leaders alive. Set your weapons to stun, switch to kill as a last resort only."

"And if they drop the ship into the launch tube before we achieve the objective?" said Vasquez.

"It's been real nice knowing you both."

The back ramp of the spaceship popped open then folded out. We could see the red Martian soil, making my adrenaline pump. I was back on the job for my last time and was determined to go out strong.

"Take final position now," ordered Blue.

We lined up on the ramp, each gripping the steel loops above our heads, waiting for Blue to give the countdown. The ship slowed down, banked right and we knew it was time.

"Arriving at Medusae Fossae jump point in five, four, three, two, one—jump."

We leapt out in different directions. DeMartin to my left side, me right out the middle, and Vasquez to my right. The initial free-fall toward the surface never ceased to be fun, but we were pros and kept calm and quiet as we torpedoed downward in the Martian night. Words were unnecessary because our suits had heads-up display and monitored the fall, indicating when we should fire the jetpack engines. Vasquez fired his first, blasting out in front of us. DeMartin followed right behind him, and they drew closer to one another before diving down toward the launch tunnel at full speed and with great agility. I used my jetpack to rotate onto my back so I could unhook BigBoy from the shoulder strap I had it locked into. The weapon was long and bulky. With the safety line firmly attached, I gripped it, rotated over again, and circled lower to the tunnel, just as DeMartin and Vasquez disappeared inside it.

So far so good. I moved closer, circling above so I could see if any fugitives we didn't know about tried to escape through hidden exits. Winds were blowing hard that night, creating a low-visibility dust storm that made it difficult to scan the area.

"McShane, we need backup!" is what I heard in my headset, followed by heavy blaster fire and screaming. The rebels were waiting in ambush. I throttled my jetpack and flew down headfirst, with BigBoy aimed in front of me. The inside of the tube was wider and taller than I expected. It was obvious that the Saganites had engineers who knew what they were doing. The tunnel's electromagnetic launch mechanism on the floor looked live and I made sure to stay high above. I killed my engines just before reaching the end, then gave them a little burst to blast up through the ladder tunnel to where flashing lights, smoke, and explosions were going off up above. BigBoy had multiple firing options. I switched it to blaster, knowing I was heading into close-proximity crossfire.

I landed on a platform that was right beside the rebel spaceship. Smoke made it difficult to see. The rebels were armed with twenty-first century laser guns that should never be fired in a cave like this. Beams of destructive red laser blasts bounced around. DeMartin and Vasquez held a position behind two metal crates and were in a laser battle with rebels that retreated, while two other rebels rushed past me pushing a hibernation chamber into the belly of the ship. I followed behind and had them cornered as they moved the chamber into its dock along the right side of the cabin.

"Freeze. SIA! Put your hands up and back away from the hibernation chamber!"

They turned around and started shooting. I dove out of the way and returned fire, wounding one's leg while the other charged right at me. I kicked him in the jaw; he fell back and reached for his weapon while two more rebels arrived with another hibernation chamber, saw us fighting, and didn't fire on me because I was right next to the first chamber now. The wounded rebel got away while I pushed back on the new chamber, using it to steer them back out of the ship so they couldn't complete their objective. The chamber was heavy and got stuck halfway out. Laser fire came at me through the smoke, followed by a huge explosion, and part of the rock ceiling caved in and fell to the ground just outside the ship. A heavy boulder smashed into the jammed chamber, knocking it clear of the door, while I fell back head over feet, tumbling back down into the main cabin of the ship.

I heard the doors close. The launch systems initiated, and I felt the ship drop down into the lower launching tube. I tried calling out to Vasquez, DeMartin, or Blue, but nobody heard me. The ship flooded with intense light, and the sound was like a loud metallic scream that was turned up slowly. I raced out of the main cabin to the loading doors to try to get out the same way I got in. They were sealed shut, with all signs indicating that the ship was about to launch. I still had BigBoy, so I switched it to full blast and aimed at the doors.

My finger came off the trigger when my body was thrown hard against the back wall of the ship. I hit with such force that I felt both of my shoulders dislocate at the same moment. I was helpless and had to keep my eyes closed as the rebel ship launched out of the tube at

God knows what speed. It was terrifying. I tried to scream, but nothing came out, and I couldn't breathe for a couple of minutes. My body became paralyzed from head to toe; it felt like I was being melded with the spaceship wall, and there was nothing I could do about it. Then I just blacked out.

At some point, I must have dislodged from the back wall because I awoke to find myself floating aimlessly around the ship's small cabin. I remained physically paralyzed, but my eyes and brain still functioned. I didn't know it then, but when the rebel ship reached superluminal speeds with me not in a hibernation chamber, it locked me into a time dilation standstill that meant time was no longer having an effect on my physical state. I was stuck in the same everlasting moment and this new reality drove me from sanity to insanity hundreds of thousands of ways. My mind was alive and present, but my body felt nonexistent. I felt no hunger, no pain, just the agony of knowing I was conscious and trapped inside a rogue spaceship heading somewhere forbidden.

I'll never forget what it was like seeing that strange, mysterious planet out the viewport for the first time. It was just a speck at first, but I knew it was a world and not a star. And I knew that I was very far from home. I stared at the terror world and watched it slowly growing closer and closer as the rebel ship sped toward it through space and warped time.

Those never ending years were the only period in my life I ever sincerely wanted to die. Getting trapped in a faster-than-light spaceship with no hibernation chamber to protect me and no rest for my mind was a hell I had read about and feared. Endless consciousness with no rest is not peace. If I had the power to fire BigBoy and end the journey, I would have, but it never came to me. And then one moment (there was no way to measure time; it was all the same monotonous feeling) I remember being in awe of planet Omega's mysterious atmosphere. As the years went by, my paralyzed body floated aimlessly. I had no control over it, couldn't right myself if I was upside down, couldn't push off anything to get to a better spot. I was just there, seeing and thinking about how it had to be a miracle that I was still alive, but that my life had to be over, and this was all just a new state of existing. How long could I remain alone like this? Each time the ship adjusted course, I moved a little, and when I passed over the two pilots' seats, my shoulder became lodged between the control panel and the viewport, so my helmet was pressed up against the window, looking out. The alien world was huge now, and it was clear to me that this ship was not stopping until it crashed into it. We were now close enough that the whole planet seemed to fluctuate between purple and whitish-yellow cloud cover that vanished and reappeared quickly like a light switch was responsible.

By this time, I was getting excited to have a slow-motion front-row seat to my own death, knowing it was far better than the millennium or so I spent facing a corner, losing my mind completely, finding it again, losing it again, over and over. It felt like a cruel joke that I was supposed to be retiring and done with the life of an SIA agent, but as the saying goes, "the universe had different plans."

I noticed lights flashing that were reflected in the viewport. A whole wall of systems was turning on behind me, and very slowly I felt my body start to feel heavy again. Soon I was lying on the control panel, and my faceplate started to fog. I instinctually reached up and wiped the moisture away, realizing at the same moment that I could move my body again. It was such a relief that I started to cry. Everything was sore like I had been beaten with a steel rod. I rolled back and let myself tumble to the floor beside the pilot seats. There was artificial gravity on board now, and it made my heart race. My breathing became difficult, so I rolled my faceplate up and was hit with a blast of fresh air. The ship was producing oxygen and a stable environment. Whoever modified this ship was a master engineer and probably an insider who secretly aligned with the Saganites.

I was too weak to move, so I just lay there taking deep breaths, trying to make sense of the situation. Lights around the hibernation chamber right above me started to flash. I used all my strength to drag myself closer to it. So many systems were kicking on all at once, but I stayed eyes locked onto the chamber, which was lying flat like a casket and fastened to the side wall of the main cabin. The relief in knowing that I was not alone and would soon get some answers from the person inside it flooded me with such feelings of hope that I started sobbing uncontrollably like a child. The journey to Omega was an absolute mental prison and torture chamber for me that was coming to an end. I pulled myself up, so I was leaning against the end of the chamber, waiting for it to complete the reanimating process.

My desperation to see another human being was extreme. I watched like someone witnessing creation as a sweet-smelling steam poured out of small side vents around the top. I could smell! Lights flashed, and health monitors gave vital information about the other human being inside. I could read it clearly from here. The heart rate was normal, lungs functional, body temperature was normal, and then, without warning, the top translucent cover popped up with a small hiss, then slid down so that half of the chamber was wide open but the human was still shrouded in steam.

I used my arms to hold my weak body up even higher so I could see inside. When the steam cleared, I saw the most beautiful young woman I have ever seen in my life, sleeping peacefully. Her golden hair was wrapped under a white silky cloak. There were odd markings from the Saganite cult on the chest area of her garment. It looked like a point with golden lines of various lengths shooting out of it. The name Lilith was right above it. Very odd and simplistic. Her lips parted, and she exhaled. Hearing the soft air leaving her mouth like that made me nervous. Then her eyes fluttered, having a hard time opening at first.

I was speechless.

When her eyes finally stayed open, she was looking right at me, and her expression quickly turned from angelic beauty to murderous wench.

“Help,” I said with tears running down my cheeks.

“Where is he? What did you do with Moksha?” she said, but before I could answer, she kicked me across the chin and knocked me to the floor. I was weak and pulled myself back while she climbed out of the chamber and grabbed after BigBoy, from the floor nearby. She held it like she knew how it worked, put her finger on the trigger, and pointed the barrel right at my forehead.

"You better start talking fast, mister, because I'm about to blow your head right off."

I held my hands up, focused on the golden letters "We Come in Peace" stitched onto the shoulder of her cloak.

"Please don't shoot that in here. We will both die."

She flipped the dial so it would shoot short energy blasts instead of a full wave.

"No. Just you. What happened?"

"My name is Adam McShane. I'm in the SIA, and I was sent to arrest you and Moksha the Seer for illegally trying to launch this ship… and somehow, we got trapped in here together, and it took off. Please don't kill me."

She knocked me out cold with the butt of BigBoy instead. When I came to, she had me strapped into the copilot's seat with my hands behind my back. The worst part was that she space taped my mouth shut too.

I could see out the viewport that we were closing in on planet Omega, and it was a really magnificent sight to behold. The oceans were vast and blue, just like back home. The clouds were multicolored but in a way that blended as if being painted by a great artist in real time. Lilith was in total control of the rebel ship and started telling me what was about to happen and what was expected of me from here on out.

"I will never forgive you for what you did back on Mars, but this mission only works if a man and woman of peace are the first ones to make contact—and you're not stopping that."

I tried to hum a question, and she understood me.

"Who are we making contact with? The intelligent beings of Omega who sent the signal of 2024. We are answering their call for help and arriving in peace for all mankind."

I tried to scream through the tape. She reached over and ripped it right off, taking a little chin skin with it.

"Ouch!"

"What were you trying to say?"

"I will not go along with your harebrained plan! This is insanity of the highest level and irresponsible to the people of Earth too."

"Fine. Then I'll offer you as a sacrifice to the first hostile creature we encounter."

"Are you crazy, woman? Any hostile creature will eat you too. You're naïve to think otherwise."

"I'm naïve? Ha! You system jacks don't think for yourselves; you let some computer do the thinking for you."

She had a point, but I wasn't about to give her the satisfaction of knowing I might sympathize with her just one bit. Blue was the AI that set human policy, and nobody knows who programmed Blue or why it directed society the way it did, away from God and towards science.

The instrument panel started to beep and flash. She focused on it and adjusted course according to data that was pointing her to the Southern Hemisphere of Omega.

"Where exactly are you taking us? I have a right to know."

"Oh, do you?"

"Damn right. Where are you taking me?"

"To the coordinates, as specified in the signal."

"What coordinates?"

"You don't know there were coordinates in the message?"

"No. Enlighten me, O peaceful one."

She slapped me in the back of the head like I was her misbehaving child. It was so irritating, but I had to bide my time. It's not like I could just get out and call for an SIA ship to come intercept us. I didn't know how far across the galaxy we were, but I was positive it was too far for any ship in the agency's fleet. Only an eccentric trillionaire could afford to develop something like this rebel ship, and if I were home, whoever that is would be arrested and locked up in the lunar far-side prison mines for life.

With her new course set, she looked at me in the eyes for the first time, appealing to me like she was recruiting for her cause.

"The signal of 2024 was an SOS, and it came from planet Omega."

"I see."

"With precise directions on where the senders could be found."

"And that's where you're taking us?"

"Yes."

"But that was more than a thousand years ago. It's probably too late."

"Despite what you believe and have been taught, it is never too late to do the right thing. Instead of locking down the human race to maintain control over the population, we should be free because the whole universe wants to connect."

"Hey, I don't set the rules. I just enforce them."

"Like a trained dog."

"We all have different masters."

"I am Lilith of planet Earth. I am a free spirit who can be in contact with other beings to spread peace and love throughout the universe."

"And you're attempting to do so with bad information. Who taught you that the signal was an SOS? That's false, and we're probably both about to die thanks to your fantasy about saving God knows what kind of aliens we're going to meet."

"God? There is no God. How childish are you?"

Her response was expected, yet I was still disappointed. I knew the Saganites were all atheists, but I wasn't prepared for the genuine hatred for God that she had in her tone. It was fine not to believe, but those views always become hostile eventually. She goes in peace but rejects that there is source of good in the first place.

"What if the aliens lied?"

"What if the aliens are true and kind, and everything we humans have such a hard time being?"

"Then they wouldn't need to send out an SOS… but I hope you're right. I really do. And if we survive, I hope they can help us figure out a way to get back home. I don't even want to be here trying to stop you right now. I'm supposed to be retiring in six months!"

"Six months was a long, long time ago."

"Trust me, I know."

The ship started to bounce as it entered the upper atmosphere. The clouds had giant holes in them, and I could see, plain as day, a gigantic volcano that stretched down to the ocean. Lilith thrusted the ship down and to my left; it felt like we were falling toward the ground. The engines clicked off.

"What's happening?" I shouted.

"I don't know. Moksha was supposed to land the ship."

"I'm a pilot, let me help."

Alarms wailed. She looked panicked and started hammering on some buttons one after the other. "C'mon, c'mon… override!" She got up and started cutting away my restraints. I rubbed my sore hands.

"Grab the controls. We're going to have to glide it down, and it takes two people."

The ship bumped and fell faster. Omega was huge and getting too close too fast as we plummeted through thick purple clouds. We could no longer see the horizon and started burning through the atmosphere. I'll never forget it, the way the flames were purple and yellow, cascading over the viewport. Omega was a wonder to see out the viewport, even if we were about to crash right into it. Everything looked familiar and totally different at the same time. For a moment, I thought maybe it was a dream. Maybe I was about to wake up back in SIA sickbay. The ship jolted hard, and I looked over at Lilith on the controls. She was stunning and real; this was no dream.

"Grab the controls!" she shouted.

The ship broke through thick yellow clouds. Turbulence came on strong, but we were oriented enough to know that we were heading straight toward solid ground like a speeding bullet. The instrument panel was calculating our time to impact, and we had less than five minutes.

"On three, I need you to throttle forward control number two then push the parachute release right after."

"Copy!"

She grabbed the main set of flight controls with her left hand and reached with her right over a switch where her finger hovered. The bumping turbulence intensified and came with wide sways left and right like we were skating across the atmosphere and it was full of potholes. It felt like we could be flipped upside down any moment now. The clouds started to dissipate, giving small glimpses of the surface below, but the whole time I was disoriented and had no sense of place.

"Three! Two! *One!*"

She throttled her controls forward and flipped her switch at the same exact times as I did the opposing set. The ship buckled as parachutes zipped out the sides of the wings and filled with air. The winds on Omega overwhelmed us and flipped the ship upside down. We started spinning out of control from high altitude, heading straight for the rocky shores of a continent at the base of the volcano. The ship made a whistling sound as it shot toward the ground, then, as if by miracle, a powerful Omegan gust refilled our parachutes, setting us straight, and we were able to get control of the glide function and begin circling in to find a hard landing spot. With the ship somewhat stabilized, it was now about survival, so we were a team with the same goal. Instant trust happened because it was necessary.

"We have less than three minutes to pick a landing spot. What looks good to you?" she asked, still searching out the viewport at the alien world below.

Various on-board cameras showed the land in a 360-degree circle below us.

"Can this baby make a water landing?"

"Yes. She floats."

"That's the safest option; we mess up on solid ground, and we could die a million different ways."

"Look over there."

To our right was a raging river, a rapid wide enough to give us plenty of room to land in the water. The river was lined with jungle foliage. Rocky cliffs created a ledge around the volcano, which was also covered with plant life.

"We don't know how deep it is."

"We're going to find out."

The ship was still traveling way too fast for an easy water landing. Guiding the controls with small nudges, she was able to get us in line over the river. We were dropping fast like a stone, and keeping the nose of the ship up became difficult. Gravity was a little different on Omega, and we didn't understand how to use it to our advantage. Crosswinds rocked the ship side to side the lower we got. She was unafraid and determined to land.

"You got this," I reassured her.

"Almost there..."

I could see into the river water now. It was clear, teeming with life, and appeared fairly deep. When she gave the final nudge for touchdown, the nose dropped first, slapping the water at high speed. We flipped high into the air and then plopped upside down with a huge splash. I was still strapped into my seat and only shaken a little. Lilith was not strapped in and slammed her shoulder against the hibernation chamber to her right. She was in serious pain when the ship stopped rocking. I was hanging upside down in my seat, and she lay directly beneath me on the ceiling.

"Hang on. I'm also a trained medic." I let myself out of the seat and then hung from my feet until I could jump down and land upright. The ship rocked in the water, making it difficult to balance. I squatted over her; she was moaning in pain, lying in the fetal position. I activated my fedcom's X-ray feature that we used for treating battlefield bone breaks and scanned her shoulder.

"Good news—your bones are intact." I gently rolled her over, and she looked up at me with tears in her eyes. Sobbing, but not really sad.

"Are you in pain?"

"No... I'm just so happy."

"Good job keeping us alive."

"Don't you get it? Don't you feel it? We're here. We're on a planet with life that is not Earth." She started to get up, and I assisted her because I am a gentleman. She waved off my help, scoffing at me. "I don't need a man to save me." She stood, adjusted her cloak, then climbed up to look at the instrument panel and out the viewport.

"The oxygen levels outside are higher than back home. The air will be breathable and life sustaining for us."

"How are we going to get out of here?"

"We have to get the ship right side up."

As the ship bobbed and glided down the river, she jumped back down beside me, looked around the cabin, and pointed to the wall behind me.

"We can run up the side, get it rocking until it flips over."

"Primitive. But whatever works."

We stood side by side about six feet apart, and on *ready, set, go*, we ran to the wall and tried climbing up the side. The ship rocked in our direction and then back even faster.

"Again and again until it flips," she said.

As we kept running and jumping, I couldn't help but think how absurd it was that the first two humans to land on another world were now trapped inside their own hamster wheel that they rode across the stars.

WE COME IN PEACE

After a bunch of tiring attempts, we finally got the ship right side up. I sat in the pilot seat, looking out the viewport as the river pulled us along. Lilith was running a computer tracking system that was designed to determine our location according to her original plans. Turns out the Saganites knew quite a bit about Omega and spared no expense to arrive prepared to survive for the long haul. The ship was packed with critical supplies, including medicines, tools, camping gear, and seeds for foods that can sustain humans. I had no doubt in my mind that the man who was supposed to arrive here in my place was also supposed to start a human family with Lilith. She was all of twenty years old and, despite her hard-edged attitude toward me, she was quite beautiful and innocent underneath it all.

While she performed her mission duties, I did what comes natural to me and kept guard, looking downriver, eyes scanning everything outside. This world was obviously full of life, but nothing that looked intelligent, no cities, no technology was visible outside the viewport. It was just nature. Speaking of nature, I should have known that rapids usually lead to waterfalls. Why would it be any different on Omega than on Earth? And by the size of this river, which felt like a fast-moving lake, the fall will be treacherous. Its bubbling white froth and the sudden drop-off in the land had me more concerned than when I was melting out of light-speed.

"Heya, Lilith, there's a waterfall straight ahead. We might need to jump ship and try to swim to shore."

"What?" Her focus was still on a small computer system set in the side panel of the ship. That's when I heard a pinging sound.

"Yes!"

"Yes what?"

"We are in proximity to the rendezvous point that was sent with the signal. Do you know what this means?"

"Nothing if we die going over that waterfall."

"What waterfall?"

"That one!" I said, pointing out the viewport. She looked up and gasped.

"Why didn't you say something?"

"I did. You weren't listening."

"Well what can we do?"

"We can jump out now and have a good chance of making it to shore before going over or we can ride it out and hope for the best."

"We have to ride it out. We need this ship. Get strapped in!"

She was right, we needed to stay with the only vessel with human supplies on it. We both got strapped in and braced for the unknown. The closer we got to the waterfall, the more the ship bounced and swayed in the waves.

"I've got a really bad feeling about this."

"You men of faith all have no faith."

I couldn't believe she would mock me in this moment, but she did. My mind was more logical and forward thinking than her emotional state of being. We had no way of knowing what's on the other side of the falls until we got there, but Lilith remained calm and determined to survive, even if by magic.

"We are right where we're supposed to be. It will all work itself out."

"How do you know?"

"Because I can feel it. The universe didn't bring me this far so I could drown in a river."

"You do know the universe doesn't revolve around you?"

"Why are you such a pessimist?"

"I'm a realist. We're maybe about to crash to certain death after traveling clear across the galaxy. The more I think about it, the more I realize jumping out and swimming to shore is probably a better idea."

She picked up and pointed BigBoy at me again. "You're taking orders from me from now on, remember?"

"How could I forget?"

Another huge bump rocked the ship and BigBoy fell out of her hands. We didn't have time to react when the nose poked over the crest and we were looking down at least fifteen hundred feet to a lake of blue water so clear that it didn't appear very deep. The nose tipped, and over we went, covered in rain and mist, then came the freefall sensation, which seemed to happen in slow motion, before the whole ship dove nose first into deep, clear water and we got our first look at alien sea creatures.

The diversity swimming in the waters of Omega was mind-blowing. I was spooked by a sea thing that resembled a starfish, but the tentacles were tiny humanoid legs with feet and toes instead. One of them brushed past the viewport as we sank deeper. It made my skin crawl.

"Why aren't we rising back up to the surface yet?"

"Different gravity, I hope…"

The ship moaned and creaked under the intense pressure of the water. It felt like we were descending into hell. Then the downward motion stopped, and we slowly started to rise again.

"Hallelujah" I said, and she laughed out loud.

The ship started to rise faster. As we neared the surface a wobbly image of the surrounding stone ledges that made the gorge came into view. I noticed bipeds standing up on the ledges right before we surfaced and came crashing out of the water.

"My God, do you see all those—"

"Omegans! I see them!"

When the rebel ship settled, we unbuckled and moved close to the viewports, looking everywhere for the creatures that resembled pale grey monkeys standing upright.

A humanlike head, completely bald and with large black eyes, appeared on the other side of the viewport and scared the living daylights out of us both. Its face looked old and tired, but its body was young and strong. It was primitive, wearing a brown cloth wrapped around its middle. I fell back, reaching for my backup blaster, but Lilith was already pressing her hand on the glass, smiling at the humanoid on the other side.

"Hello. We come in peace. We come in peace." Tears were rolling down her cheeks. She wiped them away, smiling and quite frankly, obnoxiously careless about the situation we were in. The alien's eyes grew wide and excited like a humans. Its mouth clearly showed an expression of shock. It turned around and waved at something before jumping off. Seconds later, I heard others climbing on top of the ship. The ship moved quickly now, and I readied my blaster.

"What's happening?"

"They're pulling us to shore," said Lilith in an excited little-girl voice.

"How do we know they're friendly?"

"Because this is the planet where the signal came from. Intelligent life is here, calling out, and humanity listened."

"Yeah, but it doesn't mean it's those… things out there."

"They're sentient beings from planet Omega."

"It doesn't mean they are friendly."

While she looked out the viewport, I had my backup blaster in hand and pointed it into her back.

"I hate to do this. No more games. Hand over BigBoy. Now."

She turned around and pushed the blaster away.

"You put that away. You are not going to make first contact walking off this ship with a blaster in your hand."

"Hand me BigBoy."

"What are you going to do? Shoot me? That would be typical. The first thing two humans do when they land on another world? One murders the other."

"I'll just hit you with my stun gun if I have to."

She grabbed the long gun from beside her and handed it over.

"Please don't be like this. We are ambassadors of peace. Please... look with your heart at the intelligent beings out there."

"Fine. I know you're here to make discoveries and be the first human to make contact, but the minute I sense danger, I am not going to hesitate to defend you and me."

"This was a one-way trip. There's no going back now."

"I understand that, but I'm still not going down without a fight. You do your thing and I'll do mine, and maybe we will last."

There was a sudden jolt as the ship had been pulled ashore somewhere. She became tearful again, emotional, and pleaded with me. "Will you please just trust me? Something good is going to happen when I open the door. Something incredible and beautiful. Real first contact!"

"How about you trust me just a little? I am a trained federal space agent, and I know how to keep us alive in a hostile situation."

"And I am Queen Lilith Sands of Mars, and you're my bodyguard. That's our story from now on. Can we stick with that?"

"Queen?"

"That's right. From the house of Sagan."

"Good grief. Whatever you want to do is fine with me, princess, I mean your majesty."

She looked toward the exit, straightening out her cloak, ready to meet the Omegans. Satisfied, she exhaled deeply then moved to the side doors of the ship and put in the code to make it open. I had BigBoy strapped across my shoulder and my side blaster in hand.

"When I open this door, you must be kind to all strangers you encounter and go in peace for all humankind," she said in the smuggest voice.

"Lead the way." I said.

The doors parted, and the first thing I remember is the hot air hitting my face like a ton of bricks. Omega was extremely humid and warm where we landed. Sweat ran down my forehead immediately, but the feeling was so good compared to the time I spent frozen in the rebel ship. The sounds of Omega were familiar too—wind blowing foliage, wildlife making strange noises, water lapping up against the side of the ship. Life was life, but the beings outside the ship were definitely unexpected.

Lilith held her hands at her side, palms out, as she started down the short ramp that led out of the ship. The bright light from the Omegan sun made her briefly look like a glowing angel. I followed right behind her, blaster ready to protect her—us—the only humans here on an alien world.

When I stepped out and my eyes adjusted, I counted no less than thirty of the little gray Omegans waiting along the shoreline, staggered about and hidden between the jungle growth. The one that looked at us through the window was standing alone, the obvious leader, waiting to greet us. His outfit was easier to see now. The Omegans wore pants that looked like culottes made of patched-together textiles, hand stitched and basic, reminiscent of pictures of poor country farmers on Earth from a long, long time ago.

"Greetings. We are from planet Earth. We come in peace," proclaimed Lilith with her hands out, palms up. Another reminder that the Saganites are a religious cult.

"*Hello*," said the closest Omegan. It kneeled and bowed its head to us. I was dumbfounded.

"*Guten tag*," said another Omegan, stepping out of the jungle and taking a knee.

"*Hola*," said another.

"Lilith… what's going on?"

"*Shalom*," said another.

"I don't know, but it's beautiful."

"*Bonjour*," said another.

"This is a most unexpected discovery," said Lilith with tears forming in her eyes again.

The Omegans started to emerge out of the jungle in large numbers and were not threatening at all. They looked like little old people with arms slightly too long, legs too short, and faces eerily human but old looking. The main difference was the blackened eyes. The entire pupil was black.

"*Konichiwa*."

"How is this even possible? Are we in some parallel universe?" I asked out loud.

"The real question is how long has this world—and these beings—been hidden from us?" she said as the first Omegan got up from his knees and held out both hands.

"Planet Earth. Answer call. Come in peace," said the Omegan. Lilith reached out and hovered her hands over his, looking directly into his eyes. The large group of Omegans watched silently as they touched hands.

"Yes. Planet Earth. We come in peace," she said.

The whole group of Omegans got on their knees now. They clearly worshiped Lilith as if she were a deity. I just stood silently trying to assess our surroundings and safety as the little Omegans drew closer to our ship, curious and inquisitive.

"Peace," said the Omegan.

"Peace," replied Lilith.

As we stood there, I noticed a ripple in the water that splashed up on shore. A deep vibration started to move the ground that felt like a small quake. The Omegans noticed too and didn't like it. They all looked up in the sky and not at us anymore. The leader pulled his hands back and seemed frightened.

"Omim," he said.

"Omim. Omim," repeated the Omegans, who started to retreat back into the jungle.

The leader stopped and looked back at us. "Run!"

Just as he said that, I felt my entire body vibrate as a large shadow was cast over us, accompanied by a sound that is impossible to describe. It was a deep vibrating buzz, like an electrical hum, but somewhat musical. I looked up behind me and saw a giant flying barge ship with long, black, snakelike tendrils shooting out from the bottom. The tendrils had the form of a powerful hand at the end. One tried to grab Lilith and me. I dove and moved her off the ramp just in time. The hand grabbed me by the jetpack, and I felt myself lifting into the air. I unhooked from the jetpack and fell back down, landing on two feet.

"We better follow their advice!" I helped Lilith up, and we ran as fast as possible into the jungle. Black tendrils zoomed past me and grabbed fleeing Omegans by the necks, arms, feet—whatever it could grab—before yanking them up and into the floating ship's center, where a quick hole would open as if the disc was made of liquid. It looked like it was eating the Omegans.

Even with BigBoy strapped across my shoulder, I was a faster runner than Lilith and had to pull her along. Our situation quickly went from peace to panic, and Lilith was the only one who seemed confused by it.

"What is happening?" she cried, frightened as screaming Omegans were rounded up. One went flying by, being held by its head. "Help us!" it screamed as it passed us.

"I'll tell you what's happening. The laws of nature are happening!"

"What does that even mean?"

"It means you should have never come here!"

A tendril flew past us but stopped in mid-flight and turned and looked at us. The hand morphed into a black hole at the end and appeared alive. Before I could react, it wrapped around Lilith's leg and pulled her, but she grabbed a tree and held on. I fired my blaster at the tendril, and all it did was flare up red in that spot as if nothing happened.

"Don't let it take me, Adam!"

"I'm trying."

I swung BigBoy around and fired a high-intensity laser beam that sliced the tendril in half. It flapped wildly out of control and then zipped back to the disc above the treetops. I helped Lilith up. Her whole peace thing was obliterated, and she looked shell-shocked.

"Whatever that Omim thing is, it's going to come back for us. We have to keep moving."

The leader of the Omegans poked his head out of a thick growth and called out to us. "This way, Earth saviors!"

We followed him into the overgrowth. The flying disc continued to pick up Omegans all around us, and I couldn't take my eyes off the sky. The Omegans moved fast, darting around trees and jungle growth, bringing us closer to the base of the volcano. The Omim disc appeared overhead again. Its vibrations were painful.

"Cover your eyes, Lilith!"

I flipped BigBoy to micro-nuke, pointed it right at the center of the disc, and pulled the damn trigger. I turned around and threw myself on Lilith as a small ball of light shot into the sky and was swallowed by the center of the disc, creating a hideous sound like a million voices screaming all at once. Explosive energy waves cascaded out from the disc, and it flew, uneven and wobbly. All of its tendrils now limp. Whatever it was, I damaged it pretty good.

The leader of the Omegans couldn't believe his own eyes.

"Peace!" he yelled while waving for us to follow. He was rounding down a well-worn path that led to a large, flat rock with a wide crawl space under it. He disappeared into the crawl space. Lilith was in hysterics, shaken to her core.

"Lovely planet you've brought us to. Everything is so nice and peaceful, just like you expected."

"Just stop. We don't know exactly what's going on here yet."

"Well, I know one thing: that flying spaghetti monster wanted to kill us both, and I don't like that. Did you like that?"

"I like that the sentient beings we encountered speak our language. That alone is a universe-shattering discovery of galactic proportions, but you're too dumb to appreciate it."

I had no words. This day started all wrong and just kept getting worse. This was the first time she left me flabbergasted and optionless, but definitely not the last. I held BigBoy, got on my stomach, and looked in.

"I'm not staying out here to find out what comes next."

There were a handful of Omegans waiting for us in a deep cavern. The leader waved me in and I went headfirst and slid down a short ledge. When I touched the ground, I was able to stand up. Lilith came right behind me.

The Omegans looked up at us, but only the leader spoke. "You are savior. You see Lord Drade. Follow." He turned around, and they all walked into a carved-out hole big enough for them to pass through, but Lilith and I had to crawl.

"Get your finger off that trigger."

"Sorry, kid, you lost all authority when I had to laser that tentacle from pulling you into the mouth of hell. You will follow me from now on and you will do as I say."

The hole was really a long, crude stairway that wound down and around a corner. The smell was hideous below, like we were heading toward a giant pair of old socks. I squat-crawled ahead of Lilith. When I rounded the corner, I could see flickering light at the bottom and heard the loud sound of Omegans talking to one another. It sounded like a spacious place on the other side.

I stopped and looked back at Lilith. "Hey."

"What?"

"What if they want to eat us?"

"You're too sour."

"No, really."

"I don't know. Are you asking for permission to kill?"

"Only if I have to in self-defense."

She gave me the dirtiest look. I turned and continued down the stairs, my feet slipping on the loose rocks until I reached the bottom and could stand up straight.

"Oh my God."

The inside of the volcano was a massive, sprawling underground world. Homes were everywhere, carved into the sides of the mountain. There were roads and stairs leading to higher levels, and a town center right in the open space. If these Omegans didn't resemble humans, I would swear we were inside a sophisticated ant den. Lilith stepped in behind me and was speechless. When we looked out, thousands of Omegans were all bowing down on the ground throughout the place. The leader we'd been following came walking toward Lilith and me, bowed again, and then spoke.

"Welcome, inhabitants of planet Earthlings. I am Madu. I take you to Lord Drade. We have all been praying for this day to come, and now you are here."

Lilith elbowed me in the back and whispered, "Not going to eat us."

"They prayed." I replied.

"Why are your people bowing for us, Madu?" I asked.

"You come in peace. You come to defeat Omim and fulfill prophecy. You are savior."

"Who told you that?" I added.

"It is the prophecy. Please follow me to Lord Drade."

Madu walked us through the town center, which was more like an open-air market in the middle of the open space. Some of the same strange sea creatures we saw underwater were for sale and laid out in baskets. Curious fruits and what I assumed were vegetables were also on display. For an alien tribe of underground tiny old people, life was pretty familiar, except for the whole city-in-a-volcano thing. Their black eyes made sense because they lived by firelight. The pale alien skin was also a symptom of not living on the surface.

After we crossed through the town center, the pathway hooked right and led directly to a beautiful and intricate four-story temple carved right out of the stone. Lit with torches that illuminated its alien-gothic design, the building was an obvious holy site and the center of their entire underground world.

Madu led us past rows of Omegans lining the sides of the path, all kneeling and bowing their heads. It was odd being greeted like a deity and not something I wanted to get used to. Their expectations were too high for us humans. Lilith, on the other hand, waved and smiled and whispered "peace" to Omegans as we passed them. She took herself way too seriously.

The doorway to the temple was open; darkness and flickering torchlight were all we could see, then Drade hobbled out, old and frail. He stood in the doorway, smiling at us like someone who couldn't believe his own eyes. He was wearing a purple-and-gold robe and carrying a large staff with a golden disc suspended between two prongs on the top. I had to squint to see if my eyes were playing low-light tricks on me, because I could swear it was an old-fashioned antique record album from the twentieth century.

"The saviors have arrived, my Lord." Madu bowed at Drade and stepped aside.

Drade looked so much older than the rest of the Omegans. He was taller, his jaw was sharper, and his nose was crooked and imperfect as if were severely broken and healed wrong. It gave him a look that was at odds with his soft and peaceful nature.

"*Namaste,*" said Drade.

Lilith put her hands together and bowed in return. "*Namaste.*" She looked at me, making her eyes big, prodding for my greeting.

"Hey."

"I am Drade, leader of the people."

"I am Queen Lilith Sands of Mars, and this is—"

"Special Agent Adam McShane, Federal Space Intelligence Agency."

"He's my bodyguard."

"She's my tour guide."

Drade didn't react to our bickering; he remained serious and calm. "We've been waiting for this day to come for many ages, and now you are here at last to free us from the Omim."

Drade fixated on Lilith's soft skin and big green eyes. He reached up to touch her.

I drew my blaster. "No touchy."

Lilith slapped my hand. "It's okay. He's just curious." She then held out her hands to him, and he grabbed them like old friends do.

"Tell me, Drade, how did your people learn to speak our language?" I asked.

"From the golden sky disc you sent to our world."

He pulled his hands back and held the staff with both, looking at us. That's about the time Lilith and I looked up above the entrance to the temple. In the center, right where a cross or star of David would be found was a giant golden disc with strange writing and scribbles etched on it.

"What is it?"

"*Voyager Two*." she said.

"*Voyager Two*?"

"The golden sky disc is the record Carl Sagan sent into space on the *Voyager Two* probe back in the late twentieth century. This encounter between us was meant to be. It's fate."

She looked at Drade, who was hanging on her every word. "Do you have the real record?"

"It is our most precious artifact."

"Can we—"

I put my hand over Lilith's mouth to cut her off. She was going about it all wrong. The Omegans viewed us as their long-awaited saviors. As gods.

"Take us to the record, Drade."

Drade bowed his head and stepped back, using his arm to welcome us inside.

"Right this way, Earth lords."

Lilith and I had to bow down to pass through the archway, but once we stepped inside, we were like giants in a playhouse with very tall ceilings. The Omegan cathedral was magnificent, with arches stretching from floor and converging in the center, where another golden disc was suspended. Drade called out to his people, telling them to prepare for a feast in our honor. Then he closed the doors and led us to the back.

The temple was lit by torchlights along the walls. Under each torch were murals depicting life on Earth. The first mural was of a little girl licking an ice cream cone, the second one was a fat man eating a grilled-cheese sandwich. A little further down was a man pouring water into his mouth from a glass pitcher. Lilith and I looked at the murals and then each other. I had to pull her back and whisper. "Tell me how any of this makes any sense to you."

"Oh, it makes perfect sense and confirms all of my beliefs. These images were encoded in analog form on the golden disc. We put them there to show what life on Earth was like."

"And now this is religious art to them."

"I'd call it spiritual, not religious."

"When was that record sent from Earth?"

"In 1977."

Her eyes were drawn to the next mural of a twentieth-century interstate highway, four lanes, crammed with cars and trucks, followed by another of an African hut home with a roof made of bound sticks and mud.

"Highways... homes... they must have used our civilization as a blueprint to build their own."

"Except we don't live in volcanoes."

"These images could mean anything to them. We don't know the full context of their faith in Earthlings yet."

"I hope it's not a strong faith, because I didn't come here to save anyone."

"Besides yourself. I know."

Drade reached the large throne at end of the cathedral. It was big enough for a human to sit in and made of stacked stone blocks with intricate carvings of constellations on it. The word "PEACE" was in big, bold letters on the back. Drade kneeled before the throne and said some prayers that were hard to hear. Then he pushed in a series of small trigger stones on the throne itself, and the floor stones began to pull apart, revealing a hidden chamber below. Drade stayed in the kneeling position, head bowed. There was a glowing light inside, and we saw stone stairs leading down to a deep square chamber.

"After you."

I stood halfway and let Lilith go down alone, ready to react if this was some kind of trap. When she called me down, I joined her around a stone table with a crude-looking device with the golden record balanced on a peg in the middle. Two glowing stones on either side of the table kept it lit.

"What is that?"

"I believe that is a very basic record player. It's how recordings were stored and listened to in the twentieth century." She searched around with her fingers and found a crank. Spinning it made the record start to rotate at a steady pace.

"They had to build the player themselves. That was the test of intelligence for whoever discovered the golden record and the Omegans passed."

"But how?"

"The instructions are on the back of the disc." She pulled a bent piece of smooth wood with a sharp crystal at one end over the record and set it down on the grooves. Strange, eerie music started to play and echo all around us, creating a crude surround sound inside this stone box. The song came to end and then after a short moment of silence, sounds of raw nature started to play. The crack of lightning, a boom of thunder, earthquakes, an erupting volcano. I recognized them all, and they made me really miss Earth. A strong howling wind sound faded into footsteps of people hurrying about. Next was the sounds of twentieth-century city traffic which sounded like grinding metal, horns, whistles and horse clops. All of that ended and the last sound was an SOS.

"That's it!" she said. "That is how the Omegans knew to send an SOS."

"The signal of 2024 came from Drade?"

"Or his people. Eons ago."

"How?"

"Interstellar space has a network of wormholes that the government hid from you, but we Saganites know they exist. Voyager must have been pulled in and brought to the Omega system through one.

"If Voyager launched in 1977, when did it leave the sol system and enter interstellar space?"

"In 2018."

"But that's just 41 human years."

"Wormholes are thought to lead to the past. Now we know for sure that they do. Another huge discovery."

"But we didn't arrive in their past."

"We arrived in our future because we traveled faster than light, faster than time. It's been at least 500 years since we left Earth."

"What do you think the Omegans really want from us?"

"To be liberated from the Omim."

I laughed. Based on what I saw of the Omim, I too would like to be liberated from them. Lilith was cleverer than I anticipated. She already knew how to pacify me with some far-out hope.

"The Omim are obviously the more advanced beings on this world—they might possess ships capable of getting you back home," she said.

"And what about you if such a miracle were to happen?"

"I'll stay here until I die. It's my destiny to help and educate the Omegans. That's why I came." She lifted the needle off the record and stopped it from spinning with her finger. When the disc stopped spinning, she picked it up and turned it over, revealing a solid gold platter with detailed engravings showing how to build the machine to play it. There were lines and scribbles; none of it made any sense to me, and I was from the planet that sent it.

"What are those lines right there?"

I pointed at the lower left-hand corner of the disc to what looked like a dot with fourteen lines of various lengths shooting out from it.

"That's the location of our sun in the universe."

"Now we know how the Omegans knew where to send an SOS. It still doesn't explain how they sent it."

"I sent it from Omim City," said the gravelly voice of Drade, who had come down into the chamber with us. Lilith placed the record down on the player and stepped back.

"Where is Omim City?" asked Lilith.

"It is far from here, at the very top of the world. We stay hidden from the Omim so they will leave us alone."

"Why do they attack you?"

"To gather slaves and drain us of our life force."

I shot Lilith a look of *I told you so.*

"Are the Omim from your world, or did they arrive here?" I said while inspecting the record.

"They arrived many generations ago and have ruled over this world ever since. They drove us underground to avoid their wrath, but when they want more of my people, they send out the collectors."

"Is that what came after us—a collector?"

"Yes. But you are powerful and sent it back."

"What about our ship? I have important supplies on it. When can we go back to it?" asked Lilith.

"After nightfall is the best time to safely venture out around here. I will have Madu take you to your ship later."

"We humans can't live down in a cave like this for a long time. We need sunlight and fresh air to stay healthy." I said.

"I know you are gods of light whose power comes from the light. We are simple creatures with simple needs, and we are begging you to liberate us from the Omim."

"Oh, that's all you want?"

I looked at Lilith with an expression of disbelief. She saw the highly advanced flying machine, and she knew that the Omim, based on that alone, were too advanced for two small human beings to defeat. My mind raced. They wanted us to save them from advanced oppressors who subjugated their entire world, but the two who crashed in the river and almost died are the gods they've been waiting for? It was too much to process, and I knew there was no way to escape this world without a working spaceship, so I had no choice but to entertain the idea of playing the part until a better option came to mind.

"How far away is Omim City?"

"It takes ninety suns to reach it, but you cannot travel there alone without supplies and a guide. It's a dangerous journey now that the Omim have their monsters running wild."

"Their monsters?" Asked Lilith, her voice quivering.

"They populate the planet with beasts that attack us. A predator we didn't have until they arrived."

"Aren't you lucky I'm here with you?" I said to Lilith while pulling on BigBoy's strap while patting my blaster with the other hand.

"I do not understand," said Drade, moving around me to get a better look at BigBoy.

"It's a weapon. Do you know what a weapon is? It's used to attack and kill an enemy. With one wrong move, your whole city in here will go up in flames—boom—big fire."

Drade's eyes were wide as he listened to me. I could see my reflection in the black of his eyes. Drade was looking at me but also into me in a way that I felt in my heart.

"Your soul is tired and your body is hungry. You need rest and preparation before traveling to Omim City. You need a place to call home, and we have one waiting for you—our saviors—it has always been waiting for you to arrive."

"Thank you," said Lilith. She bowed and threw me another dirty look, so I bowed, then we all left the chamber. Drade seemed relieved when the stone floor sealed again. By this time, I had become oblivious to the smell of the Omegans, and my eyes were adjusting to the dim lighting from torches and lamps.

Madu led us back through the center of the village. We walked past the entrance, over to a long set of stairs carved into the side of the volcano. Every Omegan we passed greeted us in different languages. Lilith bowed her head and said, "We come in peace" every time. I just strolled by like a king, nodding slightly. My mind was elsewhere, delirious, exhausted, and thinking about how I might get off this world and back to my own.

We followed Madu up the stone steps, which were wide and smooth and lit with torches that led up high to a darkened cave with a stone ledge in the side of the wall. Madu used his torch to light another one outside the cave before going into the darkness, where he lit a lamp hanging in the center. It was a deep, warm room, laid out like a basic African hut from the example on the *Voyager* record. Rugs made of dried plants created bedding on the floor. There was a cooking area, a small fire pit in the corner of the cave and a bowl overflowing with Omegan foods on the counter. I've slept in worse places on Earth.

Madu lit the fire pit in the corner, and smoke was sucked out through tiny natural vents that went up to the surface. The last thing I remember was lying down on the bedding to see how comfortable it was. For a six-inch layer of dried flowers and leaves, it was damn comfortable, and I passed right out.

I was awakened later by a stick poking me in the shoulder. It was Madu letting me know it was time to go see if we could recover items from the spaceship. I woke up Lilith, and soon we were heading out into the darkness with a large group of Omegans in the middle of the night. This was how they gathered food without being hunted down by collector ships, and being on the move with them felt primal, like we stepped back in time to the caveman era. When we slid out of the rock and I stood up in the fresh air again, I was struck by how beautiful the night sky was. It sparkled as if not even real. The density of stars in this part of the universe made it feel like we were in a dream painting come to life. We moved in a straight line down well-worn paths that led right down to the water's edge, where the rebel ship should still be moored on the pebble beach.

I stayed close to Madu and kept reaching my other hand back for Lilith to use as a guide. At one point, she just slapped it away and said that her eyes adjusted and she could see just fine. When we broke through the growth and stepped onto the pebble beach, a large indentation where the rebel ship once sat was all that was there. Starlight danced on the clear water as it lapped against the shore. Lilith moved forward and stood with both hands at her side, disappointed. I found it comical, but Madu and the gang saw it as the behavior of an angry goddess.

"What does this mean, Madu?" She asked him while he scanned the horizon with his eyes and nose.

"It means the Omim know you are here, and they will be back stronger and deadlier."

"That's not good," said Lilith.

She glanced at me out of the corner of her eyes. I could see the stars reflected as tiny points of light in her pupils, and despite her ignorance, she had a charming innocence that was endearing even to me, a cynical veteran of the SIA.

"I don't want to be standing here when they come back."

"Omim only come hunting for us when the sun is up," said Madu.

The sounds of Omegans diving into the waters and then climbing out again with splashing and thrashing creatures in hand was oddly comforting to hear. Survival was survival, and these beings were all taking part in it. Lilith, on the other hand, seemed lost without the ship and remained there observing the action with slumped shoulders.

"It's going to be okay."

"How do you know?" she said.

"I have faith."

She turned away from me, removed her boots, and sat down on the pebble beach dipping her toes into the water. It soothed her in some way, and I understood it. The simplest familiar thing can take you millions of miles across space to the home you miss.

"I've never been to Earth."

"Never? It's a lot like this place. You'd be surprised."

I squatted down beside her and ran my fingers through the water, back and forth, creating small lines that faded away like time. We sat silently as the fishing continued beside us. It was a strange moment because I think we both realized we only had each other.

We didn't talk on the way back to the volcano. And when we returned to our cave she turned away from me and fell asleep.

PLIGHT OF THE OMEGANS

I AWOKE TO THE smell of savory cooking. To my surprise, it was an appetizing roasted yet salty smell, not that different from pretzels. Very similar, in fact. Lilith was already awake and fixing her hair over by the firelight. I watched for a moment. Her body was fit, curves any young man would have a difficult time resisting. I wondered what might be happening right now if I hadn't been on the ship. Would she and the other guy be in the same place, or would the Omim have already killed or captured them both? She seemed empowered and excited to be in this position as one of the first humans to make face-to-face contact with aliens, despite the fact that our ship was gone and we found ourselves living in an underground kingdom of small beings that reeked of farts and cheese. I remained fixated on what awaited us outside the safety of the volcano, and I was worried.

BigBoy was nearby against the wall. I sat up and gazed out across the volcano as the flickering firelights of Omegan homes, huts and caves started to wake up and stir.

"So… none of this is a dream." I said.

"No, I'm afraid not."

"How long have I been asleep?"

"I wouldn't know. Time feels different here."

"How about in Earth time? Approximately?"

"About ten hours, I guess."

"What have you been doing?"

"Listening. Observing. Meditating."

I noticed some movement outside the cave and instinctively reached for my blaster.

"It's Madu. He's been assigned to stay by us." said Lilith.

"For what?"

"Anything. We're strangers in a strange land."

"Can I tell him I need a cheeseburger and a spaceship that can get us back home?"

"Anything within reason."

I squinted to focus in the low light and saw Madu sitting alone like a small child. His humanlike shoulders were hunched forward, and his head was down. From my angle, he resembled a demon child perched on a shadowy cliff, but something about the Omegans was inherently peaceful, like it was part of their DNA. There was something mystical about them that I couldn't place, but I felt it, despite the way they looked.

Down below, someone started to beat a deep drum, soft and repeatedly. Madu looked out and then stood up. The drumming meant something to him, and then the lights of many torches lit the common area outside the temple. Omegans down below started to chant, and it sounded familiar, but I couldn't place it.

"Navajo…" Lilith whispered while walking to the cave entrance for a better view. I stood up and got next to her.

"American Indians?"

The musical chanting grew louder.

"They're doing the Navajo Night Chant… from the golden record. I know every word and sound." She then started to chant along in a hushed, irritating human voice. I stood up just as Madu walked in and bowed his head.

"Saviors, the feast in your honor is about to begin."

Lilith stood beside me and bowed back at him, but I pulled her up before she could bend.

"What are you doing?"

"You don't bow to your own subjects. Don't confuse Madu."

"Please follow me, my saviors."

Lilith and I started after him, but when I reached the cave entrance, I remembered that I was not in Texopolis anymore. I walked back and grabbed BigBoy and threw him over my shoulder. Wherever I go, BigBoy goes, and that's how it's always going to be from now on.

I caught up just as they were heading down the long stone stairs. Madu was holding Lilith's hand and leading her down. All the Omegans were on the ground, singing and chanting together as we made our way. The strange tone of their alien voices echoing off the volcano walls with the drumming was dizzying. I started to feel slightly nauseated, so I took in some slow, deep breaths as we descended to the bottom.

When we reached ground level, we were met by thousands of Omegans. They parted and made a path down the middle that led across the center of the volcano and over to a wide-open space beside the temple. Madu led us, and as we passed by, the Omegans followed until the entire community was gathered outside the temple, with Lilith and me in the front row. These beings truly believed we were going to liberate them from the Omim. I remember thinking how wrong they were and how I wanted nothing to do with it.

We stood in the open space roped off for us in front of the stage. It filled in with Omegans all around us. The ones close to Lilith and me would reach out, smiling, and touch our legs or hands. When I looked back, they would shy away, giggling. The children had a look of hope in their eyes that was difficult to evade. I didn't want to let them down and show that I already knew it was a hopeless dream to think two humans could overthrow whatever designed that flying machine of death, but I played the part of hero for now. I went along.

Dramatic music began to broadcast through a row of angled cut-out openings in the temple that were aimed at the nearby walls of the volcano so the sound bounced off and then back at us in the audience. A hush fell over the crowd. Madu bowed before us again and brought us up onto a stone ledge that acted as the stage beside the temple. The music was from the golden record. For Lilith, being a Saganite devotee meant being a student of the time and life of their spiritual leader, Carl Sagan. The modern war between science and religion on Earth really took root in his era too. For her, this was like a celebration of everything she believed and loved; a confirmation of the self-evident truths she was taught. She was absolutely clueless, but every time music played, Lilith knew it right away.

"Sacrificial Dance (Rite of Spring) by Igor Stravinsky," she whispered into my ear as we climbed up. I had no clue what that was, but the song is like a soundtrack from a very old movie and grew increasingly more dramatic.

Madu was handed two small stools and set them up for us on the left side so we could have the guest-of-honor view. As the music intensified, Omegans in costumes began to assemble on stage. They were putting on some kind of educational show for us. When the music slowed down, the Omegans started to dance like Native Americans. It was bizarre—even though I knew this was an ancient form of storytelling, I had no idea what the story was. Lilith seemed to be following along much better with fascination and a connection to the Omegans that felt fake and disingenuous to me. I leaned close to her.

"What is happening?"

"They're telling the story of how they became oppressed by the Omim. It's tragic and beautiful, isn't it?"

"And what does that story have to do with us?"

"We're part of their prophecy. They believe we're here to save their race from extinction, but mostly you are going to save them."

"You're getting all that from this?"

"Yes. You're the one they are all counting on." she declared.

"Wonderful. Just freakin' wonderful."

The costumed Omegans looked bizarre yet strangely familiar as they danced and told their story to us. Despite what Lilith believed, it was becoming obvious that the laws of nature are constant throughout the universe with only slight variations. The acting out of history looked like a coping mechanism employed by beings of a certain level of intelligence. It was primitive, this song-and-dance show, and pointed toward their belief in something controlling, mysterious, and greater than themselves. I saw the opposite of what Lilith did—I saw beings calling out for God and mistaking Him for us humans.

Drade appeared in the doorway of the temple, dressed in a full costume that made him appear like half-man, half-insect. His robes were golden, and his head was covered with a mask of some hideous beast with rounded bug eyes and a mouth full of teeth that were pointed straight out. If I didn't know this was a show, I would have hit it with my blaster already. The drumming intensified as he moved toward the center of the stage. One by one, he pointed at the Omegans near him, and they would fall to the ground and pretend to be dead. While Lilith watched the show, my attention drifted. In the Omegan village beyond us, little huts were arranged like a museum scene of life on Earth. It suddenly hit me hard that I might never see home again and that I could die forgotten on another world. Someday archaeologists might dig up my human bones and wonder how they got here. If I'm going to be trapped here with only one other human being, I need to make that relationship work, no matter how different we are—and we are as different as humanly possible. If we're both in imminent danger because we answered the call of the weaker race on Omega, then I need to accept that we may die a very painful death. Instead of being afraid of it, I need to be ready to face it, to play the hero until I physically can't anymore.

The dancing and the drumming faded into my subconscious as my gaze into their village turned into a stare because I noticed something moving around in the shadows. It was too big to be an Omegan. It was bigger than me, a large moving shadow, creeping closer and closer. There was a low hissing growl, and then the show stopped. The Omegans all turned toward the sound, terrified, as the beast leapt out of the shadows and dove toward the crowd. It was a hideous creature that looked like a bear with a thinner coat of scaly fur and a bat's head. It charged right toward us, screaming, then jumped for the nearest

Omegans as they tried to flee. It was a vicious predator that wanted to eat the Omegans. I pulled my blaster and nailed it dead center in its chest, one shot. The beast fell to the ground with a loud thud and a horrible, hollow moaning sound.

Omegans descended on it and finished the kill with their bare hands and tools, bringing a gruesome and violent end to the beast's life. The whole thing was horrific, savage, and bloody, but nobody died except the beast, which they called a wrath. Madu sent a group of Omegans to go and find where the thing got inside. It was clear to me this was not the first time. Survival on Omega was not going to be easy, but sleeping with one eye open was something I arrived good at. When the body of the wrath was cleared, the crowd gathered around for the rest of the show. Drade spoke to Lilith and me directly.

"My saviors. You have traveled far from home to sacrifice your lives for our world."

"No, we didn't," I said. Lilith elbowed me hard. "I mean, we didn't know… how bad it was for you here."

"Our world is a dangerous one, but the greatest danger to all life is the Omim, who arrived after the golden sky disc and have enslaved our people and taken over the planet. No Omegan is free anymore. We are all living on borrowed time."

"What exactly does the prophecy say we will do?"

There was a strange silence as I felt the eyes and hopes of thousands of desperate Omegans upon me. I didn't want to let them suffer, but I doubted there was anything we could do as two Earthlings. If the Omim arrived here after the golden disc, that means they had the ability to travel across the stars in large numbers—and that was the only reason that compelled me to try to find my way to Omim City.

Drade bowed to me in reverence. "The prophecy says you and only you, Adam from Earth, will end the Omim. Earthlings are the only beings in the universe who can defeat their reign of terror."

The Omegans whooped and hollered like a primitive tribe, communicating with sounds instead of words. Drade called Lilith and me close to him on the stage area. We stood on both sides of him. He held the staff up high with both hands, and everyone bowed their heads, including Lilith. I kept my eyes open and my head up while Drade proclaimed, "By the promise of the golden sky disc, a new beginning has finally arrived, and peace will be established once again on our world by the star gods from planet Earth. May the spirit of all free beings be your protection and guide. And may Carl Sagan bless you!"

The Omegans began chanting, "Peace, peace, peace!" Lilith joined them, high on a surreal level that I didn't understand. She jumped down and danced among the Omegans, chanting and smiling with them while pointing right at me. I was appalled. This was torture. I wanted none of it.

Drade continued, "And now, let us have the feast to end all feasts, in honor of our savior from across the stars, before you take the journey to Omim city."

"Peace, peace, peace!" chanted Lilith and the Omegans.

I stood up and walked over to Drade. "I have a lot of questions, my friend."

"Please eat with me in the temple, and I will answer them all."

I looked back at Lilith, who was now sitting on the floor in a circle with a group of very young Omegans. They were decorating her hair with flowers collected from outside. I thought about calling to her but decided it was better for me to be alone with Drade, one on one, man to Omegan. I followed him into the temple while Omegans scurried past us and set containers of food around the altar. Drade was frail, so I helped him into the throne. The robes concealed his body, but it felt proportioned like mine. Every other Omegan was out of proportion, with long arms and short legs.

Drade took a wooden bowl steaming with something that smelled very good to me and used a wooden ladle to serve me some. I took a seat on the steps beside the throne and smelled the soupy meal.

"How do I know if this is safe for me to eat?"

"It is. And it will make you feel strong like a warrior." Drade sipped his soup, and I could see light returning to his eyes, a vigor resurfacing that made him appear more awake. I took a sip, and to my surprise, it was delicious and felt good and warm going down. I didn't realize how hungry I was until the first taste. I started to gulp it down and found there were small chunks of meat that also tasted great, although they were a strange kind of chewy. I could feel my body rapidly getting invigorated like I was well rested and had been hitting the gym daily for months. It felt like I was eating the perfect food that unlocked every point of power and clarity in my entire body.

"What is in this… manna-from-heaven soup? I have never felt instant rejuvenation from food before."

"The main ingredient is wrath penis. Very rich in a substance that heals and strengthens muscles. It keeps our people strong."

I stopped chewing for moment and thought about spitting it out, but humans eat far worse things on Earth and Mars, and it really did make me feel amazing, so I finished it all and pretended he said, "rice and beans."

"The first thing I need to know is exactly how you got the message to Earth."

Drade stopped chewing and looked me right in the eyes. They were different from the other Omegans. His large pupils were bordered by white sclera, though narrower than mine. There was something almost human about his features that allowed for a certain closeness in the moment that I didn't expect.

"I sent it from the tower in the center of Omim City. It stretches into the clouds and can communicate across all space and time instantly."

"You are the one who sent it?"

"Yes."

"How?"

"I was once a slave of Sheeol. He is a star god like you, and supreme ruler of the Omim."

"And you believe that Lilith and I can defeat him?"

"I know you will because only you can."

Lilith was led in by Madu. She came to the throne and stood in front of us. Her hair was adorned with so many colorful flowers and plants that it no longer looked like hair, but just natural flora.

"I have been looking for you," she said to me.

"I've been right here, learning about what we're up against. The mission ahead."

She got on her knees, clasped her hands together, and obnoxiously pandered to Drade, blowing up the bond we were establishing.

"Lord Drade, your people have such pure hearts, full of love and wonder. It is an honor to be here to serve you."

"We are humbled by your sacrifice."

A deep vibration started beneath our feet—the same feeling as before. Drade's eyes grew wide. Madu looked down, then up at Drade, who was now standing. The loud scurrying of Omegans in a panic echoed off the stone walls.

"Omim! You must leave now! The colony must evacuate! Madu—lead them to Omim City and don't look back—the humans will know what to do!" said Drade.

The shaking became violent now, sending chunks of the temple crashing down to the ground. Lilith looked up, angry at who would do such a thing. She understood what was happening and looked at me for leadership. Madu started to back away, waving us along.

"This way, my saviors!"

I grabbed Drade by both shoulders and looked him in the eyes. "You have to keep the golden sky disc hidden! Never let the Omim find it!"

"It is already on the move. We are always ready to evacuate to a new home, but you must run after Madu now! Omim are here looking for you!"

The quakes were dramatic and knocked us off balance as we worked our way behind the temple. Madu ran around the back where darkness led us down into a sloping tunnel big enough to run through. It was lit up with a glowing slime-like substance that seemed alive, was growing everywhere, and made sick squish-and-pop sounds with each step. The tunnel started to slope down at a steeper grade, and we found out the slime was slippery under our boots. Lilith fell and went sliding, but I was fast enough to grab her hand and hang on. Her weight pulled me quickly behind while she gasped and closed her eyes as the mucus-like stuff splattered up. The ground kept shaking in a steady, unending rumble now, as if the entire tunnel were conducting sound. We leveled out, and I helped Lilith up. Madu looked panicked and waved for us to hurry.

"This bioluminescence is so gross." She wiped and smeared it from her hands.

"Down!" yelled Madu, who was squatting low with his head covered as a white ball of light zoomed past him and smashed against the wall beside me, creating a membrane-like barrier that melted the bioluminescent material it touched. The membrane was thick and trapped us inside the tunnel. It was electrified and stung to the touch.

"Cover your face!" I yelled at Lilith. Then I blasted the membrane with one wide beam; it started to make a hole but soon became overpowered and began to self-heal. We heard the screams of horror echoing from inside the volcano behind us, where something awful was happening to the Omegans. I pulled out BigBoy, set it to high-intensity laser, and then fired again. This time it blasted open a hole big enough for Lilith to crawl through as long as I kept firing to keep it open.

"Go! Go with Madu!"

"What about you?"

"I'll stay back and fight to the end if I can't get through."

The laser from BigBoy was intensely bright in the tunnel, and we were both squinting.

"Move!"

Lilith nodded, bunched up her cloak, and dove through the hole in the membrane. Madu came running up to her side and pulled her away while I made rapid circular motions while firing, widening the hole just enough. When the size looked good, I jumped through headfirst, letting BigBoy be the lead. I landed on the other side of the membrane, and the hole collapsed around my ankle, squeezing and holding me like a trapped bug.

"No, no, no—this is *not* how I'm going to die today."

I cycled through my options and fired an even higher-intensity laser that broke the membrane and popped it like a bubble. My leg stung a little where the stuff touched me. I ran limping after Madu and Lilith through the tunnel, toward the end of the hole, where light came through. "What was that thing, Madu?"

"Omim trap. They tried to seal us in."

"Are we like insects compared to them?"

The ground shook, and Madu stopped running and held me back too. "Get down and cover."

We squatted and covered our ears, but it did little to shield us from the horrible shrieking tone that echoed around us like an alarm had been tripped. It lasted for a few minutes and ended when the ground shook again. Madu stood up and started running for the exit.

"Hurry!"

I looked at Lilith. "Having fun yet?"

"Don't," she said before running after Madu to the bottom. I followed, blaster in hand, ready to shoot at anything that moved. When we reached the bottom, Madu climbed up some jagged rocks that led to the outside. He peeked around then waved us up with him. I tried to assist Lilith, but she shooed me away.

"I can manage on my own."

"Oh, really? If I wasn't here, you and Madu would be dissolving in that slime back there, Princess."

"It's Queen Lilith of Mars to you."

"You're some piece of work, you know that?"

"I do know that. I worked hard to get here. What did you do?"

"I tried to save you from this," I reminded her.

Madu hushed us. He looked terrified and had an urgency about him that was new. He waved me next to him, and I climbed up and knelt beside him, where a clear view outside of the tunnel was possible. Through the growth and leaves, I could see one of those giant floating collector ships hovering a few hundred yards away over open water.

"Omim," whispered Madu. I showed him BigBoy. He shook his head.

"What's it doing?"

"Hunting. Waiting."

"Where do we have to go?"

Madu pointed to the right of the floating ship, down on the water's edge, where giant leaves the size of fishing boats collected under a tall, wide tree with swirling bark that twisted and broke at the ends, making it look fuzzy from the base to the foliage. The leaves were comically large and thick, making the plant look like a field of floppy-eared dogs. Using his hands, Madu quietly gestured how we could float away in one of those leaves when the Omim ship moved on. We stayed there, spying on the ship, and it struck me how quiet it was outside. The vibrations had stopped. The ship's tendrils were loose and blew gently in the breeze. How it floated in the sky was not clear; it looked like a magic trick. There were no signs of propulsion. That's when it occurred to me that it might be alive.

Madu noticed something, grabbed my shoulder, and pulled me back from the hole. The Omim ship hummed again. The tendrils slithered back to life. After a few moments, the giant thing floated up and over the cone of the volcano, soon disappearing over the other side where the destruction, terror, and screaming were still coming from.

"Now is our chance," urged Madu.

"Lilith, please grab my hand." I helped her up so that we were all crouching near the exit.

Madu looked at us, his voice quivering. "I go first. You follow me when I wave."

Madu stuck his head out, peeked around, and then climbed out and sprinted a short distance down to the water. He scurried under the giant leaf piles and, like an insect back on Earth, used one as cover that he pulled toward the floating leaves in the water. When he was at the shoreline, he popped his head up, checked his surroundings again, and waved to us.

We climbed out and ran down to join him under his leaf and then climbed onto the floating one. It was big enough for all three of us to lie down comfortably. Madu stayed in the water, pushing the leaf boat out toward the mouth of a vast ocean. The top of his head and only half of his eyes stuck out of the water. We could hear the sounds of the volcano being ripped apart by Omim collectors on the other side. I glanced over at Lilith, who looked terrified by the sounds, like it made her question her whole worldview. She lay there crying quietly, knowing that her arrival might have triggered the eradication of the Omegans, or even worse, the discovery of Earth by hostile aliens. To me, it seemed to really hit her now, the error of her ways.

I kept my eyes looking through the slit in the overlapping leaves. We were floating toward ocean waters that were moving fast and packed with giant, prehistoric-looking leaves that were heading down current away from the volcano like super lily pads. I felt Madu hop on the back. He crouched down and shook like a dog before settling down at the tail of the leaf, looking back as his home was taken apart.

"I'm so sorry, Madu," said Lilith. He looked at her bewildered expression and didn't know what to say, but all I cared about was knowing where this escape route was taking us.

"How far will we ride the water?"

"By morning we will be halfway to Omim City. The next half is the hard part."

The leaf boat jostled as it reached the fast-moving ocean current. Unlike Earth, this water seemed to be moving like a steady glass river, taking us to a fast pace that sent cool air running through the center. It felt so refreshing compared to the stink hole we escaped from, so I took deep, calming breaths and felt Lilith looking at me. Her tears were gone, her hair matted with the remnants of wilted flowers. She looked soft and helpless for the first time.

"Are you okay?" I said.

"Yeah, just a little shook up. Don't know what I can do to help."

"We have to find the communications tower Drade told me about and send a warning back to Earth. That's the only mission I'm on right now, besides protecting you and staying alive long enough to achieve that goal."

"You're gloomy," she said.

"I'm a realist. We don't stand a chance of long-term survival here."

"I know."

"Coming to this planet was a really, really stupid idea."

"I know!" she repeated.

Madu slid closer to us and whispered, "No talk. Omim hear everything. Sometimes even thoughts."

I continued but in a soft voice. "Just admit that this is all your fault."

"You didn't have to climb on board the ship."

"I was just doing my job."

"Shhhhh!"

We both looked at Madu and nodded. I lay down so that I could still see what we were heading toward. It looked like nothing but ocean to me. Many hours later, the sun was setting, and for a brief moment it felt exactly like I was on Earth. Clouds and a sky full of burning color were magnificent to see. I looked over at Lilith, and the way the setting sun hit her face made her look like an innocent child or the daughter of Mother Earth. She really was beautiful beyond description, especially after she pissed me off. There was something so pure and innocent about her that it made me feel sorry for what I said hours ago. I just wanted to protect her. Perhaps it was my natural instinct as a man, or one that I take more seriously because I failed in the past. She looked at me and smiled as if reading my thoughts. I was starting to find myself needing her in a way that went beyond physical looks or my deep loneliness. She was one of my kind. I laid my head down, closed my eyes, and let the sounds of ocean water soothe me to sleep.

Sometime later I woke up in the pitch blackness and had to orient myself. The leaf boat was so comfortable, like a waterbed—and it was nice and warm under the top leaf. Madu was curled up asleep at the end, Lilith by my side. I craned my neck back and peered out at the night sky, struck by the view from this part of the galaxy. Nothing looked the same, all the familiar constellations and beacons known to Earthlings in the night sky simply did not exist over here. No Little Dipper, no Orion, no North Star. A genuine lostness overcame me as the vast incomprehensible distance between here and home weighed on my mind.

The hardest part was that so much of Omega was familiar, yet strange. Looking up at the alien sky and not knowing where home was wasn't a feeling I enjoyed. For the longest time, I lay listening to the sound of the leaf boat skimming over water, desperately pretending to be back on Lake Michigan. But I could not escape the nagging thought that if the Omim were ever to find Earth, there would be no freedom to enjoy its natural beauty. The end of our species in space and time would be a tragedy of intergalactic proportions. Our little three-world system would be taken over and subjugated just like the Omegans' world. All the history, battles, wars, and peacetime that enabled my kind to build a human civilization would be gone. I didn't spend my entire SIA career protecting humanity for nothing. We've known life was abundant on other worlds, but in our hubris believed that no other worldly life would ever be able to find us. Even the signal was thought to be a shot in the dark that just happened to find Earth in its path.

My eyes adjusted to the night, and I could make out the dark shadows of what looked to be a mountain range of some kind—big, bold, and dark against the starry sky. There were probably millions of giant leaves being pushed by the currents along the shoreline, and they were starting to gather closer together as the water flowed toward a new inlet. That's when it occurred to me again that my sense of size could be way off. The flying Omim ship was about the size of a football field, but adult Omegans were half the size of the average human. Maybe the Omegans are the insects of this world and the Omim are giants? The size of the leaf made this premise more likely. Lilith, Madu and I were like ladybugs gathered on it. Being small might be an advantage to making it out alive too. There was a little hope, no matter how far-fetched, in that moment. I raised my right arm and pressed the emergency call beacon on my fedcom. I knew we were too far from it being picked up but it still felt good to try. There was no connection.

Something bumped and slide under my backside. It was too solid to be liquid and made me nervous when it happened again. There was a long period of silence and no movement before the whole leaf suddenly lifted high into the air and I had to hang on to avoid sliding out.

Lilith was sleeping face down and stopped herself just in time. Madu scurried toward us as the leaf plopped back down in the water with a splash. There was another loud splash and a crunching sound just in front of us, loud and animal-like. Something was eating the leaves.

"What is that thing, Madu?"

"Nightspore! We swim to a new leaf now!"

The leaf boat became destabilized, and we had to all hang on to each other as it was lifted high and then slammed down again. I could feel the massive snakelike body of Nightspore thrashing below us. We were riding on its favorite snack. The water grew turbulent, and frothy, heavy splashes and chortled gurgling were hideous in the dark. More rocking, and then I saw the head of Nightspore rise in front of me and open its mouth to chomp on our leaf. I drew my blaster and started shooting into its mouth. The sea beast screamed an ear-shattering roar as bits of its head exploded around us. I held on to Lilith as we fell back into the fast-moving water. It was disorienting, but we held each other and kept our heads above water. Nightspore thrashed and screamed, taking the rest of the leaf boat under water. The waves settled, and it got very quiet. I had my blaster above water, ready to shoot. BigBoy was waterproof and secured to my back.

"Madu!" I called out.

"Madu!" cried Lilith. The water was unsettled and fast; leaves were passing us by.

"We have to get on one!"

"Why did you shoot it?"

"It was going to eat us!"

"It could have been a vegetarian, for all you know."

"Will you cut it out already? If I didn't act, you would be snacked."

The water made us bob up and down; sometimes our heads would go under for a second. I felt something rub underneath my feet, and that was it. I grabbed the next leaf with one hand and pulled Lilith to it with the other.

"Climb. Now."

It was difficult to get on. The water pulled, the leaf folded, we kicked, slid, and shimmied until we were safe in the middle of the leaf. This one had no cover, so we just lay there like exhausted bugs, hoping not to get eaten. I pulled BigBoy around, ready to shoot.

"What are we going to do now? We lost Madu," said Lilith.

"He fell off and swam away if he wasn't eaten. But this is his world; he knows where we're going to end up. If he survived, he'll find us."

"I hope so, because we are really lost without him."

"I used to think I knew what being lost felt like. Now I do, and it's not something that I'm enjoying." I said.

"But we're free. Free from all the other humans, everything we ever knew and did. Two humans have never been freer than you and I."

I turned my head and looked over at her. She was gazing up into the stars and showing me her true self again. She was a constant dreamer, a mystic, and her views were starting to make a little sense.

"Shh. Let's talk about this later. I don't want to have to kill another innocent Nightspore vegetarian."

She slid closer to me and held on to my arm. The leaf bobbed and floated on its way. The ride felt smooth and calm again. We stared at the star formations in the sky, saying nothing. About an hour or so later, an imposing landmass came into view right at daybreak as the water moved us closer to the shore.

STRANGE LAND

Just like Madu had promised, the giant leaves we used as boats dumped into a large round bay, where they rotted in the water and littered the shores like a mushy, seaweed-like goop. The sky had been slowly fading from black to a dreamy purple hue from the clouds up above. Something about their chemical makeup made them appear purple until sunlight hit directly, and then you could see Omega in all its beauty. The sunlight punched dramatically through the purple clouds in wide golden rays, spotlighting everything they shined on.

We stepped off our leaf and into the shallow water—the only sounds were of our legs passing through the thick muck. A low-lying fog on shore severely shortened the distance we could see. I placed my hand out and stopped Lilith. We stood together in silence, listening to our surroundings. It was quiet except for the water lapping in and out. There were no sounds of wildlife.

"What should we do?" she whispered.

"We're going to find a place to hide, so when the sun is done rising, the Omim don't find us. Then we can figure out our next steps."

I pulled out my blaster, let the water drain off it, then double checked that it was operational before leading us across the beach and into the fog. We moved slowly across orangish-colored sand that soon turned to solid ground. The fog was even denser the further we walked inland. After covering some ground, I would grab Lilith's arm and force her to stop while covering my own mouth so she knew not to speak. I made us stand there and listen for a moment, using our best available sense to determine if any danger was nearby. A few distant birdlike and other strange noises seemed to be coming from waking wildlife, which was a good sign of normalcy. None of them sounded threatening. I nodded to Lilith, and she followed me again. We walked in a straight line from where we started, slowly, methodically, looking down and forward, always listening.

I knelt down about every five feet and marked the ground with a small x to keep track of our path. My blaster was ready in case of a hostile creature, but BigBoy was always an option too, and I made sure he was one quick maneuver from being aimed and ready to fire. I sensed that Lilith was starting to appreciate me at that moment. She held my shoulder, and I could feel her squeezing it to make sure not to lose me as we walked into the unknown. Over time, the fog thinned, and we could see a little more of our surroundings. We found ourselves in some kind of dry setting with stony ground and wicked-looking trees and shrubs, if you can even call them that, scattered about. Very dry and open with the ocean behind us and rocky cliffs many miles ahead. We moved to a set of nearby shrubs that created a small place to hide and knelt down.

"I don't really see anyplace safe to set up camp, do you?" whispered Lilith.

"No, I don't. When the fog is totally cleared, we have to be careful and aware."

"Maybe we should stay by the water's edge where Madu knows we would end up."

Right after she said that, the first strong daylight broke the clouds above us, and it was like someone turned the lights on—the same effect I saw from space when we approached Omega. The fog evaporated instantly, and the sky became clear, and that's when we saw for the first time exactly where we were. A distant mountain range loomed hundreds of miles away. By my estimate, it was twice the size of Olympus Mons, and at a certain point, it disappeared into the clouds.

"Have you ever seen anything that big before?" I said.

"Not even on Mars."

"Omim City is up there? There's no way we can scale that. Look at all that snow at the higher elevations."

"There's probably less oxygen up there too."

"We need to build a shelter and camp in this general area for a while. This is where Madu will most likely come look for us if he survived."

She looked around at the barren, dry trees. "We need to head inland some more." she said.

"I agree."

We had this conversation though our gaze was held on the mountain range, clear against the alien daytime sky. I grabbed her hand and held it like a teammate. She allowed it for only a second before pulling away and slapping my arm. She thought I was trying to be romantic, when really, I was trying to hold the one thing I knew to be true—human companionship.

"No."

"I… I'm sorry. What should we call it?"

"Friendship only."

"Not that. The mountain. We get to name it because we're the first to discover it."

"I'm sure the Omegans have a name for it. It's their world."

"There's no Omegans to ask, so what do you want to call it?"

After a long silence, she said, "Mount Impossible."

"Mount Impossible," I echoed back. We were the only two of our kind on this world, and just knowing that created an unspoken closeness.

The sun grew brighter, and the air felt hotter. I surveyed the landscape before us and spotted a couple of familiar-looking plants growing in thick patches that were covered with small orange berries in clusters like grapes. We picked some of the fruit but didn't eat it yet.

"There has to be groundwater for this plant life to exist."

We started in the direction of the stone cliffs, where it looked like we might be able to find shelter. I looked back at our footprints in the sand and decided to leave them in case Madu or other Omegans came searching for us. We walked in silence for a long time, aware that the Omim might see or even hear us. After nothing came I decided to take the risk.

"We've only been here for a short time, and it looks to me like the laws of nature are constant throughout the cosmos, aren't they?"

"That was one long-held theory, and now we know for sure that it's accurate," she admitted.

"Laws have to be written by someone. Order is not the natural state of being."

"What are you saying?"

"Does life on Omega feel… random to you?" I asked.

"Yes."

"Really?"

Yes, really. When the ingredients for life are present on a world located within the habitable zone of a star, you will get life."

"Out of nothing?"

"Comes something." she said with a sarcastic tone. She was stubborn and I decided not to press the topic any more. Lilith and I were the same species but we had opposite views on how human beings came to be. It was the big dividing line in society on Earth and Mars, with Mars being the home to most of the radicals who declared God dead long ago. The further you were from Earth's nature and countryside, the less likely you are to believe in God. The religious communities that existed in the Earth-Moon-Mars Zone were very small and far outside the mainstream, but that didn't affect our mutual need to survive on Omega and try to warn humanity that truly dangerous evil awaits in space. In her mind, the whole plan to go in peace for all mankind fell apart, and it was my fault. To me, it's fate that brought me here, and my faith is what will save us—even here on another world, far from every human reality we have ever known.

I looked around. There were no defined pathways, but lots of open space in between jagged-edged shiny black boulders that protruded from the ground. Patches of blueish Omegan grass and odd little plants grew in scattered clumps as we rounded uphill away from the beach. It felt like we were in a setting similar to the high desert of Arizona. We started to walk in the direction of the berry bush and mountain with no real idea where we were heading. I kept my right hand casually over my blaster, just in case. Lilith noticed.

"Please don't shoot everything we encounter on first sight. You don't know what possesses intelligence on this planet." "I know that I do, and it's proven by this blaster."

"So, the Omim are more intelligent because they are better at killing?"

"They clearly are, but it's not the killing, it's the ability to control an entire race of native beings that should tell you what real power is."

"Real power is force. And I don't want to be forced to walk a million miles in one day. Let's take breaks."

"Of course. We're only human."

From that point, we hiked and talked for about twenty-five miles in a straight line without seeing or hearing any life forms. We were heading up a slight incline the whole time, away from the water and toward the general direction of the stone cliffs and Mount Impossible. The inlet behind us was protected by tall, rocky ledges on either side, and it felt as if time were standing still because we had no sense of time anymore. When your body wakes up on a new world, orbiting a different sun, with different cycles and intensity, it can really shatter your internal clock in ways that are impossible to explain. We both agreed that although we were heading somewhere, it really felt like we were standing still and getting nowhere. Like walking on a treadmill made of hyper-reality.

I learned a lot about Lilith on that walk. She came from a very wealthy Martian family. Her father was a notorious aerospace tycoon with secret military contracts, and that is how she was able to smuggle the parts needed to make the rebel ship with a functional FTL drive. If she were arrested and tried in the Lunar Criminal Court, her sentence would be death for that crime. I have no doubt about it.

The man she loved, the man that I killed, was one of Mars's most-wanted criminals too. He went by the name Moksha the Seer and started as a street preacher in one of the open-air markets and later became the leader of the Martian Saganite cult that was determined to break out of the Earth-moon-Mars bubble. Moksha's real name was Gerard Matos, also from a wealthy Martian family, but he rejected it all after claiming to have been contacted by aliens personally. He was the family outcast who created his own cult family in an abandoned Martian mine. She described him as good-looking and charismatic (like all charlatans are) and confided to me that she was a virgin who volunteered to come to Omega and start a human family with him to live as a minority among the locals. The look in her eyes and the sound of her voice told me that she regretted a lot of what she did in the cult. Lilith was really new at adulthood, which explained a lot of her passion for ideas that were not even close to being true.

As we hiked further, I noticed that her cloak was a mess, ripped along the bottom and one sleeve missing on her left side. It was then that I realized she had boots on her feet but no pants. Deep sleeping in a hibernation chamber was usually done naked. The fact that she wore a religious-looking cloak just shows how self-important the "we come in peace" crowd thought they were. They wanted to land here and become the pastoral teachers and leaders of the helpless Omegans, but now she's being taught, literally step by step, why that was such a wrong-headed understanding of nature.

We hadn't passed any bodies of fresh water or even a puddle yet, and I was starting to get concerned. Many hours later, when the day-light started shifting, we parked ourselves for the night in the shade of protruding boulders that were surrounded by thick, mostly yellow, shrubby plant life. There was plenty of room in the middle where we could lie down on the ground and see the vista to the right and left through the reeds, both sparse scenes except for clusters of black stones and more yellow brush. The mountain itself remained straight ahead, way off in the distance, beyond lush foliage. Behind us, the closer we looked to the ocean, the less abundant foliage there was, as if the area did not get much rain. Omega had rapidly changing microclimates, depending on the topography. I scooted close to the base of one of the plants and started to dig with my bare hands.

"What are you doing?"

"Looking for groundwater. We can't last long without it."

"Do you have hydro tabs?"

"I do not. Groundwater would be like a godsend right now."

"Pray to find some," she said with a slightly sarcastic tone.

"I have been."

Lilith scooted over and helped me. The ground was soft and was made of light-brown dirt with specks and fragments of black rocks that looked like glass. Earth and Omega were both made from the same elements but arranged differently, just like people.

We zoned out, clawing, digging, and pulling in search of a pure substance we cannot live without. The exhaustion of the hike and the mental toll of being lost on another world were getting heavy for us both and dehydration was a risk. Omegan dirt covered my hands and got under my nails, but it felt good and calming to do that most basic activity. And just like back home, the ground started to feel a little moist the deeper we went. By the time we were both elbows deep, the first trickles of groundwater started to puddle up. We looked at each other, smiling big. It was miraculous.

"Water." I proclaimed.

"Oh, thank goodness." cried Lilith.

"Thank God," I corrected her. She pretended not to hear me; then we both sat back on our knees and watched the water seep into our small well between us. The daylight on Omega had a strange glow about it at this hour, making everything it shined on become vivid and lively; heavenly is the only word. Lilith's hair was like plentiful golden silk that hung around her cheekbones. Her green eyes were bright and inquisitive. She overflowed with life, and I hated that she wasted it in a cult that brought her here.

"Do you want to try it? It's cool to the touch." she said.

I snapped out of my stare. She had cupped some of the water in her hands and was examining it in the light. It was crystal clear, odorless, and looked like exceptionally clean drinking water. The ocean water was salty, just like on Earth, and this water appeared to be from a spring. I dipped my finger into the well and tasted one drop. Water is water, and knowing that it welled beneath the ground on Omega gave me confidence that we could survive long term.

She lifted her hand up and took a sip; some of it spilled onto her chin and neck. Her eyes lit up. She looked relieved and drank it all, then wiped her mouth with a generally astounded look on her face.

"That is delicious, clean spring water, better than anything I have ever tasted imported from Earth before," she said.

I dipped two hands in and cupped a big swig. My whole body felt a shiver as the elixir of clean water shocked my tired and dehydrated system. We drank handful after handful until we were full and woozy. Falling back, feeling hydrated and normal headed, we giggled for no reason. Everything made sense again.

"Wow," I said.

"Wow is right. A little Omegan water really perked me up."

"I can only imagine what brewing some coffee in that would taste like."

Lilith looked past me, through the shrubs. "How far away do you think the mountain really is?"

I leaned over and peeked out toward the mountain. "Let's see… we hiked about twenty miles today, so I'm going to guess we have four to five hundred miles to go. It'll probably take us thirty to forty days, depending on the terrain ahead."

"Would we even notice? The days all blend into one for me."

"Me too, but once we reached the shore, today became long and uneventful, and for that I'm grateful. It's better than yesterday."

"I agree with you on that."

We stared up at the sky together, both daydreaming and reflecting. The sense of well-being from drinking the water was profound and allowed me to start considering important survival details I otherwise may have forgotten before it was too late.

"We don't know anything about the weather on this world. As we approach Mount Impossible, the climate is going to change, and we need to find you some better clothing. A peace cloak and boots are cute now but won't cut it in snow and ice."

"I have more outfits on the spaceship."

"The Omim have that now. We have to use what's available."

"You do know that I lived in the mine caves of Mars for two years."

"And?"

"And I can handle more than you think. I'll be fine like this."

She turned away from me and watched through the leaves as the sun set over the ocean on another Omegan day.

I lay back down and looked straight up through the opening in the bush to see the strange star-filled sky coming into focus again. Nighttime arrived fast, and as expected, temperatures plummeted. Lilith had her back to me, and I knew she was both mad and sad that her mission was foiled, but she needed me, and we had to work together. I decided the best way to apologize for my sarcasm was by asking for her expertise too.

"When you look up at the stars, do you know where we are?"

Lilith rolled her head back and looked up with me. She was silent for the longest time. "I do. That's… Andromeda right over there. The night sky looks unfamiliar to you because everything is upside down and further away than when we're on Earth."

"Andromeda is a different galaxy, right?"

"Right."

"Are we still even in the Milky Way galaxy?"

"We're closer to its center. Earth is way out on a spiral arm by comparison." she said.

"Do you think there's more life closer to the center of the galaxy?"

"I do because it's older. One of the things we used to talk about while planning this mission was how the center of the galaxy was probably the seat of power and that Earth, being so far from the center, was some kind of prison planet."

"So, in your mind, you were breaking out of jail?"

"We were breaking free to return to the core. And I still believe there's more peaceful intelligent beings than bad ones out there."

I decided not to argue with her and felt very small and pointless looking at the infinite mysteries of the universe from a perspective no man or woman had ever seen before. The temperature dropped some more, winds started to pick up, and Lilith curled up into a ball, pulling her robes tight around her, fighting back a shiver. I was warm because the SIA uniform was thick and insulated, designed to work on Earth, the moon, and Mars under extremely different conditions, hot or cold. I pulled my under-uniform thermal hood up from behind my neck and put it over my head.

"Lilith?"

"What?"

"I can keep you warm. You have to let me hold you."

"I'm not weak and helpless."

I could see that she was shivering but trying to hide it from me. She curled up tighter in a ball and rubbed her bare legs with her hands.

"You're human. I'm human, and I'm sorry how it all played out… but here we are, and you're going to freeze to death. Let me do my duty as a man and protect you."

There was long silence before she rolled towards me and scooted into my arms without ever looking up. She curled up with her head buried in my chest and I placed my legs over hers to act as a blanket while wrapping my arms around her shoulders. The two of us locked together and created heat. It was the first real warm non-sexual embrace I had felt since my true love died long ago. I was starting to like Lilith in a different way, a survival way—I never wanted to lose her, the only other human being here with me.

TRAX

Deep, heavy beast-breath panting right behind my head woke me up. It was predawn, and there was just enough light for me to see that the fog had returned thick. Another sniff and grunt right behind my head, and my whole body stiffened. I tried to reach for my blaster, but Lilith's leg had crossed over mine while sleeping. There was another deep inhale, and I was sure something was only inches away now. I worried that my head could get bitten off. I caught glimpses of hooves and clawed feet to the front and beside me, realizing that multiple beasts were circling our shelter.

Lilith started to stir, and I gave her two tight squeezes to let her know something was up. At the same time, there was a loud animal grunt in the distance that got her attention real quick.

Another long sniffing sound and grunt followed but this one behind us again. She looked up at me concerned. I motioned with my eyes that I needed access to my blaster. She pulled her leg back ever so slowly. I moved my hand past her thigh, unclipped the blaster, and pulled it out. She slid back away from me, and I got into the crouching position. There were now multiple beasts gathering around, and I caught glimpses of giant lizard-like legs and feet through the thick fog. Grunting and communicating with one another, sniffing around, curious about what they found in the shrubs. My only option to try and get a good look was to poke my head up through the opening in the center of the shrubs. I remained ready to pivot and shoot in any direction. The daylight was spreading, but the fog was still so thick, I couldn't really see anything unless it was a few inches away. More sniffing and grunting in the fog; whatever they were sounded big.

I was just about standing tall now, slowly turning my head around when a huge snout with three slits at the end moved very close to me and then stopped. The slits opened, and it inhaled deeply. A large mouth filled with jagged, uneven teeth opened.

I stayed frozen, not breathing.

The beast leaned its head back and made a loud braying sound that echoed across the land. It cried out over and over again. I could hear multiple beasts answer the call from far away. It sounded like more beasts were galloping toward our position. The ground shook exactly like when a pack of wild horses run by.

The fog started clearing fast as the Omegan sun blasted down through the clouds. I could finally see the beasts and was surprised by the many different species in various shapes and sizes that had gathered around us. The creatures were all making sounds, some musical, some terrifying and guttural, but none attacked us. I reached down and pulled Lilith up by the hand for her to see for herself, hoping she'd recognize that I didn't shoot first and ask questions later.

Some beasts were the size of dogs and covered in a thick fur, and some were the size of horses, but what struck me was that all of them looked like familiar versions of wildlife on Earth, just arranged differently. The way they stared, it was as if we were discovered by all the Omegan wildlife that hid from us the day before. Some of the beasts were on all fours, while some stood upright as they checked us out. It was clear that these wild creatures could rip us apart limb from limb, but they just stood there, blocking us in, grunting, breathing, sniffing, gawking like we were the zoo animals.

I remained ready to kill them all—there was no way to tell if an attack was imminent or we humans were just a curiosity.

"Be still," I whispered to Lilith as a ten-foot-tall dinosaur-looking beast emerged from the back and strolled up to us closer than the rest. It was the same one whose terrifying leg I saw through the fog. It reminded me of a kangaroo and had a head like a German shepherd dog but with longer hair. The hind legs were powerful and thick, but the front arms were short and muscular, with giant talons, like an eagle. Part bird/part dinosaur/part dog—it was bizarre and unsettling to see it approach. One of its eyes was missing, and it had scars all over its body like it had been whipped. I held my blaster up to my side as the beast stopped short, knelt down, and looked right into my eyes with its one good one. I felt my mind open up, and a bright light blinded my vision as I was transfixed by a spell. Lilith had no idea what was happening to me.

"*I am Trax. You are savior,*" is what I heard in a deep subconscious voice that was mine but sounded like two of me were talking at the same time. Trax had broken into my mind somehow and was communicating to me with vivid images and a few words. I saw a mountain pass that cuts through the middle of Mount Impossible with such clarity that I could have sworn I had been there before. Trax imprinted my memory with his own, and I knew the direction we needed to go from here. Trax lowered his head away, and I was free. He lay down, exhausted and panting.

"It's okay." I holstered my blaster and stepped forward through the shrubs with my hand out. I touched Trax on his forehead to let him know I received the message.

"What are you doing, Adam?"

"It's okay. They are friendly creatures, and I know the way to Omim City now. We must ride with the herd."

"And you know this, how?"

"Trax just showed me, in my mind."

"Trax?"

"This is Trax. He's going to escort us."

"How did you receive this information from him?"

"In my mind… I saw images of a mountain pass that leads to

Omim City. I heard my own voice talking to me, but it was not me saying it. The words came from Trax."

Trax turned away from us and made some movements with his head. Most of the beasts dispersed, running away back into the wild while two more of the dog-headed dinosaur beasts trotted over and got down low before us.

"They want us to ride with them."

Lilith pulled me close and whispered, "Didn't Madu warn that the Omim can read thoughts and have beasts that hunt for them?"

"He called me savior."

"You don't think that's strange that it just implanted thoughts in your mind?"

"It was more like a shared vision. But this isn't Earth. None of the rules apply."

"What if it's a trap, Adam?"

"I'm still armed and ready to defend our lives. If anything goes afoul, I'll be the first to act, but a beast to ride is better than walking."

"You trust him?"

"I'm going to give him a chance."

Lilith looked past me to Trax standing idly by like a dog awaiting its master. She studied it for a long time before agreeing. We walked out of the bushes and into the circle of beasts. It was good that Lilith was skeptical for a change. We climbed onto the kneeling beasts, which were partially covered in a rough fur, but around the neck, their skin was bare and itchy like an elephant's. When they stood up, it felt like trying to ride a camel with no saddle. Trax spoke to them with grunts and throat sounds before looking at me. I nodded to him like I would my dog, then I held on to thick, rope-like hair in the area where the shoulders meet the back. BigBoy was slung over my back, safe and secure, and my blaster was right in my chest holster, waiting to be pulled. Lilith adjusted herself as well, speaking gently to her beast in a respectful tone. Before we knew it, Trax started a light run in the general direction of the mountain, and our beasts followed.

At first it was hard to hang on, but after a few awkward moments, it was clear they didn't feel us gripping tightly with our hands. Trax led us across the barren landscape at a high speed, but their backs were stable and easy to stay balanced on. It looked like we were riding giant ostriches. The first two hours were exhilarating and raw. We galloped through shallow rivers that sparkled from underwater gems where plain rocks would normally be, and through fragrant woods where colorful and delicious-smelling flowers and fruits grew wild. No wonder the Omegans could live in peace and harmony before the Omim arrived. Their world is one of abundance and beauty many times grander than is found on Earth.

After many more miles of steady movement, we started up the steep rocky hillside for about an hour of zigzag climbs. The beasts used their powerful front claws to grab solid ground and pull us upward. We had to lie down flat, hugging their sides tight so we wouldn't fall off. When we eventually reached the plateau, and could see down into a vast green and brown valley on the other side that appeared to lead all the way to the base of Mount Impossible. Our beasts stopped moving and let the mountain breeze cool their faces while Lilith and I looked on.

The usual clouds around the top of Mount Impossible were not present, revealing something very shiny and bright reflecting light at the peak. It sparkled like a diamond; huge beams of light shot out in all directions. If we didn't know better, it looked like a star had landed there.

"Look up there! Do you see the light?" cried Lilith.

"Omim City."

"Or the communications tower."

"Whatever it is, if we can see it, it can also see us."

I heel kicked at my beast, patted him on the neck, and spoke plainly. "Get us out of here. C'mon, let's head down now."

We started down into the valley behind Trax. Lilith was on the move again beside me, and our beasts descended slowly, taking loose gravel leaps and hops down from one stone ledge to the next as we navigated a stony mountainside that looked like black glass shale was underfoot. Omega appeared to be packed to the brim with natural resources, and evidence of it was visible everywhere I looked. I wondered if this was the main reason the Omim came here—and ironically, it's the main reason we don't want any visitors to arrive in our part of the sol system too. Life-sustaining resources are limited. Planets formed in the razor-thin habitable zone where life can flourish are ever rarer, and worlds like Omega and Earth really are special and probably less abundant than once imagined.

I looked one last time at that gleaming light and felt a shiver of pure fear run right down my spine. I turned away, and the feeling went away. I kept my head down after that. The foliage in the valley was enormously tall and mostly shades of brown, light green, and gold. The dominant plants on this side of the hill were wispy trees that shot straight into the sky like a palm, their tops fanned out into millions of blades to form a grass ball that was somewhat shiny like a succulent. Wind blew through the valley and shook the treetops, which rippled like underwater plant life and not leaves in the air. The deeper we traveled, the more wildlife and nature sounds we could hear around us. Flying creatures fluttered by and disappeared around rocks that blocked our view.

"Are you okay?" I called out to Lilith, who was ahead of me now.

"Hanging in there!" she yelled back.

"Pretty amazing views!"

"Otherworldly!"

"What?"

"I have to pee."

I kicked at the sides of my beast and tugged on his fur to make him run up beside Trax.

"Trax, we need a break. Humans need a break."

Trax looked at me with his one good eye. He understood and veered off the path. Lilith was embracing the adventure we found ourselves in, and she was right, it was otherworldly. I couldn't understand how Lilith could be in this moment and still think what we are experiencing is just some accident of chemical reactions that arranged themselves across space and time. There must have been a true seed from which everything grew. Some true power. Some God creator of life.

The human race had become home to a majority atheist society after it was established that intelligent aliens did exist in the cosmos. God worship ended on that day for many who still believed, but some of us were raised to keep the traditions alive, and we made up a mostly underground community of believers. Most of the SIA were religious and became members of secret church communities. If Lilith ever learned the depth of my true faith, I don't know how she would react, so I kept it to myself and wrestled with the big questions in my own head as we rode through thicker grass.

Maybe there isn't a God after all. Maybe the Liliths of the world are closer to the truth than those of us who stick to tradition and the ancient story of where mankind came from. It's true, I had very little reason to believe any of the creation stories I have been told on Earth now that I've walked on Omega, but I couldn't just accept pure randomness. It wasn't part of my DNA to think that way. None of it made any kind of logical sense.

Trax slowed, navigating the last couple hundred yards down another rocky area carefully. The ledges appeared to be brittle shale as well, ready to force a slip or crack in two. Some of the rock were embedded with of dark-green glass. Trax seemed to know where he was going, hopping to avoid certain rocks. Then at the end, he leapt down the final hundred yards, disappearing over the edge, I wasn't expecting it.

"Hang on!" I cried out to Lilith as I watched her disappear over the side a few yards before me. She screamed all the way down and landed right next to her beast, flat on her back and gasping for air. The beasts were able to land like cats but had no idea what the long fall would do to us humans. I was able to hang on to my beast's neck and flopped back down hard on its back when he landed, so I slid off and moved over to Lilith. She was taking shallow breaths, and her face was all red. She looked surprised.

"Can you inhale?"

"Trying..."

"Go slow and easy."

She sucked in some air, exhaled choppily a couple of times, but then after a few more difficult pulls of oxygen, her breathing returned to normal and the redness faded from her cheeks. I helped her up and she found a place to relieve herself out of view.

Trax and the other two beasts were unconcerned about us and gathered around a small river that flowed past a nearby cluster of the spindle trees. Lilith returned, and looked up past me, to the bizarre geometric canopy made by the spindle leaves above. They overlapped like a dancing green snowflake canopy above us. A living kaleidoscope. It was mesmerizing. Sunlight trickled through and projected beautiful patterns on the ground. Lilith focused on me. "I'm sorry."

"Sorry for what?"

"For attacking you the minute I laid eyes on you. That was savage of me, and I was wrong. I'm not a primitive."

"Don't apologize. You're human, and I am too. I understand why you reacted the way you did."

Lilith smiled. She was just a lost girl from Mars, stranded with the type of guy from Earth she never really liked or ever got to know until now.

"I understand why you do what you do too," she said.

"That means the Omega to me." I finally made her smile.

"Good one," she said.

I helped her up, and we walked over to the watering hole where Trax was lying down with the other two beasts. The crunch of the gravelly ground underfoot was reassuring. The sound of a babbling brook running through the trees and the gentle valley breeze that blew past us created a sense of comfort and calm that was missing until Trax showed up and shared those visions with me that brought us here. I don't know if Trax was delivering us right into the hands of the Omim or if he was sent by Drade, but I was grateful for the ride nonetheless.

"I guess we're stopping here for now."

"They can rest as long as they like. I like it here," said Lilith.

"Here, on Omega? Or here—*here*?"

"Here here. I mean, look around. It's… wild but feels peaceful and normal. I could live in this very spot."

We walked a few yards from the beasts and sat down in silence under a tall spindle tree, shoulder to shoulder, and just gazed around at all the odd plants like the short bush with human-ear-shaped leaves that were so detailed and real, you would think the tree was growing parts for transplants. Or the big-eyed flying things, basically insects, with one comically huge eye, that buzzed around these yellow stalks with one giant clear dollop of liquid on top, like a dewdrop as shiny as a glass orb and big like a basketball. When the little bugs would fly behind one and start sucking out nectar, its already-large eye became magnified to ridiculous proportions. It cracked us both up. The sky through the trees was shades of light red, orange, white, and blue. The setting was serene and transferred that serenity to us by just being present in it. This kind of moment was few and far between in both of our past lives in the human world. We both silently absorbed the mysterious beauty.

A loud, familiar roar echoed in the distance, and Trax's head popped up. I pulled BigBoy from my shoulder. His ears fixed on the direction of the roar and stayed focused, but there were no more roars that followed, and Trax put his head down, satisfied and unconcerned, so I felt the same way too.

"That sounded pretty far away." said Lilith.

"Sounds like a wrath. That thing I killed in front of the Omegan temple."

"The monster that hunts Omegans for the Omim?"

"And now humans too, I presume. If you want to rest, I'll stay awake and keep watch."

The roar echoed again, sounding even farther away, but Trax still seemed unconcerned and kept his head down. Looking around, I took note of the steep cliffs and hilltops that created this valley. If not for the uncanny plant life and bizarre color combinations, it could be mistaken for somewhere in South Dakota.

While Lilith closed her eyes, I poked around the watering hole and located quite a few small amphibious creatures. I stepped around a tall, fat tree and came upon a small section of short bushes that were covered in bright-green fruits, about the size of a plum. The smell was intoxicating and sweet. I recalled seeing a pile of them on display back in the Omegan village market, so I picked a few and dropped them in my side pockets to bring back to Lilith. I stood there for a moment and gazed out across the alien forest with all its bizarre sounds and noises. Although I could hear all kinds of life, I saw none of it.

A loud ripping sound cut my focus, and I ran back to find Lilith standing and tearing bark off the base of a spindle tree. It looked and behaved like leather. She was invigorated by her discovery.

"I think I can make clothing with this soft bark."

"I thought you were taking a nap."

"I tried, but I can't sleep."

"Here., I found some fruit." I broke the fruit in two and handed her a chunk. She popped it right in and started chewing.

"I had these at the feast. So good."

I joined her and inspected the curious bark with my hands. It was thick, yet very flexible and shiny like a maple leaf on one side and rougher, with a fine root structure on the other, soft to the touch. She banged the swath on the ground, and the roots fell off like little dust bombs. We backed off as the dirt cloud settled. She was left with what we jokingly called vegan leather since it came from a plant and no animals were harmed. The spindle tree didn't mind because the bark regenerated right before our eyes. The only thing close to this on Earth is found in bamboo, which can grow up to three feet within a day, but this regrowth only took seconds.

I helped her harvest more than enough strands for a blanket and pants to be stitched together. It didn't take long to find suitable fibers that we used to weave with. We spent the next hour or so stitching together a pair of vegan-leather pants, and with the remaining material, we made a cape that doubled as a blanket. The material was incredibly versatile. She looked like what I imagined Mother Omega would look like if there were such a thing. White cloak covered her chest and partially hung down around her waist while the brown vegan leather pants and cape that contrasted with her golden hair. I wasn't worried about Lilith staying warm now.

Trax and the beasts awoke soon after and relieved themselves where they stood before coming over to us. Trax looked at me and shook his head, telling me it was time to move. I helped Lilith climb onto her beast before climbing on my own. Again without warning, Trax ran off, and we followed.

The beasts ran faster on the flat ground. There was lots of space between tree bases, so keeping in a straight line was possible. Now that I was accustomed to riding, I decided to guide mine closer to Lilith. I tugged its mane to the right while kicking gently with my feet and making a clicking sound with my mouth. The beast responded and moved where I wanted.

"Well, all right. Good boy."

"How do you know it's a boy?" said Lilith as she had good control of her beast and made it run parallel to mine.

"I don't. You're right. But I know you're a girl. Look at how you ride."

She smirked and kicked her beast hard, and it ran faster than mine, carrying her away from view momentarily. I caught glimpses of her galloping through the passing trees. Her beast leaped and dodged, and she handled like it was her natural calling. She looked free and happy in the thrilling moment.

I kicked too, and my beast ran to catch up. We've been galloping at high speed for about four miles now, and the trees were starting to thin. I could see tall, stony cliffs overlooking us on the right that faded away. The left side of the valley gave way to a big rolling hill, too big to see over and covered in plant growth. Straight ahead was a field of bright, tall, golden-orange grass and we all ran right through it. Trax and our beasts picked up the pace even faster. So fast that it became unsafe.

It wasn't until we crossed into the golden-orange grass that I saw it was not a plant but living long worms that tried to stick and attach themselves to us with their round, razor-sharp mouths. Lilith screamed and pulled her legs up. I flicked my blaster to flamethrower and burned off any that were stuck to my boots and legs. When the fire hit, they would explode and leave a yellow dye everywhere. I don't know if I accidentally burned my beast or what, but next thing I knew, he threw me off his back. I landed dead in the middle of those attack worms, and he kept on running to safety without me.

Lilith looked back and saw me struggling. She tried getting her beast to turn around, but it ignored her. I focused on killing as many of the slithering bastards as possible before they overwhelmed my body. They looked like above-ground sea anemones. Sliding up, they tried to penetrate my space suit. Thankfully, they could not jump from the ground up. My titanium boots keep me safe, but there was an acid the worms secreted that started to burn small holes in my pants. It was exhausting and tedious to beat them back. The whole field, about the size of a football field, was swelling up and closing in on me. They made a constant high-pitched hissing sound that was painful to hear. I thought I was dead right there, in something worse than Martian quicksand. I pulled BigBoy around while worms spit acid on my hands, fired up its core power, flipped the dial to shockwave, and let it rip—I was like a pebble left standing in a sea of yellow gut-splat. The ground sizzled and bubbled like an acid pool at the base of each obliterated worm. My hands itched like hell and were covered in burn marks. I was unable to stop scratching and clawing at the skin, and I started screaming. I was on my knees, intense pain throbbing, hands bleeding, and the acid worms started to regenerate at the base, bubbling up and growing again. Lilith ran toward me, but I waved her back.

"No!"

"Get out of there!" cried Madu.

I looked around and spotted Madu up high on a cliff. He waved his arms to get my attention.

"Run! Run away from there!" he cried again.

"Run to me!" cried Lilith.

When I tell you the burning on my hands hurt, I mean it. The pain felt like someone was blowtorching my skin at the highest setting. Somehow, I flung BigBoy over my shoulder and got up and ran, screaming all the way with my hands in front of me like appendages I wanted to throw away. Madu finished scaling down the cliff at the same time, racing to get to me. It felt like it took forever to run that short distance to Lilith. I collapsed on the clear, worm-free ground in front of her just as Madu arrived. He made some clicking sounds, and Trax came running over and nudged me with his snout and opened his mouth wide—I thought he was going to eat me—and started licking my hands all over instead. The pain subsided. Trax had thick, foul-smelling saliva, but it gave me relief, so I didn't mind one bit, except for the dry heaves that followed.

"Don't wipe it off," said Madu.

"Madu, we thought you died in the ocean," said Lilith.

"I am here. I have been tracking you."

I was watched in horror as those above-ground sea anemones were sprouting up anew. "Are we safe right here?"

"Deathfinger stays where it is rooted."

"Deathfinger? That sounds about right."

"I'm happy that I found you. Now I can take you the rest of the way."

I stood up and felt Madu grabbing for my blaster. He pulled it out of the holster and started turning it over, trying to figure it out.

"What are you doing?" I grabbed it out of his little grubby hand.

"Is that what you attacked deathfinger with?"

"No, I used my more powerful weapon, the one on my back—don't touch it."

"Can I try the small one?"

"That's a weapon of war, Madu," said Lilith.

"And self-defense," I barked.

"Please, savior, may I try your weapon?"

I could read any man, and I could read Omegans too. Madu meant me no harm. He was curious about the great powerful weapons that I possessed, but he had a reason he wasn't saying. I set it to stun and handed him my blaster.

"Sure. You just point at what you want to hit and then squeeze..."

Before I could finish my sentence, Madu nailed Trax right in the back of the head. Trax tumbled forward like a tranquilized elephant and fell face-down on the ground. The other two beasts took off running in opposite directions.

"Hey!" I grabbed the blaster.

"Why would you?" said Lilith. She didn't like seeing Madu's aggression.

"Relax. The blaster was set to stun. He's just knocked out for a little while."

Madu clasped his hands together, fell to his knees, and begged our forgiveness.

"Please, my masters, I had to. That is an Omim scout. We must get away while it cannot see us."

"That beast is named Trax. He spoke to me in my mind and was taking us to Omim City."

"And Trax will bring you directly to the Omim ruler. You would be tortured and sacrificed. I will show you secret way in and how to get to the tower unnoticed."

"Is that what we saw atop that mountain when the clouds were not there?" Asked Lilith.

"That is Omim City. It shines like a star sometimes."

Trax grunted in his sleep, and his front arms started to move, like when a dog is dreaming.

"We don't have a lot of time before Trax wakes up, and I really enjoyed not walking, but I trust you, so show us the way, Madu."

We followed him out of the open valley and back to the cliff wall he scaled down to join us. We worked our way back up as the Omegan day became bright and warm. One thing that is the same throughout the cosmos is the feeling of sunlight. I don't know how far Omega's sun is from the planet, but the rays felt the same, and it made me happy. Its environment was clean. Perhaps it's the fact that Omegan civilization never became industrialized before the Omim arrived. The groundwater and the air felt cleaner and more refreshing than anywhere I have been on Earth.

When we reached the top again, we stopped to catch our breath behind some rocks. Madu explained that before the Omim arrived,

Omegan towns were along the coastline below us, and by traveling from abandoned town to abandoned town we'd have enough hiding spots where Omim didn't really send scouts anymore. The risk of being seen from Omim City and discovered over here was lower than taking the mountain pass that eventually led right up to the city gates. After a brisk walk/run down the other side, we made it back to the water's edge that was on the opposite side of the inlet where we first came ashore. Our mistake when we washed up without Madu was in walking straight ahead, instead of just heading to the right and hugging the coast.

"How did Trax find you?"

"We were sleeping, hiding behind some bushes, and woke up surrounded by all kinds of wild creatures. Trax was one of them. He did his mind trick, and then we left with him."

"This is bad. Very bad," said Madu.

"Why?" asked Lilith.

"Omim can see what Trax sees. Omim knows you are here."

"I shot one of their ships, Madu, and then they attacked your home. Remember?"

"Omim now can see in your thoughts."

"What do you mean?" asked Lilith.

"What Trax saw in his head, now Omim sees it too."

"I don't quite follow..."

Lilith turned around, walking backward so she could talk to us both.

"I think he's saying the Omim have some kind of shared consciousness. Like a computer network but of memories. And now your consciousness is hooked into it too."

"If that's so, how did I see what's in their thoughts?"

"Mind-bridge," said Madu.

"What's that, like some kind of connection into your head?"

"Yes. It's their power."

"God. That's not what I wanted you to say."

"I'm no god—you are descended from the God."

That stopped me dead in my tracks. Lilith and Madu kept walking ahead as the coastline rounded, but I stood there wondering if the Omegans knew the same God as mankind does. Why else would he say such a thing? Why didn't Lilith even notice? I snapped out of it when we came upon the ancient ruins of an Omegan fishing port and what was once a major hub of Omegan life. There were rickety docks, some still intact, simple little boathouses, all with collapsed roofs and plants retaking them, just like what would happen on Earth. It was easy to imagine Omegan life before the Omim arrived. It was simple and peaceful. The kind of community Lilith would thrive in. They fished and traded with each other and lived in general peace until the arrival.

We trailed close to the water's edge for hours, where the last remnants of a walking path still existed. The old fishing village was thickly overgrown and difficult to pass through, but I understood why Madu chose this way, staying close to hiding spots and more important, secret supply sheds that were used by Omegans traveling to and from Omim City over the centuries.

We hiked on without saying a word to each other. Madu led; Lilith and I followed. We passed the outskirts of small, ravaged villages and old Omegan infrastructure projects that revealed a society that was reminiscent of 1900s America, with long rural roads connecting small coastal towns.

He turned down a road and started leading us inland at an angle instead of going right toward the mountain. The day was hot and humid, and this part of the planet was alive with insects that behaved exactly like insects everywhere else in the known universe, which was just another coincidence of evolution, according to Lilith.

"I have never heard of this word… evolution," said Madu.

"Evolution is the slow change from one physical state to another. Life is not fixed in one place. It evolves. That's how life began on Earth, and here on your world too," declared Lilith.

"You can't prove that."

"We are not created?" Madu looked confused to see the human gods disagree about where we came from. His whole understanding of how he came to be in the first place had just been put into question by Lilith, who he believed was some goddess from the heavenly world.

"We're begotten, not made. That's our legend from the sky disc, Madu."

"Speak for yourself. Do you still truly believe in an all-powerful god, even after seeing all this?" prodded Lilith.

"As a matter of fact, I do, maybe even more so than before we got here."

She turned her back on me and moved closer to Madu. "Don't listen to him, Madu. There is no God, only science and scientists."

"What is scientist?"

I couldn't let her roll over me like this. I had to butt in. "A scientist is someone who thinks they know everything—all the answers to life—and should be worshiped. Like a God."

"Not true, not true. Scientists try to understand how things work. Saint Sagan was a very famous scientist. He is the one who sent you the disc, and he didn't believe in one all-powerful god because he knew better."

"Bless Saint Sagan, the sacred Carl. May peace be with him forever and ever," said Madu.

"Amen." said Lilith.

"C'mon, you guys. That's enough," I barked, and they both hushed up then walked ahead. I could hear them giggle like schoolgirls as they rounded a corner and were out of my sight for a minute. When I turned the corner and caught up, I stopped in my tracks and stood right beside Lilith, who was also stopped cold, jaw open, looking down into a valley that resembled a booming old Wild West American town in the early 1800s.

Buildings, homes, everything about the layout resembled old pictures from history books. It was as if the apocalypse happened, and all that was left was an empty wasteland of rotted buildings, overgrown roads, and the faint remnants of bustling life in the valley. Not far from where we stood was a giant hillside water tower made of wood. The top was missing, and there was a giant nest of blueish-yellow grass overflowing from it.

"What is this place, Madu?" I asked.

"Welcome to Ciria. The old capital of our world. All can trace a relative back to this place. It is holy land and where Omim struck first."

"How big was the population at the time?" asked Lilith while I kept scanning the valley, trying to develop a sense of the surroundings.

"I don't know how many lived in Ciria, but most of us are from the smaller towns across the land."

We were up above the town, looking down. It wasn't obvious until now that we followed old roads from the fishing village to here. Looking out across the valley, the colorful forest got thick with trees and plants miles away on the other side. To the right of the town, about ten miles out, there was a small, rocky mountain path that looked like a shortcut to Mount Impossible, which loomed larger in the distance.

"I'm deeply sorry that this happened to your people," said Lilith.

"I'm blessed to be alive when the prophecy is being fulfilled."

"Me too, Madu," she said as we started down the path, which wound down into the town center. Madu believed every word of the prophecy, foretelling that we would arrive one day in a chariot across the sky and then defeat the evil that has fallen upon their planet. And we did arrive in a chariot across the sky. And we were on our way to see the evil up close, but it was not some random accident that we were here. Lilith and her Saganite rebel pals were the reason we were here now. Knowing the reality gave me a strange detachment from my Earth life and made my survival instinct dominate my mind even more. I could feel the weight of my old world on my shoulders, knowing that if the Omim ever arrived there, humans would be history just like the Omegans, and who could we call out to when the whole world denied God but accepted unseen aliens?

The walk down into Ciria was breathtaking, like hiking down a path in some kind of dreamland of an abandoned, sweeping alien boom town. The plant life that took over was pretty and vibrant. We passed through overgrown wild orchards taken over by stubby plants that gave off unsavory odors. You could tell that this valley was the Omegan cradle of civilization for a reason—it was buoyed by natural resources and what seemed to be a perfect climate with ocean air rolling over the hillside, set against the giant mountains on the other side, creating a pleasant valley. The main road and ground were covered in a lush, thick, light-blue grass. Our feet made loud scuffing sounds as we pressed our way into the center of the town.

Ciria was a ghost town, devoid of life except for whatever nested up in that water tower. The buildings were square and basic but more detailed than the fishing villages we passed. Omegans crafted their windows in a circular shape, but there was no glass, just a curtain made of plant material woven together. Behind the main road, homes and huts spread out into the countryside along twisty paths. Most had collapsed inward, leaving a rotted pile of materials and a memory of how charming it once was. I tried to imagine what life was like when Ciria was populated. Smoke from home cooking filled the mountainside. Young Omegans probably ran on the side paths and played in the hills. I imagined the buildings on the main strip busy with Omegans, just like in their volcano market, buying and selling items needed to live, and in doing so, they created an economy that thrived and obviously had a religious order.

We passed one slanted old structure that looked like a schoolhouse where the young were taught their faith, based entirely on the knowledge learned from the golden record. Madu led us a little further to a very large hut at the end of the main road that was somehow still standing, albeit also a little slanted. It was ornate and heavily damaged above the door. The spot where the golden record once sat was a big, jagged hole.

"We shelter here for a rest and continue into the open lands after nightfall."

We followed Madu inside the hut, which was a long, empty room except for an elevated area with a throne crafted of tangled woven wood at the end. This was their original church, the place where the golden sky disc was used to establish order to the Omegan civilization, where the Omegans gathered, learned and worshiped an object from Earth that taught them math, language and showed them what life could be like.

Madu led us to a side room beside the throne, where an Omegan crude record player sat displayed on a stone table. "It's safer in here. The wrath caves are in these mountains, and they will come down if they sense us."

"No place seems totally safe on this world or any world," said Lilith.

"What do you expect? You grew up on Mars. Your whole life was spent in a planned community with planned outcomes. This is your first time ever in the wild, where the laws of nature reign supreme."

Lilith stared at me, and I could tell my words stung. She had no quick comeback, just a look of disappointment in the acceptance of the truth about life, especially when it's free and wild like her spirit. "You look shocked to learn that survival of the fittest is a cosmic truth." I added.

"I'm talking about personal safety."

"Safety is an illusion that is secured by people like me. This is about survival, survival of the human race and the Omegan race."

"Why can't all creatures great and small learn to love and appreciate one another?"

"Because the laws of nature are the same throughout the cosmos, and the law says that survival is ahead of kindness. Kindness comes from a source outside of humanity. It's unnatural, not part of the instinct."

"Intelligent beings are all capable of kindness. It is one of the marks of intelligence, according to Saint Sagan."

"Are you sure about that? The Omim are clearly more intelligent than the Omegans and far less kind. They tried to kill us, in case you forgot."

Madu watched for her reaction. Lilith exhaled, plopped down with her back to a wall, and closed her eyes.

"What are you doing?"

"Meditating. Can I still have that?"

"Whatever keeps you at ease."

Madu interrupted by stepping between us. "I gather food for us without being seen. I'll be back quick. You both stay here."

He left, and I stood behind the throne, watching him go. He

crossed the main road and ran out toward the grassy neighborhoods in the hillside. I lost him as he darted between the dilapidated structures and tall weeds. The sun was starting to fade a little, but he was the native; he knew what he was doing and how much time there was left.

I walked back inside the smaller chamber room, and Lilith was still meditating, able to generate a moment of peace that was lost to me in this place—and just about every moment of my life, if I'm being honest. I existed in fight-or-flight mode even when doing nothing.

I looked at Lilith with her eyes closed and her face at peace. Even though she smelled funny and was generally a mess, she still radiated. Her unshakable desire to love had its charms. She would make an excellent mother if that love could ever be selfless instead of what I think is selfish. Lilith wants this world and all worlds to conform to her peaceful values, but that's not at all how things work and she now knows it.

I couldn't relax, so I sat in silence, picking dirt off my blaster and listening to the sounds of the wind picking up speed as it passed over the thatched roof, whistling between crevices. The gusts on Omega always intensified as it grew dark. I heard a repetitive scratching sound come from somewhere inside the main room and got up to investigate. It was the sound of furious digging, but I couldn't place exactly where. When I thought I located where it was coming from, I walked toward the scratching, at which moment it sounded like it was coming from the other side of the room. The digging grew louder until I started to move closer; then it stopped.

I kicked a piece of fallen roof wood away from a corner and before me was a pink reptilian creature, the size of a dachshund with a long, slim body and multiple short arms ending in five-finger, human-looking hands. It was so bizarre that I jumped back. There was no apparent head, just a body with arms and hands. Both ends of its body stretched and recoiled like a worm, then its hands started to dig into the ground. It hurried out of sight, and I was just as glad to see it go. Stepping back, I accidentally flipped another board over, tripping on a nest of gelatinous bubbles, gross and wobbly. Each cell held tiny sets of human hands attached to a wormlike body floating inside. These were eggs, and I kicked it as far away as possible, pulled my blaster, and zapped the nest into oblivion. The eggs screamed while they burned, and tiny human hands on little arms reached out to me—it was so unnerving that I shot some more, wanting the gruesome vision to disappear as fast as possible. Lilith heard the blasts and came out just as the mother critter and a hundred of her friends crawled out of the ground and surrounded us. Both ends of their bodies grew large and red, and then the hideous creatures arched in a U shape and shot tiny needles out like a porcupine.

I went berserk.

"Get out of this building! Move away!" I shouted to Lilith as I stomped, blasted, and tossed the hell spawns away as they climbed on me. Their needles burned little holes in my bare skin, sending up a white vapor that nauseated me and made my eyes water. The tiny hands were so powerful. One of the monsters climbed all the way up to my face and latched onto my eyes. I screamed and fell to the ground, trying to pull the thing off while its body started to swell in my hands. It was going to poke out my eye and crawl right in, no doubt about it.

Lilith picked up a shard of wood and batted it off my face with one vicious slap. Blood squirted from my nose. I scrambled for BigBoy, eyes bleeding water so thick all I could hear were the sound of hideous hissing critters as Lilith plunged the stake into their backs one at a time. I fumbled with the controls, but I knew them by heart.

"Clear!" I yelled to Lilith. Then I burned the whole place down. I had no choice. My eyes started to clear up as we ran outside. The temple was as dry as a tinderbox and engulfed in flames. The winds picked up and sent sparks blowing out into the countryside where they landed and started small subsequent fires on old homes.

"Uh-oh," I said.

"Where's Madu?" said Lilith, looking out toward the hillside, the evening in its last bit of light before darkness fell. I spotted him running toward us with his arms full of fruits. He looked panicked when he noticed that the temple was in flames. He stopped running, dropped the fruit, and fell to the ground and wept.

"Nooo!" he cried.

Lilith and I ran up to him. She was trying to put out small fires with her boots while I knelt down to look Madu in the eyes.

"We were attacked by some crawling thing that tried to kill us. I used my weapon, and that's how the fires started."

"What did it look like?" asked Madu.

"Like giant worms, with human arms and hands. It was disgusting."

"Omim," said Madu.

"They control all the life on this planet?"

"The evil creatures all come from Omim. They create and send them into the wild to keep track of us."

"The Omim are present in the trees and in the animals?"

"Sometimes."

"They're creators," stated Lilith. "Gods."

ESCAPE FROM CIRIA

THE OMEGAN HOMELAND burned as we hiked out of the valley and up toward the stone mountain ridge in darkness. It was easy to see where we were going from the glowing light of the fires behind us. Nobody said a word; we just followed Madu at his hurried pace up a path that hugged the side of the valley, cutting around the ruins of countryside homes. After about an hour of hiking, the plant life started to thin out, and we found ourselves at the base of a wide stone plateau with jagged cliffs jutting out all around it, creating the look of a wide-open mouth full of fangs. It was a terror to see against the starry backdrop.

Madu stopped and looked back at the fires. His little shoulders slumped, and his body language was the same as any human witnessing loss. I felt horrible as the fires raged, and it was obvious that the whole of what was still standing in Ciria would burn to the ground before daybreak. Even the Omim didn't burn their cities to the ground; that's a human tactic. But in my defense, the valley was bone dry when we arrived, and it just needed a spark, which I provided free of charge. Some savior I was.

Lilith walked up and put her hands on his little shoulders to comfort him. Madu leaned closer and hugged her thigh like a dog wanting to be picked up. It was a very human moment between two different beings, and it made me consider that being human was not simply a physical state, but a kind of mind set too.

I couldn't help but feel for the first time a little bit of what Lilith believes—that we should aim for peace among the stars and peace among all creatures. Why not aim for it? The contrast of their embrace against the backdrop of the burning town and glittering stars allowed me to see that love was the most powerful force in the entire universe, always finding ways to surface and ripple out against the painful consequences of existing in the flesh. Love was universal, felt by sentient beings, and served as a common language too. I was seeing it with my own eyes in real time, but that moment was shattered by a terrifying roar that echoed behind us, startling me right into self-defense mode. I looked up on the cliff and saw the shadowed outline of a huge wrath beast standing tall on its hind legs, roaring into the night. More roars echoed from around us, and when I circled around, I could see no fewer than six of the beasts gathering and looking down from the cliffs above. They had us surrounded.

"What are they so upset about?" I asked.

"The fires drew them out of their caves and led them to us," said Madu.

"Now what?" said Lilith.

"Now you both get directly behind me."

I pulled BigBoy around and aimed at the wraths. BigBoy was the Swiss Army knife of SIA weapons, and without it we wouldn't be alive now. Lilith knelt and held Madu close while more wraths gathered around, and we were quickly surrounded by more than twenty of the growling monsters. Their roars and snarls told me that the pack intended to rip us all apart limb by limb. *Kill or be killed* erased any peaceful fantasies I was entertaining just moments ago. I had to decide the best way to kill them first. Without looking, I thumbed the settings until I heard the familiar click I was waiting for—the multibeam direct-energy ray.

"Stay as close behind me as possible," I ordered them one last time.

As if on cue, the first group of wraths jumped from their vantage points and scaled down the mountain pass walls. We were rushed by the pack from all sides at once, like muscular black shadows, the dark of night coming alive to murder us. Their roars were bone rattling as they drew closer. A sound I never want to hear again. I held my ground.

"Stay real close," I urged while moving in a slow circle as BigBoy's lasers targeted the wraths one by one until it looked like they were connected to me via laser wire. The red dots distracted the beasts just long enough for the aim to lock in. "Cover your eyes," I warned and then pulled the trigger—the target beams became supercharged and hit the wraths like red lightning bolts, dropping a few straight to the ground, screaming in pain with a giant hole blasted out of the center of their chests. Lilith screamed at the bloody horror that surrounded us. Death by laser was messy. More wraths came running at us, and I started to pivot and shoot. The beasts went crazy. I tried to hand Lilith my blaster, but she didn't want it.

"Take it!"

"I will not kill!"

"You will be killed!"

"No!"

"I will!" said Madu, his hand out, eager for my weapon. I handed it to him, then had to turn and shoot wraths that leapt and clawed at us from all sides. Each time I hit one, the maimed beast would fall to the ground, screaming in uncontrollable pain. It was not pretty, but I put them out of their misery one by one with a head shot that looked savage but saved our lives.

Madu was happy to cover us from his side. He got the hang of it and started to shoot and holler like someone tasting revenge for the very first time. I looked up and noticed more wraths scaling down the walls. Then one that towered over the rest appeared on the ridge, and my heart sank. This wrath was the biggest beast I had seen on Omega. It was dinosaur big, twice the size of Trax, and its angry deep growl made my skin crawl. All of its brood lay dead, maimed, or crying out in pain around us. Dumb animals, an easy kill for a class-five laser marksman like me, but their big momma was not happy. The sky was unusually bright and starry, making the monster looking down appear as if a terrifying constellation came to life that intended to eat us all. Madu moved to my side, pointing the blaster right at the giant wrath. I flipped BigBoy to its most powerful direct laser setting. My heart was pounding in my chest; something about this beast was different than the others. It didn't wildly come at us. Instead, it stood there, blocking us from the mountain, with its heaving body. There was a distant sparkle of bright-white light flying toward us from afar, coming up behind the wrath. It was growing brighter and bigger very fast. Madu ran away, and he still had my blaster in his hand.

"OMIM!" yelled Madu.

"Hey, get back here!"

The beast stood tall, jumped off the cliff, and landed with such force that I felt the ground shake. It jumped high again and came down right behind the fleeing Madu, swiped him up with one arm, and bit his head clean off.

Lilith screamed. I grabbed and pulled her behind me with BigBoy pointed right at the giant monster. We back stepped as it lurched at us in a slow and menacing fashion, snapping its shark-like teeth and moving its claws in a pre-attack dance that didn't make sense to me. The beast seemed to not want to kill us, just corner us. That's when I noticed the silver collar on its neck that had a flashing light on it. This was someone's pet—an Omim attack dog.

The wrath lunged at me, and I fired one shot that missed and trailed off into the night as I fell back and out of its way. Lilith ran the opposite direction. I didn't have time to see the deep gorge behind me.

"Lilith!" I cried as the beast sank its teeth into my shoulder, trying to bite my head. I jammed the butt of BigBoy into its chest, just as the wrath and I tumbled over a ledge and into darkness while a large bright ball of light chased down Lilith.

As I was falling backward into the void, the last thing I saw was the glowing ball of light plop down and swallow Lilith before speeding away just as fast as it arrived with her trapped inside and trying to get out.

I kept falling. Wind whipped by with no knowing how far down I'd go before I'd hit bottom. There was a sudden terrible crunch as the wrath smacked hard against a sharp rock that jutted out from the gorge wall. It whimpered, thwacked on something else, and then went quiet. I held on to BigBoy with my entire body through the pitch blackness. I could see nothing around me, and the thought of my impending splat when I hit bottom made my heart race.

I was in full get-ready-to-die mode, anticipating an uncertain and painful death at any moment. My heart banged against my chest, a thick lump of terror swelled in my throat. I started to pray for Lilith's safety and my survival—and that's when something unexpected happened. I felt the falling sensation transition to more of a floating sensation, as an invisible force swooped me in a new direction. Did I already die? I clung to BigBoy, and the winds rushed loud against my ears as I raced fast forward in upward direction. Feeling around with my fingers, I located the switch to illuminate the barrel lamp, shooting bright light out in all directions at once. It was designed for lighting up lunar caves and Martian bunkers. I flipped the switch with my freezing thumb and saw that I was being carried by a powerful updraft that pushed me through a wide gorge like a feather in the wind. The steep and rocky walls went so deep that I could only see blackness far below while I was in the middle of a V shape and had to be moving at least one hundred miles an hour. I kept looking around, anticipating that I might splat into one of the stones jutting out, but since I was so small, I stayed right down the middle as if by miracle.

Part of the cliff wall moved as I neared it, but it wasn't a cliff wall. Four huge wings of a flying creature spread out as a beast with a bird-like head, two dark-red eyes, and tentacles where legs should be, rose high above me as I zoomed by. It chased after me. I tried to control my flight, but I couldn't, while gripping BigBoy. The monster lunged, wrapped its tentacles around me and squeezed the air out of my lungs. BigBoy's light was still shining, and suddenly I was over treetops, the rocky land moving fast beneath me. The monster pulled me through a mass of abrasive plant material and thick sticky cobwebs that stuck to me and reeked like burnt rubber and vomit.

Sticky tentacles moved fast and stuffed me into a muddy wall, forcefully pushing on my forehead and midsection while encasing half of my body in mud and excrement, even though I was still holding BigBoy between my legs the whole time. The monster grunted and hissed while it worked on packing me away for a later snack. Juices oozed from its torso like an acid that helped seal me in. Its noxious odor caused me to hallucinate, and I began to envision myself as an insect with swollen eyes and metallic skin.

The monster left the nest to go hunt some more. I rotated my insect head and could see all kinds of creatures stuck in the side walls around me, dead, dying, or decaying. The smell was horrendous. I used my antennae to sense the situation, and I felt dread. The muddy walls tightened around me, squeezing my spine, and I thought that was it, I would die as a pathetic snack in a cave. But BigBoy was still wrapped up in my legs and arms. Struggling, I stretched my free claw as wide as possible, trying to fit it inside the trigger. I didn't know what setting it was on, but I was not going out without doing some damage to the monster that dragged me in here. The wailing cries of dying creatures stuck in the walls with me was a symphony of demon sounds straight from the depths of hell. We were dinner, and through the web of white slime, plant material, and rotten corpses, I had never felt so helpless, even when I was stuck in the time dilation effect of intergalactic superluminal space travel.

The beast broke through the nest wall again, this time carrying the half-dead wrath in its tentacles. The wrath struggled and resisted, but the beast broke its back and then stuffed it into the mud wall right next to me. The torso and arms of the beast were hard to look at. It started taking account of its meals and crawled up and around so that it was right above me. An awful, guttural, wet throat sound repulsed my entire being as it crunched a skull above me, its blue-green blood dripping down and landing on my cheek.

My thumb. I came out of the hallucination and felt the tip against steel… a little more. I pressed down on the damn trigger. The nest exploded outward, cracking a hole in the side of it, sending its tentacles, meat chunks and its dead smorgasbord downwind. I was still stuck inside the mud wall, but the wind rushed past and peeled away the dried nest that encased me. The monster had built a mud nest against the side of the gorge wall. I broke loose, and the wind tried to pull me away, but I managed to keep BigBoy close to my chest while climbing up and out of the nest, which was on a long overhang. It took forever because I hugged the ground the whole way. I could see the top ridge of the gorge, so I kept going. Each move across the gorge wall drained me, but the farther up I went, the less wind I could feel pulling at me until it was nothing more than a distant howl in the darkness.

SEEKER

By the time I made it to top of the howling canyon ledge, the sun was coming up and burning off the clouds, revealing a new day and a dramatically changing terrain ahead. My heart was heavy from being separated from Lilith and I had no idea where to start looking for her. I said goodbye to the stars and pulled myself up and over the ledge until I was standing on flat ground again. Looking back, it was a miracle that I made it out alive. I could hear the distant whistling sound of that incredible wind down in the depths.

I was stranded somewhere between Ciria and Omim City, looking at a landscape before me made mostly of stone. Who knows how far the wind carried me off course? I'm sure if Madu were still with me, he would say not to go this way, but there was no other choice really, so with BigBoy at the ready, I started into the desert landscape and hiked as far as I could by day, praying and thinking about Lilith every step of the way. What happened to her in that ball of glowing light? My gut told me she was alive; I don't know why I felt that way, but I did. I also felt it inside my heart with certainty, and so I pressed on in faith that I would eventually find her if I could survive until that time.

I crossed into a colorful canyon of massive boulders that looked like they were piled up by giants. Peculiar stacked shapes shot high into the sky, creating a city of improbable stone towers that stretched on as far as my eyes could see. There were small caves and out of the ordinary formations of plant life in the most random spots too. My guess was that it was once an ocean that was now dry. I studied one tower and found small fossils embedded, confirming my suspicions. It was clear to me now that unless the wildlife was instantly aggressive, it wanted less to do with me than I with it, and that's how I liked it. Even the smallest thing could kill me, for all I knew. Most of the creatures I passed on the first day alone looked like they were well adapted to the harsh environment with an abundance of lizard-type life forms that were very small, walked on their hind legs, and had no tail, making them look like little marching soldiers running away. If this was my home world, I would try to have one as a pet. When they moved in large numbers, they looked like synchronized dancers scooting and moving left and right. It was hard to imagine how these creatures evolved to behave this way, but it fascinated me to no end and helped pass the time. They were cute, to say the least, like upright frogs who danced with each step.

This was the hottest day so far on Omega. I kept close track of the temperature as I hiked into the dusk hours and could see a shimmering heat coming off the ground many miles in the distance. I was sweating, and my SIA suit's environmental controls stopped functioning, so I decided to slow down and camp out when I found a suitable location with shade.

Hours later, I came upon a cave that looked too small from the outside, but I knew enough about this world from the Omegans, so I got on all fours to look in. When I did, I could see something glowing and sparkling somewhere out of sight, around a bend. I shined BigBoy's light around and saw that the cave was much bigger inside, so I pulled myself in and stood up, ready to kill anything that came from the glowing area. I was living minute to minute, knowing and accepting that I could run out of time before reaching the base of Mount Impossible. I stepped forward, and the closer I got to the turn, the louder I could hear the sound of trickling water. What a refreshing sound! By some crazy good luck, I found an underground well that felt like something out of a dream. The ceiling arched upward and had beige stalactite drip stones hanging down, with droplets falling from their tips into a pool of illuminated crystal-clear water. The well was nothing short of enchanting, and I seemed to be the only living thing in there. It was the perfect place to camp for the night. The cool temperature inside was ideal, and I could get some real rest. I found a sloped corner about five feet from the water and lay back against it with BigBoy in my lap. I snacked on some of the dried fruits that I had picked and sipped handfuls of the water just until I felt refreshed.

As I lay there being soothed by the sound of water drops, worry about Lilith and our home world crept into my imagination. I started to assume the worst and felt a sinking feeling that I was never going to make it to Omim City, and who was I fooling to presume otherwise? I felt lonely, with no one to talk to, no one who knew life like I did. I steeled myself. One thing I won't do is quit trying. I'll keep going to get there and find her, but in the back of my mind, I was bracing for either death or slavery at the hands of the Omim, no different than the Omegans. Or being the oddball adopted member of an Omegan tribe that knows my language but not my faith. A man without a planet. I could preach to the Omegans and lead them to the true God of life, and who knows, maybe that's what really brought me here. The thought made me chuckle. I don't know how long I remained awake after that.

The pool's glowing light was gone and the cave was pitch black when my eyes opened wide. I couldn't see a thing but heard a large creature climb out of the water. Its ear-shattering screams hurt, and I could hear similar screams echoing across the stone valley outside of my cave. I sat frozen with my back against the stone while something enormous pulled itself past me, making long, sloshing, sliding sounds. Flashes of light came from outside that must have triggered the thing in my cave, because it lit up like a lightning bug as it pulled itself out of the cave. I could see that it was a shapeless, transparent, moving blob. It was only bright for a second, but that was enough to burn into my mind the image of a jellyfish-like creature. Lights were flashing outside at regular intervals now, but not according to any kind of pattern. It looked like lightning bursts, and I could hear a strange zipping and popping sound over and over again too.

I moved to the entrance, knelt down, and saw these glowing, translucent blobs had climbed to the top of the rocky formations and were expanding and contracting to catch black flying beasts as they were passing by, presumably migrating somewhere. Each time one of the glow slugs would get hit, it would absorb the black thing until it was gone. I figured it was a good idea to avoid touching or being touched by it, and since it looked like tens of thousands had climbed to their perch, I slid out and found a spot away from the entrance to sit back and observe. The flying creatures made a zipping sound as they went through the air that ended in a muted pop when it hit the glow slug. The winds were gentle and the stars were clear and bright against a night sky. The cosmos in the background started to merge with the translucent slugs in the foreground, making it feel like I was hallucinating, watching the sky melt and drip in a cosmic dance. This show went on until the flying creatures stopped passing by in droves. When it was done, the glow slugs made their way back to their caves, lighting up at odd intervals, then slid into the dark water and lit up bright again, blending in with the water. They were invisible to the naked eye, and it was just another reminder that nothing is what it seems to be on Omega. I was just thankful that drinking that water didn't make me sick.

A new day dawned as the glow slugs returned to their caves, and I stayed where I was outside and took a few bites of the fruits I still had. I had been existing on this world just long enough to start enjoying my breakfast routine and the strange energy boost I got from it.

Keeping Mount Impossible in front of me was how I chose which direction to head, and so I set off, hiking though an unchanging landscape for three more days.

I crossed into a gradually expanding green forest that was hilly and thick with knotted tree growth. At first it seemed like the ideal area to pass through because of the shade of trees and lots of places to hide if I had to, and by now, I had grown accustomed to all the strange little life forms I encountered. Just like back home, most life wants to be left alone to live in peace. But with more plant life around than in previous areas, I was careful not to touch anything with my bare skin. My beard was really starting to come in now, so that was an extra layer of protection. The only real exposed parts of me were my hands and face.

Hours after hiking one day, I came upon a fast-moving river before nightfall and decided to camp next to it on the banks. I was almost out of the fruits I picked on my own and knew that I could probably fish something out for a more nutritious meal. I broke off a long stalk from a plant I had seen in many places since landing here. It was like wood but not quite the same texture. I unwound some of the threading from inside my suit's lapel, where there's always some extra threads, and used that as a fishing line. For the hook, I found a jagged rock that I could wind up to the thread and then stick a small bite of fruit on the end. It was my next-to-last piece, so I needed it to work. When I dropped my line in, the river pulled it downstream, and it went taut almost instantly. I tugged back, but it was not a catch, just the power of the river, which happened to be flowing in the direction I needed to go. While I was busy building a small raft to use, the real tug came, and I almost lost my rod.

I grabbed hold of it with both hands and pulled something fighting and struggling out of the water. I was relieved to recognize it as a big version of a long fish that I ate at the Omegan feast, but I was horrified to see that it had human arms and hands again. Hundreds of them this time, like a centipede, all reaching and clawing at the river banks as I ripped it from its watery home. Some of the tiny hands had a power grip on something just below the water and wouldn't give. I had to beat the fish over the head with BigBoy until it let go. I never felt so put off by food (besides the wrath penis), and it was difficult to gut and skin the fish with all those human arms and hands. I clipped them off one by one, and each time I felt an odd pinch in my own shoulders. While the skinned and cut fish hung out to dry, I went about making a quick lean-to out of the familiar fallen trees and plant life around me. I was shrouded by plenty of shade and felt good about not being seen.

By sundown, I had assembled a one-person raft using the same materials. That night, for the first time on Omega, I made a campfire, and I cooked the fish, seasoned it by squeezing some fruit juice on it, ate its oily meat, and then lay back and gazed at the stars. The crackle from my fire made me long for home in the worst possible way. Something so primitive and earthy that my senses knew and that triggered deep memories of camping in the outer lands when I was a kid. The odor from the wood was different here—sweeter, almost like burnt cotton candy.

Looking up at the stars, I saw a bright light streak by out in space while I played with the soil with my bare hands, taking a deep breath of air, thankful for my life and for witnessing this miracle on another world with all my senses, even though it was a death sentence for me.

I fell asleep right there and slept hard, having lucid dreams of being chased by a mouth of fire. It was one of those dreams where the flames and heat seemed to be closing in on me, but I was running in slow motion. It was no ordinary fire either. There was a black hole in the center where sounds of people wailing came pouring out and looked like it was going to swallow me whole.

I woke up well rested, despite the nightmare and the day began with weather I had yet to experience on Omega—rain in a slow drizzle that built into a heavy downpour. Low clouds hung over the land. I sat in the shelter of my lean-to and waited it out, using the time to pray for Lilith's safety until I could find her.

The rain lasted two days, but the river I camped beside never flooded and was now flowing like whitewater rapids. I wasted no time hopping in the water to ride my leaf-and-branch raft held together by palm-like fronds woven into rope. I plopped down cross-legged on the raft, which folded up slightly and hugged my legs like a semi-flat inner tube. BigBoy laid across my lap, ready to be drawn and fired. My hope was that the river would save me from walking for a day and deliver me closer to Mount Impossible. There was enough room for me to lie straight back and recline, so that's what I did in an attempt to blend in like a floating log of wood.

It was a pleasant and scenic river ride once the weather moved out and the clouds broke. I remained on the lookout for an unexpected waterfall or water creature, but for the first day it was smooth, fast sailing down a long and ever-flowing river. Lots of different flying creatures made their homes in the trees along the riverbanks, which were always lush with bushes and trees. It made sense. Again and again, I was reminded that life was life, water was water, and gravity was what held everything together on any planet. The rest is up to the nature of the living things that grow out of those perfect conditions, and what is most incredible to me is that the Omegans consider themselves to be spiritual brothers and sisters with humans. If that is true, then our souls all come from one source, but that would mean the same is also true for the Omim?

THE BOOK OF OMIM

PRECIOUS FIND

An Omim flying orb with a glowing liquid-filled body descended on and absorbed a fleeing Lilith, capturing her inside it. She struggled to break free but stopped and froze in a clawing position as the luminous ball bounced straight into the air and zoomed at high speed in the direction of Mount Impossible.

Lilith remained conscious, but she was physically paralyzed. Her eyes were wide open and terror filled, but all she could see was bright cloudy water all around. She felt the liquid filling her lungs, but there was no pain or difficulty breathing. Her heartbeat sounded as loud as a drum, and she looked exactly like a baby in the womb. Her clothing dissolved until she was naked. An umbilical cord formed at the bottom of the orb and slithered up through the cloudy water and attached to her belly button. Lilith's body jolted then relaxed.

The orb looked like a shooting star, racing across the land, passing over great valleys, lakes, waterfalls, between a deep rocky canyon and up steep, snow-covered hills until it reached the base of Mount Impossible and came to an unnatural solid black wall sticking out of the ground with snow packed around it. The orb hovered there while a hole opened big enough for it to pass through—it was pulled in and the hole closed again as if no hole was ever there.

The orb floated up through total blackness. Lilith's body settled on the bottom, so she was lying on her back, looking straight up. Through the smoky liquid, she could see a very bright speck of light far away, slowly getting bigger until it shined too bright and, like a disinfectant, cleared up all the fogginess in the water, leaving her suspended in a clear bubble that attached itself to a blinding bright circle. Looking through it, everything was fuzzy. She felt control of her body return, and she could move again. She tugged on the umbilical cord then swam upright, pressing and clawing at the bright light spot. The hole started to widen, and the entire orb was pulled up and in. Lilith panicked, swimming down to the bottom again to get away. The orb popped through the hole and came to rest balancing on a wide pedestal in a vast open room with shiny turquoise-colored walls. Her eyes adjusted to the light and fixated on other clear bubbles on pedestals with different trapped creatures inside them. Her heart raced. She was caught like a wild animal and didn't know what to do. The creature closest to her had two oblong eyes set far apart, a curved orange beak, and spiky yellow fur. It stared back at her.

Lilith looked down and realized she was naked and still attached at the cord, which grew into her body. She banged and clawed at the orb walls until she ran out of energy and resigned herself to sitting cross-legged on the bottom, where she eventually curled up in a ball like a baby. She lay there with both eyes open and her hair floating upward and then fell into a deep sleep.

Many hours later, she felt a presence and opened her eyes to see an angelic-looking human, neither male nor female, just mesmerizing and radiant, wearing a shiny golden cloak, staring at her through the orb. The being was taller and broad-shouldered compared to a human. It's perfect Omim face was long, with dark green eyes illuminated from within. Its head was bald, with a face that was hairless and smooth, not a pore to be seen, making the Omim appear to be a superior humanoid race that look identical to humans but without any flaws or obvious gender.

She stood up, appealing to it, one human being to another.

"Omim? You're human? Let me out of here. Help me, please!"

The Omim said nothing. It just watched the curious naked woman freaking out inside the orb and talking with her hands.

"Please let me out of here. I come in peace for all mankind. Look at me! I look like you. This is an amazing discovery. We are both human. Please."

The Omim placed one of its long fingered hands on the orb and Lilith sank down and pulled her legs up, reacting to a sudden feeling of doom that made her not want to make eye contact with this being anymore. Her fear grew as the golden cloaked Omim walked around the tank, inspecting her from every angle like she was some piece of meat on display. She was humiliated. The Omim lowered itself down and looked her in the eyes, but this time she couldn't look away. Instead, her mind was filled with images of this strange and powerful Omim being and herself sitting together in the most beautiful garden—a lush and glorious landscape containing flowers and vegetation from across the hospitable planets in the center of the galaxy. It took her hand in the dream and inspected it with its long, pointy fingers. She didn't even notice because she was captivated by a quivering flower patch nearby that looked like a burning fire one moment, then red and yellow arrow-shaped flowers the next.

Holding her wrist tightly, the Omim placed its index finger in the center of her palm and slowly pushed right through the center. She cried out in pain but couldn't escape. Blood splattered on its face as it twisted and turned until the Omim finger was all the way through and Lilith let out bloodcurdling screams. The Omim recaptured her direct attention with its eyes and smiled big before jamming the long finger all the way down—the umbilical cord detached itself from her belly, and the liquid started to drain through the bottom of the orb, freeing Lilith from the nightmare vision. She flailed away and was soon above water, violently puking up the liquid that had filled her lungs. The golden Omim stood back and watched with an intense stare as the last drops of liquid ran out. Lilith shivered like a frightened animal inside the orb.

The golden Omim raised its hand, and the orb levitated off the pedestal and fell in line behind it and a hideous looking black-cloaked Omim who watched from the side. They walked through a door that opened like a camera aperture with the orb following them into a long, dark hallway that led to a glaring white room in the distance.

Lilith didn't understand why the Omim beings didn't acknowledge her, didn't see that she was the same as them and reach out a helping hand. Instead, she was horrified and afraid that despite the physical similarities, the Omim were an entirely different breed, and that made the encounter more terrifying.

The orb floated into the white room and Lilith squinted while her eyes adjusted. It hovered over a large central pool filled with shimmering black liquid and settled down onto it. The orb dissolved away, and Lilith was left floating on her back in the middle. She felt her body being moved by an invisible force. Her arms were pulled up, and her legs were pulled open, so that she was totally exposed. She cried out, but the two strange, emotionless Omim beings just watched as her body was scanned and evaluated by a bright orb at the end of a fleshy snake that dropped down from the ceiling and shined onto her body—wherever it hit, her insides were fully visible as if she had no skin. When it passed over her face and revealed a skull, the golden Omim looked closely at the size of her cranium. Its intrigue deepened when the orb moved down over her heart and stopped there. Lilith looked down and could see it beating and pumping. She started to breathe heavily and could see her own lungs inflate and deflate rapidly. She was frightened and anxious, as any creature would be in these circumstances.

The orb moved more, passing over and exposing her guts and then stopped right at her abdomen, where a small, hollow space glowed. She tilted her head and looked down, knowing it was her uterus, wondering what was so interesting to the Omim. So far, they weren't really hurting her in any real way, just thoroughly examining, and that was to be expected, despite her fear. The pool slowly tilted forward and brought Lilith to an angle, but the shimmering liquid never spilled. She tried to move her arms to cover up, but was unable to lift anything but her head. The orb swiftly and suddenly pulled up and disappeared into the black ceiling.

The golden cloaked Omim stepped close to Lilith and stood before her in all its flawless perfection, looking into her eyes like a predator who just discovered its true prey. The Omim reached out with its long-fingered hand and grabbed her skull, causing her to pass out instantly.

THE ONE

LILITH AWOKE IN the softest bed she had ever slept in. Puffy white blankets and sheets were smooth, heavy, warm, and comforting. Her mind felt very foggy; she rubbed her eyes, yawned, and sat up to discover that the bed was floating in the center of a small, dome-shaped room, like a big bubble that was transparent as if it were floating among the clouds. The golden cloaked Omim was standing alone with its back to her, looking out toward the horizon where Omega's atmosphere and the darkness of deep space intersected. Its energy radiated into Lilith's mind, captivating her with its angelic presence. It knew she had awakened.

"Do you feel rested, Lilith?"

"How do you know my name?"

Lilith pulled the blankets up around her naked body, terrified but with nowhere to hide.

The golden Omim turned around and pulled back the hood, revealing the perfect flawless face of an androgynous super-being. This time she could see its face clearly and knew that it was not merely human; but something more, far superior and advanced.

"I already know everything about you, Lilith."

"Who are you?"

"I am Sheeol. I am the One."

She pulled the covers even tighter around her body. When eye to eye with Sheeol, it held out one of the long-fingered hands to help her out of bed. She looked at it with untrusting fear. Her body remembered something occurred with that hand, but it was too foggy in her mind.

"I have no clothes."

Sheeol said nothing. She took the hand anyway, climbed off, and stood facing it like a helpless naked child. The bed shrank down into a mist until it vanished.

"I am the One. There is no life without me."

Sheeol led her by the hand to the edge of the bubble, and she soon realized that this was the highest point in Omim City, far above the mountaintop and clouds. She looked down and saw two rings magically hovering around the giant skyscraper they stood atop, like the rings of Saturn. Down below was a magnificent garden filled with green grass. Vertigo made her hold on to Sheeol tightly, and she was mesmerized by the liquid softness of the cloak, which wrapped itself around her arms like it was holding her as well.

"Who..."

Sheeol picked her up with both hands and turned in a slow circle so she could see the entire view. "I am the One, and everything you see is my kingdom."

"This world?"

"This universe."

It set her down, and she backed away, feeling dread again and not understating where it was coming from. She used both hands to press on the transparent walls and maintain balance as she walked around the large circular room, looking down at Omim City through clouds beneath the floor. Her mind raced with a million questions at once, as if touching Sheeol activated a part of her brain that she'd never felt before.

Sheeol stood in the center and watched her every move, captivated by the way her naked body moved, her eyes and lips, the back of her neck. They were all characteristics unseen by any Omim, including the One. The female body was divine music come to life as she made her way around the surreal space, trapped and unable to get away. The spires and glittering lights below made it feel like she was falling when she looked down. She looked ill and faced Sheeol, still leaning on the window for support.

"What's happening to me?"

"You are with me now."

Sheeol placed one long-fingered hand across her stomach and looked her in the eyes. She understood, the blood drained from her face, and she fainted.

When her eyes opened again, she was lying beside an exotic flower patch in a tranquil garden. This time her father was sitting on the bench, admiring her from afar.

"Daddy?"

She pushed herself up into a sitting position and looked at him lovingly. He was a sight for her sore eyes to see, and for a brief moment, she forgot where she was. The trickle from a babbling brook that snaked through green and yellow lush grass, with fruit and nut trees and exotic flowers all around, soothed her senses.

She stood up and walked over to her dad. He stood to embrace her, morphing back into Sheeol right before the embrace. Lilith screamed and backed up.

"Be not afraid."

"How…?"

"I thought you would trust me more in that skin."

"That is not skin—that was my father. What did you do to him?"

"Your… father?"

"Everyone has a mother and a father where I come from."

"How many more of your kind are there?"

"Billions on one planet alone. How can you speak my language?"

Sheeol's eyes narrowed. Lilith was powerful and threatening, but she didn't know it.

"I bridged your mind when you went dark. I can see your past life experiences as if I lived them. You come from a red, rocky world, and you come in peace for all mankind. You arrived in a starship that is impressive for its primitive design. You came alone, escaping some tyranny… the memory is a little unclear."

Lilith snapped her head up and looked at Sheeol. He didn't mention her most recent memories. Not one word about Adam. His read of her memories ended when she got inside the hibernation chamber on Mars.

"I do come in peace. And I want you to make peace with the beings of this world that were here before you. Why can't they live free from tyranny?"

Sheeol's eyes turned a darker shade. "You are a lost child of a forgotten race. You will learn the Omim way, and will be the last of your kind to ever exist."

"But I am no threat to your kingdom."

"You possess the science to make the universe inside your fragile body, and I am the master of the universe. There is no life without me."

Lilith was entranced by Sheeol as he placed both of his hands on her belly.

"Are there no women in your kingdom?" she said.

"Omim defeated gender millions of years ago."

"How does your kind reproduce?"

"We don't. I create new life."

Sheeol pulled back his hands and lifted her chin up with his finger.

"And I move souls."

Sheeol stepped closer to her, backing her against a magnificent tree with golden willows and pink leaves hanging from its branches. She became paralyzed by his stare while he unfurled his long fingers.

"But your soul exists in violation of my creation."

He pointed the fingers forward and pushed right through her chest, into her heart, where he pinched and pulled out a white, gaseous substance with tiny jolts of lightning pulsating through it.

"Who… made… you?"

The substance didn't want to give as it smoked around his fingers and glowed with an unnatural bright light. He pulled the ball of light about six inches from her chest, with its tail still deep in her heart like a root. Lilith gasped, looking on as her life force was pulled from her body and she could see it with her own eyes for the first time.

"This is your soul. I can place it inside any skin that you desire. Eternal life of Omim can be yours."

After watching her squirm uncomfortably, unable to speak, in shock, he let her soul snap back and disappear into her chest. She fell to the ground gasping, grabbing her heart, looking up at him afraid. He had just held her soul in his wicked hand. The pain shocked her whole mind and body. She felt numb and deeply afraid. This was the first time she really knew her soul was more than just an abstraction, and it made her weep uncontrollably.

Sheeol sat down on the bench and watched with a grin on his face. He pitied the primitive human being who had her first true encounter with power beyond her understanding and knew that her feeble mind couldn't comprehend what just happened. She looked up at his grinning evil smile and shrieked when she realized Sheeol found pleasure in her suffering and confusion.

She closed her eyes and cried herself to sleep under the tree with the golden and pink leaves and willows, and awoke later to find herself in large round bed that overlooked a tiny floating island with a small waterfall somewhere high up in the Omim City tower.

She sat bolt upright and glanced around at the spacious and luxurious suite overlooking the garden far below. Pushing the blanket down, she was in a silken light-blue cloak now. An enchanting floral smell tickled her senses. She stepped out of the bed and walked through the opening to the outdoor shower oasis waterfall flowing down into the small pool. Gravity defying floating stones made a short path out to the pool. She put her foot down on the closest one and discovered that it was solid. Stepping across them, she tried to ignore the fact that many miles below was the ground level of Omim City. The view made her stop in the middle because she didn't see a single being in sight. Hundreds of thousands of Omim should be coming and going in this gigantic tower, but Sheeol's kingdom was eerily quiet and empty. She continued to the waterfall and found soap, shampoo, and a towel waiting. Creature comforts left for her by Sheeol.

After an outdoor bath, she explored her suite and couldn't find a way out. She moved toward a mirrored wall that opened up automatically, leading to a wardrobe of clothing as far as the eye could see and as high up too. It was a human wardrobe vault of impossible proportions that looked and smelled like the finest department stores on Mars where she grew up, inspired from her memory.

"Take anything you like. I want you to look and feel your best."

Lilith spun around to see Sheeol standing in the doorway, handsome and dark, the perfect man. Perfect in every way except that he wasn't a man.

"Is this all a dream?"

"Life is nothing but a dream that never ever has to end."

"Never?"

"I am the One. There is eternal life with me."

"What am I getting dressed for?"

"A feast in your honor, to welcome you to my kingdom."

"How will I communicate with your people?"

"All Omim understand your language now. They share my mind, and we all learn as one. Go. Choose whatever your heart desires. All of the finest brands are in there."

Lilith looked back into the department-store-sized space, and the first place her eyes went were the shoes. The rack seemed to go on for miles into the ceiling.

"This is all… real?"

"I made it all for you. Go on now. Everything your heart desires is waiting. I'll send a servant to escort you to the feast later."

"How much time do I have?"

"Time is an illusion my child. You'll be ready when you're ready, and that will be the right time."

Lilith was utterly charmed by Sheeol's mysterious ways now, and it filled her with a sense of wonder and possibility beyond human existence. The emotional roller coaster that interacting with the One caused was strange and impossible to comprehend, but it was real, and her physical body could not help but react. She was desired beyond any feeling of love experienced in the human world, and it made her want to please him in some way, to be a good guest and slowly convince Sheeol to abandon the reign of terror against the Omegans.

"I will look my best for you, and I cannot wait to learn more about your kingdom."

"And my kingdom awaits your soul."

The One savored manipulating Lilith's primitive mind. He watched her walk into the bright and shiny store space, captivated by all the objects of a woman's desire. Toys to pacify her feeble brain from ever realizing how powerful it truly was. He backed up and disappeared though a portal in the wall that opened behind him.

Lilith stood inside the surreal shopping space and walked to a marble table in the center that had a fruit basket in the center, bright golden plates with cheese, various small cakes and sweets. The generous layout was tempting to a girl raised on Mars, and it spoke loud and clear to her inner human nature and physical needs.

She nibbled on a piece of cheese, and it was the best bite she had ever tasted. Looking up and around, the store was one tall tower with floor after floor stocked with clothing and costumery. The highest level sparkled like diamonds because it overflowed with jewelry.

Lilith knew that heaven was not real but Omim City was.

Excited and curious, she strolled across the open space to what looked like beams of light shining down and dancing around in a close pattern. She stepped into the light, and it lifted her as if by magic to the first floor. She stepped out into an ocean of fantastical gowns all in her exact size and stood there with a huge smile across her face.

Lilith was never the princess growing up, but Sheeol made sure she felt like a queen in Omim City. After trying on so many items, she felt radiant in the gold leaf and pink willow dress that hugged her figure and accentuated her curves. The pink willows danced with every step, with the golden leaves beneath it creating a watery shimmer. The material was the same as Sheeol's cloak, and it felt like smooth human skin.

She stood in front of a golden mirror and slid a decorative crown onto her head as the final touch. It was an elaborate, twisted crown made of brilliant gold with little pink roses and thorns, and one black pyramid-shaped stone set in the center that drooped onto her forehead. A perfect fit.

Despite being a stranger in a strange world and a witness to Omim horrors against the Omegans, the civilized and luxurious treatment she was receiving charmed her into forgiving what happened in the garden earlier as a consequence of two different beings from two different worlds meeting in a future not of her design. She didn't forget about the plight of the Omegans, and she intentionally kept Adam as far from her thoughts as possible—but tonight as the guest of honor at a feast to celebrate her arrival, her only option was to be present, to be the ambassador of the human race she came to Omega to be. Lilith believed she could reason with Sheeol and be the one to bring peace to all the inhabitants of this wild and beautiful planet. It was her destiny. She studied herself in the mirror some more—a mirror that made her seem even more gorgeous, and she truly loved the reflection looking back. Her beauty paled in comparison to Sheeol's flawless perfection, which she suddenly wanted to be closer to, despite the darkness that she felt inside and tried to rationalize away. When she turned around, an Omim in an all-black cloak was inside her suite, waiting for her. His head was down low, so she could not see his face. He was slightly smaller than Sheeol but still taller than most human beings.

"Oh, hello. I didn't see you there."

"The One is ready for you. Follow me."

He stepped back, triggering the hidden portal in the wall to open. Standing inside it, he motioned for her to pass through. Lilith stepped into the grand hallway outside of her suite and looked up at the twenty-foot-tall ceiling that was aglow with a light similar to sunlight that illuminated the long and rounded hall.

The Omim started walking, and she followed behind him, excited to discover what might be right around the bend in this magnificent future city. Long, thin windows went from floor to ceiling, and she could see that Omim City had one ring around it at this level. Her suite was out on the ring but it didn't appear connected to the main tower. The floor was smooth and shiny, without a smudge or bit of dust anywhere to be seen. The walls were a kind of turquoise metal that was cool to the touch and kept the whole place at a steady temperature. Omim liked it cold. Her guide didn't speak, he just led, walking right down the middle with his head down as if a mindless drone.

They rounded a big turn, and Lilith could see large doors down the hall that looked like a giant star with an upside-down pyramid in the center that was split down the middle. It was dark inside except for a faint greenish glow. The festive feeling vanished, and she felt dread the closer she got to the doors. When her guide reached the entrance, he got down on his knees and bowed outside the door. Lilith stood beside him and saw Sheeol seated atop a throne on a wide pedestal in the center of the great room. The throne was a large green stone pyramid with a V-shaped section cut from the center where he sat with his head down, obscured by the hood of his golden cloak. His arms were stretched out on the armrests, with his long-fingered hands hanging loosely over the front. He was surrounded by eleven Omim dressed in all black cloaks that were seated one level down, facing him. Behind the throne was a wall of skulls and bones stretching from floor to ceiling that looked like a fossil with millions of creatures trapped inside it.

The eleven Omim sat in silent worship. The guide Omim stayed in the prostrate position, but Lilith just stood there, small and lost, ready for a party that was nothing like what she imagined it would be.

"Kneel before the One." Boomed Sheeol's voice, echoing in the cavernous room, a voice she felt in her bones. Without hesitation, she lowered herself down into the same position as her guide. Only then were they ordered to stand and approach the throne.

The mood inside was tense and dark, despite being a vast open space. Ornate etchings on pillars reached from the floor to the ceiling. She stepped toward the throne, expecting more Omim or inhabitants of Omim City than were present. But it was just Sheeol and his twelve silent apostles.

Sheeol pulled his hood back when she stood before him. Looking down, he smiled the same sinister grin he had in the garden while watching her suffer from an attack on her soul.

"You look radiant."

"Is this the feast?"

Sheeol stood up from his throne and walked down a short flight of steps to be face to face with her on the ground level. He touched her cheek with his long finger, and she recoiled before steeling herself and smiling back. He took both of her hands in his, looking her in the eyes.

"Tonight will begin the first steps in your transition to eternal Omim life. You will receive it in exchange for giving me the universe inside you."

"How?"

"You have been implanted with my Omim spirit and now carry my only begotten child in your primitive shell."

Using his finger, he pushed her face from left to right so she was looking at a large banquet table almost identical to one that would be used in the finest dining halls on Mars. It was long, made of reddish metal, but it had legs that looked like open-mouthed snakes curled up on the bottom with their bodies flowing up as if the table was being held level by the tips of their tails.

"I did this all for you."

Lilith looked at the banquet table overflowing with every human food imaginable, prepared and presented as in the finest restaurants. She turned back around and the twelve Omim in dark cloaks flanked Sheeol now.

"Be seated." Sheeol walked her to the head of the table and pulled back the chair. The other Omim filled in the seats on the sides, but Sheeol sat across from Lilith at the opposite end.

"All this food… it looks and smells so good."

"Fuel for your organic body, which will produce new flesh. Eat."

"I am so hungry," said Lilith, who picked up her plate, which was fine china. She piled on roasted chicken, grilled fish, vegetables, and bread—oh, how she missed bread. She got excited and took a big bite of the bread while still piling food on. She looked up and saw that they were all watching her.

"Aren't you going to eat?"

"Our bodies are not the same. We feast later," said Sheeol.

One of the black-cloaked Omim offered to pour her a glass of wine, but his face was hidden in the shadow of his cloak.

"May I?"

"Why, thank you."

She watched his perfect hands take a golden chalice and fill it with wine from a bottle. His hand lacked the long fingers of Sheeol, but they were without blemish or detail.

Lilith started to eat like she hasn't tasted real food in a thousand years, which was technically true, due to the distance she traveled through space and time to get here.

"You seem to be enjoying the meal."

"I am. How did you do this? How did you make a perfect-tasting chicken? This wine? How?"

"I am the One. I can make anything from your mind become real. You have had all this food before. It was in your memories."

Lilith looked down at the bottle of wine and read the label. It was a vintage Martian bottle from Musk Vineyards. The chicken was one she had at a family get-together when Earth relatives visited.

"I want to learn everything I can about Omim. I want to know your customs, what you eat," she said with all the curiosity of a scientist.

"There is no hunger in my kingdom."

Sheeol's grin returned. He radiated like an angel as the light-green glow from his throne hit the back of his head just so, creating a halo that awed Lilith. High above him, hovering glowing orbs flowed and moved around in the open space above and were hypnotic to Lilith. There was a structure to the dance, like the orbs were keeping time.

"If you don't eat, how do you stay alive? Everything has to eat something, even if it's just plant life."

Lilith sipped the wine and then downed the whole glass. When she set it down, the sound of the glass hitting the table made a very loud clink that echoed over and over again without end, and then time stood still.

Suddenly she was surrounded by the twelve black-cloaked Omim, who closed in on her. She could hear Sheeol in her mind again as if he was whispering inside her head. *"Resist me."*

Her breathing became heavy and labored as the twelve lifted her body and laid it on the dining table. The food was gone; now she was the only thing being served. Her head moved from side to side in a haze of a semiconsciousness. She was lucid but afraid and unable to move. Sheeol stood and watched as the twelve dark Omim removed her dress slowly and methodically, chanting in a bizarre tongue that had a musical sound to it. When her clothing was removed and she lay bare, the twelve dark Omim lifted her as if by magic, and she floated in the air. Her legs were open and her arms were held tight by two dark Omim keeping her palms up.

Sheeol rose into the air and landed on the table with a loud thud. He walked to Lilith floating in the middle and stood right between her open legs, so he was looking down at her terrified expression. He unfurled both of his hands and pointed them toward her. Both of his index fingers stretched and grew until he sank one pointed finger into her right wrist and one into her left.

Lilith's mouth opened, she moaned in agony, her head flailing while Sheeol lifted her body up by the wrist wounds and held her up high in the shape of a cross. His eyes burned like emerald fire, and her soul started to separate from her body in the form of a milky gas that radiated from her heart, dripped from her eye sockets, and tried to escape through her mouth and ears. A sad wailing sound came from her, like a musical instrument stretched to its limit, squealing for it to stop before all the strings break.

They were draining her of life. One by one, the dark Omim took turns breathing in parts of her soul with their mouths close to her naked body, drawing the milky gas into their body while Sheeol sucked the biggest taste straight from her heart. His body heaved and grew with each inhale.

Omim apostles howled like aroused beasts and raised their arms up high. Lilith was limp, seemingly dead but still breathing. Sheeol retracted his fingers and let her body fall to the table where it landed with a dull thud.

They left her lying there naked, alone and within an inch of her fragile human life.

Sheeol returned to his throne, and the Omim apostles reformed their circle around him. Sheeol used his fingers to pull apart his own chest, where only darkness existed. Glowing tendrils of Lilith's soul shot out of him and connected with the dark heart of every Omim. He tilted his head back, opened his jaw, and the sounds of Lilith's tortured soul came flooding out, echoing off the temple walls and stimulating the flying orbs into a frenzy of movement.

Lilith's eyes shot open, awakened by her own screaming soul's sounds. Her jaw trembled, terror physically manifesting itself on the human animal in a way that she never felt before. She was broken in two, right at the core, and found herself back in the luxurious suite, in the bed, naked and afraid but surrounded by physical comfort. She looked across the cold and lifeless room at a small marble pedestal overflowing with exotic fruits and drinks. She was parched and felt the dryness all the way down her throat. She pushed herself up and sat still for a moment, hugging her own body and rocking back and forth, with no clear recollection of what happened, then stood and walked to the food like a zombie.

Tears from a deep, unknown sadness rolled down her cheeks. Hands trembling, she reached for the fruit and bit into it. Blood-colored juice ran down her lips and dripped onto her breast, and one small dot splashed on the floor. The splash shape looked oddly like a heart that was violently ripped apart. She devoured the rest of the fruit in a rage and was soon covered in red stains as if she had just been stabbed over and over again. She closed her eyes and screamed at the top of her lungs.

When she opened them again, she was standing in a long, dim room in front of an illuminated tank holding featureless empty Omim shell bodies. They were suspended in a pinkish-red translucent liquid like suits hanging on a rack. Lilith looked into it with Sheeol standing right behind her, both hands on her shoulders. They were all identical muscular skins—statue of David perfection, but with no sexual anatomy. She was somehow clean again and wearing a white hooded cloak, which partially covered a large, deep-red gash running down the side of her face. There was less life in her eyes as she looked down at her wrists, at the holes Sheeol punctured with his fingers that were trying to heal, and then back to the skins on display in the tank. Sheeol stood behind her, observing, as she looked from her wounds to the submerged bodies.

"Why do you hurt me instead of heal me?"

"I cannot do it any other way. Your body was not made for eternity. You will have eternal life through me when I move your soul into a new shell, one I will make just for you. But first it must be drawn out slowly."

"Do you know who made me?"

Sheeol turned her around and held her head in his hands, cupping them like she was all his and there was nothing she could do about it.

"Nobody made you. But I will remake you better than how you evolved. I am the One, and only I have this power in the whole universe."

Lilith's expression darkened. What remained of her free-spirited way vanished. She was locked under a deep spell of despair that flowed from Sheeol directly into her.

"My heart hurts."

"It is hungry for that which doesn't exist. You will feel better after you're refreshed in the garden where I grow special fruit that can relieve your pain."

Sheeol pulled her under his arm and walked her out of the Omim body lab. She held on to him, but terror filled her eyes and she looked more like a prisoner. He cradled her like an evil and abusive father as they walked down the long, featureless hallway toward a bright light at the end.

The conditions in the garden were always splendid. Sheeol picked an apple from a tree and handed it to her. It was large, shiny, and perfect. The first fruit from home that she saw growing on Omega. She took it in both hands and sank her teeth in. The juices ran down her mouth, and her eyes awakened like someone who just ingested a powerful mind-altering substance, but she could only handle one bite. The apple dropped from her hands and rolled away while she took a deep breath and looked around, smiling at all the colors in the garden. She picked one of the star-shaped flowers from a nearby patch and inhaled its scent.

"Did you make all of these too?"

"Everything you see comes from my imagination into reality."

"They're so wonderful. Your imagination is so wonderful. I want to have a mind like yours."

She turned in a circle, taking in the sights as if seeing them for the first time now. She spread her arms and ran across the open field, taking in the sunshine that beamed through the upper rings of Omim City. Then she stopped and put her hands on her stomach, remembering, then spinning around to look at Sheeol, who stood watching her.

"If you have no reproductive organs, how am I pregnant?"

"Science, as you call it. I am the master of science."

"Science is truth."

"Indeed, my child. Science is truth. Science never lies."

Lilith walked over to a shimmering pond and looked in at her reflection, noticing the gash on her face for the first time. She reached up and touched it, keeping her gaze fixed on the water. Sheeol cast a shadow that loomed beside her and looked like an executioner standing by.

"When do I get a new face?"

"After our child is ripe."

"If you can create life, why am I having your baby the human way?"

"The world you came from needs an Omim king to be bring human animals into line. Once there is Omim in the blood, your kind will begin to transition without knowing."

Lilith turned around and looked at Sheeol. He had that dark smile again—a smile that made her human spirit want to run and hide.

"What about me?"

"You will be Lilith, queen of the universe, and our son will establish the new kingdom on your home world. One that is ordered around science and Omim."

"I don't remember where I came from."

"Your world was purposely hidden from me but I will find it."

"I feel sleepy again."

"Rest now so your transitioning soul can adjust."

"Why did you hurt me last night?"

"Pain is part of the transformation. Eternal life can only be earned through pain and suffering first, which loosens the soul for transfer."

"Can I rest here in the garden? It is so lovely and warm."

"Yes. And you may eat any of the fruit. The more you eat, the faster your transition will become."

Lilith walked off through the garden, strolling and taking in the patterns of flowers and perfection in each blade of grass. Sheeol watched for a moment, always the predator eyeing his prey. He will devour her in small bites, extracting her essence bit by bit over time because in all of the millennia that had passed, nothing tasted as sweet as the naive human soul. Sheeol was determined to find every last one of them.

Sheeol turned and walked in the opposite direction, toward the long ramp into the central tower of Omim City. His golden cloak shimmered, and he cast an unnaturally long shadow across the garden, disfigured and uneven. The only way to tell the difference between a human and an Omim was by the shadow they cast.

Lilith was drawn to the shimmering pond by dancing lights on the water's surface. She sat down on a sparkling diamond rock and dipped her toes in like a lonely child. Looking at the reflection, she could see the wound on her face again, but this time it made her heart fill with sadness, a psychological memory tied to a physical experience that was cloudy in her mind. When she touched it again, an image flashed into her thoughts —she was suspended in the air, feeling tremendous turmoil and agony. One of the twelve scratched her across the face like he was peeling open an orange. She snapped out of it when a hideous face with pitch-black eyes appeared in the water like a ghost. She leapt away from the water, frightened and suddenly hungry again. She searched for fruit and spotted the apple tree.

She walked over and picked one, took a bite, and had to spit it out. The apple was black on the inside, pitch black like the darkest night. Her loneliness and helplessness only increased her despair and made her soul all the more delicious to the Omim—but only Sheeol knew that.

Overcome with a heavy feeling, she continued the short distance to the golden willow, lay down under it, and fell fast asleep curled up in a ball, sucking her thumb like a frightened, abandoned child lost in the garden of Eden.

MIND-BRIDGE

SHEEOL ENTERED THE mind-bridge lab. Diemus, his one and only semi-autonomous dark Omim, stood in front of a wall-sized opening at the end that appeared as if it looked into the Martian base where the Saganites once lived. It was Lilith's memories playing out in extreme reality before them, just on the other side of the missing wall.

Diemus sensed Sheeol's presence, turned, bowed, and kept his head down.

"My Lord."

"You harmed the human during the feeding last night. If you go too far again, I will cast you into the fire of no return and she will replace you by my side."

"I never tasted a spirit so sweet and pure. It made me feel strange, and I got carried away."

"Raise your head, Diemus."

Diemus stood and pulled back his black hood. His eyes were black, and his face looked hardened and wicked compared to Sheeol's androgynous perfection.

"There's a world full of humans like her out there. We can feed on them and breed our kind again the primitive way and stop feeding on the lower creatures whose energy is never enough."

"Why would we desire to go back into nature when we are outside of it?"

"It is our destiny to again become flesh. When an Omim mind rules every intelligent being's heart, we will have created existence as it should have always been."

"You are the One," stated Diemus.

"I am. Did you locate the human world yet?"

Diemus turned back to the wall scene and walked toward it.

"I'm still searching. These beings were cave dwellers just like the primitives that inhabit this planet. Some of her memories are unclear. Something cut them off over a long period before her arrival here. There is a mysterious gap."

Sheeol walked closer to the scene playing out as if in a room on the other side of a glassless window. Diemus moved to his side, looking at the scene too.

"My Lord, the humans look like you. How did that happen?"

"Lilith is a descendant of the Ancient One who made their kind by leaving a spark of himself in each before he was divided in three by me. I believed we eliminated every last abomination, including their vile and disgusting maker, long before I granted eternal life to you. I may have miscalculated his tenacity to undermine the Omim order."

"How did their maker escape the fire of no return? It is not possible, even for you."

"Because he made that fire. He crafted death as the passage to being reborn in his company, and for that reason, he was banished from the core by me."

"You are the One."

"I am! And I will transform these hideous hybrids by becoming a little like them in the flesh, in order to feed off of their misery along the way."

"Mortal?"

Sheeol faced Diemus and grinned that same devious smile that is evil personified.

"When Omim become human and multiply like humans, the universe will be conquered from within and all intelligent beings will worship me."

"You are the One." said Diemus. "But there is another human who arrived with Lilith. A different kind."

Diemus led Sheeol into an adjoining mind bridge where another scene was playing out.

"This just came in from Trax. He was wandering and lost when a collector found him." "How could you lose Trax?"

"Something happened. His mind shut off, and the memories failed to return until today."

The memory on display was Adam's surprised reaction when the beast started to speak inside his head.

"This one is different, my Lord. The humans possess greater intelligence than first imagined."

They watched the memory play out of Adam climbing onto the back of the beast and then the view he saw while running through the land. The memory ended with Madu raising the weapon and pulling the trigger, then it went black.

"This is the work of Drade… He summoned them here to unseat me. Where is this other human now?"

"I haven't found him, and he's yet to be trapped."

"When he is found, bring him to me unharmed and alive."

"Yes, my Lord."

Diemus lowered his head and walked back into the next room to carry out the order. Sheeol stood still before the scene as the beast's memory restarted from the top, beginning with the surprised look on Adam's face when they first met. Sheeol froze the memory with a hand motion and walked right up to Adam's hyper-real face and stood looking him in the eyes.

"Who are you?"

Sheeol kept his stare fixed on Adam. Repulsed by his imperfect nose, his bright, uneven eyes and wild hair. Sheeol saw a beast mixed with a divine being, and it made his mind erupt with rage at what the maker had done without him knowing. His eyes narrowed into focused, determined anger. Humans should not exist, and Sheeol will remake them as his own.

Adam's face started to crack and split down the middle, a small hairline fracture that moved like broken glass, traveling straight down until it reached his heart, where his body—the hyper-real image—broke apart in the center of his chest, opening the cavity. A bright light shot out that blinded Sheeol. He covered his eyes and reeled back in pain. The light hurt him before the simulation faded out and died. The space where the scene once played was now black and formless. Sheeol stared into that darkness like he saw something he never expected to see again. Like he just saw a ghost.

He turned around and walked out of the lab, across the hall to the transparent side of the ring, where he looked down and spotted Lilith still curled up, sleeping under the golden tree. His hatred for the weakness in humans was compounded by the fact that what he saw in Adam's eyes and heart unsettled his absolute certainty about his reign. The One had never seen a real human man, formed by the maker, in his own image and likeness—a creature of both flesh and spirit that appeared billions of years after the maker disappeared and should not exist. He didn't even know the cancer was out there until it arrived in his city of perfection. For the One not to know something was a crime against his sovereignty over consciousness itself.

Sheeol walked onto the portal and rode it all the way up to his private dome. He stepped inside and went to the opposite side, looking down toward the mountainous regions where Adam and Lilith were before she was captured. Way off in the distance, sunlight bounced off ocean mist and created a faint rainbow that stretched across the valley, but it was upside down and looked exactly like a smile, mocking him in the Omegan sky.

He returned to his throne determined to undermine and destroy the human world once it was found. Eleven Omim apostles were in their seats below him with their heads down in what looked like prayer but was really a temporary stasis put upon them by Sheeol.

Diemus entered the temple and walked toward the throne with his head low. When he reached the One, he knelt.

"Speak, Diemus."

"I have determined the human world is hidden at the end of a spiral arm at the farthest point away from the core. I have yet to locate its precise home star system."

"The humans were created to erode Omim power."

"Are the human beings a threat to Omim?"

"Nothing threatens my kingdom and survives. Eliminating them will take more than our science and power. It will take deception long enough to snuff out the ember of the original fire they all carry in their blood-filled hearts."

"That why Lilith's soul tastes so different."

Sheeol lifted up Diemus' head with his long index finger and looked him in his eyes.

"That is the taste of the maker who I destroyed. It can be addictive and draw you into his death cult. Do not be deceived by the false power you feel from it."

"You are the One."

"I am the One. Now go and find the precise location of their world, and do not come back until you do."

Diemus bowed, turned, and walked out of the temple. The other eleven Omim remained silent with their heads down in their seats. They were inanimate and appeared lifeless until Sheeol stood and raised his arms, making the Omim stand like marionettes controlled by invisible strings.

"Rise, my sons. The enemy is in our presence, trying to reestablish his tyranny of death into new life. Begin preparations to move to the human world."

"Yes, my Lord," said the eleven Omim in unison before turning around like soldiers and walking out of the temple in a straight line.

"I am the One!" boomed Sheeol's voice like thunder that carried out into the wind and shook the mountains.

THE BOOK OF
ADAM

PART TWO: THE MAN

I WOKE UP HEARING a voice in the clouds, deep and terrifying, rumbling like thunder across the sky. The only word I could make out was "one," and at first, I thought my mind was playing tricks on me again. I was hungry and had been riding the river that drew me closer to Mount Impossible for three straight days. The climate dramatically changed for the cooler overnight, and I was now approaching the mouth of a large, foggy lake with tall purple and white crystals jetting out of the water, reflecting bits of morning sunlight, making the whole place sparkle and shimmer. I sat up and cleared my head. The fog was low around me, making it difficult to see more than ten feet straight ahead. I listened carefully to the sky but only heard the smooth sound of my raft gliding through calmer water. When I neared a crystal, I used the barrel of BigBoy to push away, always ready to fire if the crystal turned out to be a living thing instead of what it appeared to be. I wished I had gotten out when I could see the shore, but it was too late for that now.

I floated toward a large tunnel straight ahead where the river ran through the mountain pass. I could see that it was tall and wide, with light coming from somewhere on the other side, so I decided to let the water pull me, as long as I was heading in the right direction. I had enough to nibble on for another day, and I had mastered the balancing act of urinating over the side so I could maintain my ride. The tunnel was dark where I entered, so I used BigBoy for light and had confidence that I could scare or kill anything with it. My mind was really worried for Lilith. I believed in my heart of hearts that the Omim captured her alive and that she was still alive.

My raft drifted into the cave. Water trickled down through gaps in the sides, and one large waterfall pounded into the river from a hole in the stone to my far right. There were wide holes in the top that let some light shine down too, creating brilliant pillars where flying creatures seemed to enjoy the warmth of the rays. They looked like birds from here, swooping in and out of the light beam, singing and whistling in an organized dance. When the raft got deep enough inside the cave, the river bent to the left, and I noticed a dry area to the right with an unnatural black column going from the water's edge, straight through the rock above, and to somewhere on the outside. I used my hands to paddle toward it, since the water was pulling me the other way. When I managed to get close, I used the butt of BigBoy to pull myself ashore and pull the raft onto a short pebble-and-rock area that backed up against stone walls.

The black column was not natural and not Omegan. It was very shiny and as wide as a small building back home, but also razor thin. The closer I got to it, the more I felt that it was pulling at me, so I stopped and knelt with BigBoy aimed, just observing the column in silence. The distant echo of the happy flying creatures bounced around the cave. I looked up and studied how the column seemed to vanish right into the rock, not like the rock was cut around it but like it disappeared where the two meet. I picked up a stone and threw it at the column and watched it bounce off. Next, I fished around deep in my leg pocket and pulled out my SIA challenge coin we used to verify status during undercover missions. It was made of metal that would stick to any magnet. I flicked it at the column and missed hitting the wall by about two feet. I figured that was close enough to pull the coin in if it were magnetized, so I stood up to retrieve it.

As I took my third step forward, a hole opened up on the column like a gateway to another dimension, swirling bluish-white light patterns with pull. I tried to move back, but it sucked me right in, repelling BigBoy off its strap and pulling me into a dark void, where I floated upward. My right arm with the fedcom attached however, didn't want to come in. Caught between a rock and a bizarre place hurt like hell. The force pulling me upward was powerful, and all I could do was cry out in agony as the fedcom was violently ripped off of my forearm and crashed to the ground, covered in blood, next to BigBoy and my challenge coin. The hole slammed shut and my ride accelerated, sending me tumbling much higher than I knew the column to be. There was no oxygen. I struggled to hold my breath when I really wanted to scream. All of my clothing dissolved until I was naked from head to toe. I looked up and saw a rapidly approaching white light.

To my amazement, the bleeding cuts in my arm healed as if nothing were ever attached. Suddenly I was pressed right up next to a bright white oval of light, flat against it, like a bug on a windshield. It opened like a flower and spit me out into a very large room. Dozens of globes on pedestals held wild beasts inside them, but on my pedestal, I didn't have one around me. I was lying on top of a flat, cold surface with the dark hole beneath me and couldn't press my hand back through, no matter how hard I tried. Knowing I was captured and couldn't just sit here naked and shivering, I slid down off the platform and landed on the ice cold floor.

The room was huge. I don't know how many of those traps are set around Omega, but there were so many different species being kept that I wondered if that's why wildlife wasn't more abundant across the lands. As far as I could see, there were trapped animals inside clear orbs filled with liquid, and all of them seemed shocked when a naked human man went streaking past, searching for a place to hide. My priority was simply not being discovered and finding someplace warm.

I stayed low and just kept going in the same direction, heading toward a turquoise-colored wall that stretched hundreds of feet into the air, hoping the holes lining the top were vents I could fit into. I crept down and crawled along the floor like a dog, looking for cover in any nook or little area I might be able to climb into or get behind. The floor's extreme cold temperature froze and burned my skin. My body tried to warm itself, and I broke into a sudden shiver. The cold took over my whole being. I stopped crawling and fell to my side. I couldn't believe that I might freeze to death right there.

I heard a muted banging sound coming from somewhere behind me. I tilted my head back and saw a familiar face looking down—an Omegan was inside one of the clear round orbs. Amazed and with love in its beady eyes, it banged at the bubble to try to get my attention. I was shaking violently. My ability to think straight was fading, but somehow, by some miracle, I was able to pull myself up and talk to the Omegan.

"*Bonjour*," it said.

"I-I-I… know Drade."

"Earth savior?"

"Yes, yes Earth savior. Can you help? I'm going to f-f-f-freeze to death out here. It's too cold."

"Get me free, and I can show the way."

"H-h-how?"

"Push."

With my body shaking and my hands like frozen sticks, I pushed all of my weight into the bubble, but it didn't budge. I tried again, pressing my shoulders up and into the area where it was rounded, and the thing flipped right off, fell to the floor, and dissipated. The Omegan leapt down and caught me right as I fell from being frozen. She dragged my contorted body across the room toward the turquoise wall. I have never been that cold in my life. It felt like I was no longer in control of my thoughts. Everything was moving slow, blurry. The last thing I remembered was being dragged into a section of the wall that was removed by the Omegan and then put back from the inside of a secret hollow area. When we were in between the wall, I felt warmth burning back into me that made my whole body shiver. I was pulled about a hundred yards in and then found myself inside a big open space, warm and big enough for me to stand in, with a network of different crawl spaces going in and out of it. I sat up and took deep breaths of the warm air. The Omegan sat patiently across from me with a big smile on its face.

"I Nandee."

"I—I'm Adam."

"You came to kill the One."

"I came to find the female from my planet. Her name is Lilith, and she was caught by the Omim."

"You no here to kill Sheeol?"

"What's a Sheeol?"

"The One."

"Never heard of him—it. But the one thing I need right now is something to wear. My body isn't made for this."

Nandee looked around the space, her eyes narrowing on a shadowy corner where odds and ends were left by Omegans passing through. The Omegans were like highly intelligent insects with their own secret tunnel networks and hiding spots. Nandee handed me a smelly old pile of Omegan slave garments that I fitted around my waist like a towel. Its odor was ridiculously foul, but the material was strong and held, giving me the look of a caveman trapped in a future maze.

"Thank you, Nandee. I feel more like a human again."

"You are savior?"

"I… I am. I didn't know it until I arrived, but I guess that is my fate."

"Omim rule the universe."

"I didn't say I was going to win. But I won't go down without a fight. Us humans, we're scrappy like that."

"Omim live for all time."

"Tell me more."

"Omim is energy and intelligence that rules all life in the universe."

"Immortal, all-powerful beings? And you think humans will save you from them?"

"Omim killed God," she declared with a bluntness that pierced my heart and shattered my perceptions. I felt pain hearing those words, lost for a moment in total disbelief, and the creeping horror of it being a possibility really hit me hard. Before I could respond, the whole room started to hum like some very large machine had just started above us.

"Collectors are going out, Omim are angry." she said. The decibels were ear-piercing, and I had to cover both of mine. Nandee pulled me by the loincloth to a new tunnel where, we got down and crawled as fast as we could down a long, dark, sloping tube that seemed to go on for a mile. It was completely black, but I could feel that the place was chiseled out by hand. The humming sound faded behind us down to a low rumble that lasted for the duration of our getaway. The tunnel turned and rounded down until we soon arrived someplace where the ground flattened out and became soft, made of dirt. Nandee stopped and faced me in the crammed dirt cave. "You have to be very quiet here."

"Okay."

"Stay in shadows with me."

"Where are we?"

"This is Omim City. Stay very close to me."

She crawled forward, using her shoulder to move aside a sliding rock shrouded by shrubs, revealing a small hole in the ground through which I could see the ground level of Omim City. I knew we had crawled down, but I had no idea how far down. Most of my senses about time and distance were getting harder to rely on. Nandee squirmed her body through and waited for me, her little Omegan hands calling me out in rapid waves. I had to get on my stomach to squeeze through the opening, but the minute my head popped out, I was physically in Omim City at the ground level.

I could tell that nothing I knew so far made any sense. It was nighttime. I squatted there against a vine-covered wall like a primitive man seeing the distant future of his own world. The place looked like a high tech outpost of an advanced human civilization with dazzling architecture that defied gravity. At the center of Omim City stood one soaring, monolithic, futuristic tower. The ground level where we currently were looked like a garden of Eden in the glow of starlight. It smelled of sweet perfume and floral air. The plants and trees were perfectly manicured and set among gentle rolling hills. It was as if an alien super-civilization had grown out of a piece of heaven and was balancing it all atop this mountain. I was captivated by the sheer size.

There was a distant vocal chant in the air. Some kind of ritual was going on in the middle of the garden, about two hundred yards away, where a dark and ominous red light shot up from the ground. Humanoid aliens huddled around the red light. They didn't look like giants, they appeared to be slightly larger than men.

"Is that the Omim?" I whispered to Nandee. That's when we heard a horrible, prolonged, bloodcurdling scream, horrific and sad, like a life was just violently ended in the most unjust way.

"Yes, Omim," whispered Nandee, her head down, saddened, tugging at me to follow her.

"What are they doing?"

"Sacrifice."

"Sacrifice? What?"

"Please, we must get far from here now."

"Hang on."

I crept though the garden until I could get a better vantage point and see more clearly what was going on. I came to a strange tree with white bark with golden willows and pink leaves that sparkled in the reflection of the lights from above. I jumped up, grabbed a branch, and pulled myself into the tree, climbing high enough to see what they were gathered around.

It was a hole in the ground, about the size of a small pool, and the light coming from inside was glowing orange and dark red. I saw black-cloaked Omim gathered with their heads bowed down. One Omim wearing a golden cloak stood directly in front of the hole, holding the limp dead body of an Omegan above his head like a true sacrificial offering. After a moment, the golden Omim threw the body down into the pit then held both hands up to the sky. The others all bowed their heads to the ground and stayed that way until the golden one lowered his hands.

When they stood up, I noticed one light-blue cloak among the black ones. I could tell right away that it was Lilith. I wanted to jump down and run to her, but I knew better. There's no way Lilith would participate in a sacrifice of the very creatures she came to save. Why would such an obviously advanced race of beings need to sacrifice anything?

"Please, Savior. You can't stay here."

I looked down at a panic-stricken Nandee looking up at me.

"We go now, or you'll be next."

"But that's Lilith. She's with them."

"Omim take souls. Come now. We get away from here."

Nandee took off running back the way we came, moving along the shadowy side border of Omim City, rounding through the thickest part of the garden.

I stayed hidden in my perch as the procession with Lilith and the Omim in the golden cloak in the center, walked toward a long ramp that went into the central tower. I started to make the climb down when the golden cloaked man suddenly looked in my direction. I froze, and a heavy feeling of doom crept in on me. I felt fear coming from inside my own heart, and I broke into a sweat. When it looked away, the feeling left.

I remained still until they all made the long walk up the ramp and entered the tower. Noise came from the glowing pit as a group of Omegan slaves sealed it and the bright light that shot straight into the sky was no longer. I lingered in my spot for a moment, taking in as much as I could of this garden level and making mental notes of the lay of the land before I slid down form the tree and ran off in the direction that Nandee went. She was still waiting for me, hiding along the thorny growth on the walls. She said nothing and waved at me to follow her again. We ran around to the back side of the tower and passed through a portal door.

We stepped inside a dimly lit wing where the walls looked like they had glowing blue veins running through them—thin lines of light weaving from the ground up in a geometric pattern that ended so far up that it looked like a vortex. Nandee pulled me down a darkened corridor that was also softly lit the same way.

"Where are we?"

"Shhh."

She hurried down the corridor, and I noticed how human her body was. Its curves and shape were similar to any human female as she moved in graceful silence, leading me somewhere. I ran on the front pads of my feet to make less noise. The corridor rounded, and soon we came to an arched doorway lit in a dark-red glow. Crying and moaning echoed from inside a deep, cavernous room below. Omim City was starting to feel more and more like hell to me. Nandee slowed and walked behind me, pushing gently at my back.

"This is what Omim do to us."

I stepped through the arch and was looking down into a giant pit. A room full of Omegans of all ages and sizes were lying shoulder to shoulder on long slabs. Each Omegan was affixed by a humanlike hand that grew out of the slab, its long fingers gripped each head with its tips. Each Omegan was experiencing terror and pain, unable to move freely as collars of white beams of laser light pinned down their necks. They cried out with their eyes closed, and I couldn't stand what I was hearing. I felt the need to break them all free but knew that would be suicide. Omegans were helpless, starved prisoners of a cruel alien master race that showed up unannounced, took over their world, and subjugated their people. Lilith was who I was really here for. Nandee pulled me into a dark shadow, just out of sight, so we could talk.

"What is this awful place?"

"The nursery."

"Why are these Omegans being tortured and kept down here?"

"They are sacrifice, but first they suffer nightmares."

"Why so cruel?"

"The more terrified they are, the better the Omim like it."

"Nandee! Get away from there!" said an elder Omegan standing just outside the archway. Nandee pulled me out of the shadow with her, and the old Omegan saw me and bowed down, terrified, presuming I was an Omim.

"Have no fear, Uncle. This is human savior."

The old Omegan looked me up and down and realized I was not Omim. He was dressed in a servant outfit that was different from the other Omegans, who all wore primitive clothing. It was a purple cloak of Omim design, and he seemed shocked and relieved to see me and started to tear up.

"Is it really you? Savior? We have waited so long for your arrival."

And in a very human moment, the old Omegan came close and hugged me. I embraced him while Nandee looked on, smiling.

"When did you land here? How did you find us?" Uncle asked me.

I landed about twenty Omegan suns ago and didn't arrive alone. After meeting Drade and learning of your slavery, I got separated from my partner who was captured by the Omim."

"You saw Lord Drade? May his peaceful spirit endure, oh merciful one."

Uncle said a prayer—the first prayer I saw an Omegan make to a being that was not me or Lilith. Omegans were religious creatures that understood the nature and truth of the same God as humans. I reached my hands out to pray with him. He put his in mine, and we looked each other. He said his prayer, and I said mine, but somehow, we knew we were appealing to the same being.

Uncle looked at me as if just realizing I was almost naked except for the loincloth.

"You can't be seen like that, Savior. Nandee, get him one of the Omim cloaks."

"But—"

"Just do it. We will make another before it's needed by the masters."

"Uncle, have you seen the female who looks like me?"

"All the Omim look like you."

"What do you mean?"

"They are your kind. When they first arrived, we thought they were from the world that sent the golden sky disc."

"I don't understand."

"Drade said that Omim are corrupted humans, from another line."

I didn't want to show how insane that sounded to me, so I remained stoic for their benefit. Nandee returned with a folded black cloak in her arms and handed it to me. It turned out lucky for me that she was one of the workers who happened to get trapped when she ventured too far outside of Omim City trying to gather a special herb that Omegans use to treat their mental anguish and suffering. I took the cloak, which was smooth but not like silk, more like the softest skin, but it acted like fabric and felt heavy. I unfolded it and slid it over my head while putting my arms through the holes. When it was all the way down, the cloak rested on my shoulders with the hood covering my head. It felt like a perfect fit and was comfortable beyond description.

"What about his feet?" said Nandee.

Uncle looked down and shook his head. "Ah, they are not the same."

"What do Omim feet look like?"

"Cloven." He said.

I looked down and moved the robe. It covered my feet for the most part and kept my whole body warm.

"Now you blend in, Savior. We are blessed that you are here to free us."

I didn't want to tell him that I had no idea how I was supposed to save them, just that I knew I had to try. He told me when the Omim take over, adult Omegans have to participate in the birth and then enslavement and murder of their offspring to keep the Omim alive, and it filled me with a quiet rage that deepened my desire to try to fulfill the prophecy I didn't ask for. What kind of super intelligence could evolve into this pure, systematic evil that existed on the energy of innocent souls? I accepted that making it home was improbable, and became determined to do as much damage as humanly possible to the Omim.

"If I am going to save anyone, first I need to know where they're keeping the woman from my world who arrived with me, and where the galactic broadcaster is that Drade used to send the message to Earth."

"I'm sorry, Savior. I don't know where the message was sent from as I am not allowed above this floor, but I see the other human in the garden during the day. Always alone. Always crying."

"The garden, right outside of here?"

"It is where the One likes to torture her."

My fists tightened and I clenched my teeth at the thought of Lilith being tortured by those cloaked demons I saw outside. I knew I had to work in stealth mode until I could identify a weakness in the Omim. I had to lurk around this evil towering compound without being discovered because Omim were advanced beyond my wildest dreams and so powerful that Omegans accepted and participated in the murderous sacrifice of their people because they were helpless against it. The wailing and crying sounds of the sacrificial lambs one room over was horrific and constant, but we just talked as if it was another workday in Omim City for Uncle and Nandee.

"What is that strange hand doing that is holding them into place?"

"It instills fear and sadness inside the heart and mind, to increase the potency of the soul. The more terrified we are, the more the Omim like it when sacrifice happens because it extends their own life force even longer."

Until that moment, the question never crossed my mind as to how or why the Omim existed, and I could feel the gravity of what Uncle was about to say before the words left his mouth.

"Omim feed off the souls of other beings until they die and then cast the body into the eternal fire."

"How do they feed off souls? You can't see someone's soul."

"The One has a way of draining the life force of others. It is what he's doing to the other human you seek and it is unstoppable."

"Why are you all still alive?"

"We are the unlucky who work until we are called to sacrifice."

"All of you?"

"All of us, until we are gone."

"Then what?"

"Then the Omim will find a new world."

"How many Omim are there?"

"The One and his twelve apostles."

I lowered my head and said a small prayer for Earth and Lilith, who was being kept and used by these monsters. She was young and still had a pure soul—even I as a human man could tell that she was full of life.

"This whole place, this whole towering monolith of evil only has thirteen Omim? Where is everyone else?"

"According to legend, they ate their own before arriving here."

I was horrified but not surprised because it was common knowledge among religious humans that evil is a self-defeating power and must be avoided so that it can die out. The technology that makes eternal life possible for the Omim also created the need to endlessly search for new life to consume so that evil can live. Despite their power, I was starting to uncover a weakness in their small number.

"If I could get back to the black wall that transported me here, I could retrieve my weapon and destroy this whole diabolical tower with it."

Uncle tilted his head, confused.

"He was caught by a species trap. They're everywhere again like when the Omim first arrived," said Nandee.

"Do you remember where you were when it captured you?" asked Uncle.

"I rode a river for days that led into a lake with giant crystals sticking out, and encountered a solid black wall beached inside a cave that I floated into."

Uncle looked at Nandee, said something, and they agreed that it had to be a place they called Matoon. He was suspicious of my claim about BigBoy.

"What weapon can defeat the Omim? There is nothing that can end their power but the fire of no return and Drade's prophecy says only a human being can throw them into the fire."

"I call it BigBoy. It creates the fire of no return and shoots it across a great distance."

"I will find your weapon, Savior. I know that lake, and I know all the ways in and out," said Nandee.

"You'll kill yourself if you hold it the wrong way. It's as long as your whole body."

"I will be careful."

"When you find it, carry it by the strap; that's the safest way. And don't pull the trigger. Don't even touch the middle of it."

"Trigger?"

I demonstrated with my hand, using my finger to show what I meant. Nandee understood.

"I'm going to try and locate Lilith while you search for BigBoy."

"Wearing the cloak, you will be able to ride the portals and blend in with the Omim. Your human companion is being kept somewhere in the upper ring."

I clenched both fists, and my knuckles cracked. "Show me how to get there?"

"You will find three portals in the hall. I don't know where they each go, but they will take you up into the tower."

I looked at Nandee, who was wide-eyed with anticipation, ready to move.

"If you find my weapon, where can I find you?"

"Where we snuck in, behind the golden tree. I will hide it in the tunnel there."

"Be safe, and please… don't get caught."

"I run like the wind for you, Savior."

Nandee took off around the corner before I could say goodbye.

The whole time, the moaning and crying from the imprisoned and tortured Omegans was loud and constant. Like standing there talking while people were being murdered.

"Be careful, keep your head down, and try to blend in. And thank you, human."

"Pray for me, and thank God if I succeed."

Uncle bowed to me, and then we parted ways. The fact that there were only thirteen Omim was unsettling to me, considering the size of Omim City. On the human world, there were once twelve apostles who spread a message of peace and harmony though a mysterious relationship with the son of the Creator of the universe. On Omega, it was the reverse. The evil one and his twelve Omim took over an entire world and all its creatures to feed Sheeol's life force, the One who gave them life through him. In the animal kingdom, the lesser creatures are food for the more advanced creatures, and only now, stranded on another planet far from every human reality I know, it is clear that the same food chain exists on a supernatural level, and the Omim have mastered the dark science as a means to eternal life.

Very few people on Earth kept the ancient religious traditions when I left, and if the Omim ever arrived, they wouldn't have to conquer anyone, just impress humanity with their transhumanist promise of eternal life through science. That is what the most powerful and influential humans have been trying to achieve with varying degrees of success as long as I can remember, but nobody has ever cracked the code—yet.

I began down the corridor, determined to rescue Lilith before they capture me, kill me, and find our home. Liberating the Omegans was not exactly the purpose I was seeking after retirement from the SIA, but it became my purpose, the more I learned about the Omim and their wicked way of living off the souls of others. To be born with an innocent spirit full of life-giving energy and potential, only to have it captured and milked to extend the life of superior beings was an iteration of evil I would never expect from such an advanced race with obvious scientific mastery. When humans imagine superior beings, we always presume they will have bigger weapons because this is really a reflection of who we are, but the reality is that the Omim are far more sinister than that. Their life-extending technique relies on healthy supply of new souls to drain and devour their energy. Omim City was quite literally hell on Omega for every Omegan. No wonder they were desperate for help. Theirs was a desperate situation for the future of human beings now too.

The lower corridors of the central tower were dimly lit with glowing bluish veins in the walls everywhere. The further I got away from the wailing Omegan sounds, the better. I approached three of the black slabs, which I now knew were just elevator portals. There was no sign marking them, and I risked getting discovered the longer I lingered without deciding. Since there were three options, I made the illogical choice of stepping into the middle slab.

This time, the clothing stayed on, and the ride upward through darkness took longer than I thought it would. It felt like I was standing still on solid ground, even though when I looked down, it appeared that I was suspended in black space, and I could dangle my feet. Soon enough, I arrived at the top, and my feet flattened out. The blackness opened up, and it looked like I was stepping right into clouds—it was just one big empty see-through dome space, seemingly made of glass, like a genie lived in here.

I looked down and realized I was standing at the very top of Omim City, the pinnacle of the towering structure. The mistake I made was taking that first step forward into the middle. From that moment on, I lost the portal and was trapped, so I stood still in the center, silent, looking out past the clouds where I could see the horizon where the upper atmosphere met space. The top of the dome was just touching the atmosphere, the lower half in the clouds. I had no idea what to make of it. Was it some lookout? I didn't see any kind of device that could send a signal across space in here either. The sound of my own thoughts was too loud in my head because the perfect silence inside the dome was even louder.

A lone strand of Lilith's long, golden hair floated past my face. I plucked it out of the air and examined it in my fingers. She was in here not long ago. I walked around, pressing my hands against the walls in an attempt to find the way out, and I did.

Falling into a portal that I didn't even know was there, I found myself floating down at a rapid pace until movement stopped. There was no crash, no hard fall—just the reduction of the feeling that I was moving and my feet flattening out on solid ground.

I stepped out of the portal, and this time I was standing in one of the rings. I looked both ways down the rounded hallway. The ring wall was transparent on one side, and I could see the garden and lower levels of Omim City beneath me by looking out. I figured that it was the first ring because I couldn't spot one below me, and I knew there to be two. There were portals visible down both directions. The ring itself was empty and cold and felt like a hospital in that way. The floor was shiny white, and the strange part—the ring didn't appear to be attached to the central tower at all. It just hovered in place, silently, around this gigantic structure. It was a bad idea to just stand there gawking, so I walked right and kept my head down low in case anyone came around the corner. One thing that stood out to me, that I could see up close, was that the central tower of Omim City had very few windows. There were a number of slits, about the length of a football field, in the center of the tower, arranged unevenly and in an arching pattern.

I came to the first portal and passed through it, and found myself standing inside a long, rectangular room with sterile white walls. Straight ahead of me at the open end of the room, down in a lower space, was a group of human beings doing something that was familiar to me and hyper-realistic. For a split second, I was fooled, but my eyes adjusted as I crept forward in awe. It was like looking down a time tunnel and observing a live moment where real people were on the other side, oblivious to my presence, going about their lives. I stepped closer to the scene and realized I was seeing the Saganites of Mars from Lilith's memories, probably hours before I arrived at their base. She oversaw a crew that was loading supplies into the rebel ship. They were hurrying; they knew the SIA was inbound. I stood there watching from Lilith's point of view, and it all looked real, like I could step down into the scene with them. Omim technology was terrifying. It didn't seem possible. Was I looking into another dimension and not a replay of a memory? Maybe the Omim could see back in time and only need to know where to look? If they can see back to Mars, they will find Earth sooner or later.

I poked around the room to try to find where the memory playback was coming from and couldn't locate any kind of hardware or system or projector. The scene magically existed on the other side of the missing fourth wall. I watched it play out to its end when Lilith's boyfriend kissed her before closing the door on her hibernation chamber. After that, the scene looped back to the beginning. I had seen enough and left the room, knowing the Omim were trying to figure us humans out, and they had the power see into the past somehow.

When I passed through the portal and stepped back into the hall, it was still empty, so I kept going to my right when I heard footsteps trailing me. They were not ordinary footsteps. Each one landed in my heart and felt deep as a bass drum. I could sense a dark presence approaching, like a heavy shadow that was determined to overtake me. My pulse quickened. I heard my heart beating and felt myself starting to breathe heavily, as if I had been running. A feeling of sudden dread weighed on my mind. There was no avoiding a direct confrontation, so I turned myself around, shaking, keeping my head just low enough to peek out from under the hood at the nightmare that stood across from me. It cast a jagged shadow across the floor that caught my attention because it was so strange. The Omim was broad shouldered and slightly taller than me, but I saw no face deep in its black hood. We faced one another for what seemed like a long time, and then, without warning, it grabbed my head with one giant hand. The last thing I remember seeing was glowing red eyes burning into my mind like a blinding headache.

When the pain subsided and my vision returned, I was standing across from my fiancée, Maura, in our very first apartment. She was sitting at the kitchen bar with a glass of wine, working on her interplanetary law degree, and I was about to run to the store. I felt a presence with me, only I couldn't see it, and I knew that I was dreaming, but I couldn't snap out of it either.

"I left some gear at the space academy that I need to pick up. Do we need anything while I'm out?"

"Just you to come back. It's getting dangerous downtown."

"I'll be quick, in and out."

I kissed her on the cheek and then left the room, walked out of our apartment, and took the elevator down to the garage, where all the car pods were. I ordered one from my fedcom on the way down and couldn't shake the feeling that someone was with me. I was in that middle state where I could no longer tell if I was dreaming or awake. In that moment, I had no memory of the Omim that had a grip on my head, but I felt some darkness lurking near me, ever present, probing, and dark.

The car pod rolled up, and I got in. That's when I glimpsed the Omim's reflection in the windshield, sitting in the passenger seat, looking straight ahead. I said nothing, sat still, and let the car pod roll out into traffic. I was starting to regain my mind as the Omim looked out the window of the car pod, searching for a clear view of the sky, which was impossible to see this far down in lower Texopolis. The car pod sped along and then turned onto the mid-city ramp. (This was years before I was issued a personal drone.) I pressed the button on the music console and blasted tech metal that made the perfectly acoustic car pod dome feel like we were riding in a sound wave.

The Omim looked confused, not comprehending what was happening. The music seemed to alter its powers, and he had less of a grip on my mind. When the car pod reached the highest section of the byway, about fifty stories up, I took over, jammed it into manual control, and started to weave the pod side to side, making the Omim brace itself against the dashboard. Going about 200 MPH, I knew the sharp turn was coming.

"Get out of my mind, alien!"

"You have a strong will, human."

"Stronger than you know, asshole!"

I pulled the emergency brake, sending the car pod into a violent spin, and pressed the button to open his door. He was sucked right out and fell off the byway, tumbling down into the abyss of shops that made up the space market industrial zone below.

Somehow, I remained trapped in this dream state but fully aware of it at the same time. I gunned the car pod and took the next exit ramp back down to the ground level, which let me out right in the congested traffic of the spaceship-parts district. I was planning to circle back home to see Maura, if only in my dream. At least I could be with her for another real-feeling moment.

The car pod died, and the world outside froze, but I could still move, so I hopped out and started to run though the crowds of still-life characters from my memories. This part of the city was always packed with spaceship mechanics shopping for parts, and every one of them drove big rigs to haul those parts. It was always chaotic, but I moved into a clearing and saw the Omim standing in the middle of the road, looking around at the human world like a machine taking a reading. Then all the people around us vanished. He was altering my dream state somehow, narrowing in on just me, so I stood my ground.

"You like what you see around here?"

"Kneel down before Diemus, and point me to your home star."

"I don't kneel for demons. You're going to have to make me."

Diemus started walking toward me. He pulled his hood back, and I saw his pitch-black eyes and the bitter expression of evil locked onto his face. Each of his steps sounded louder and louder, like drums in my head. I could feel myself getting stuck in place, so I turned and tried to run, but it was one of those runs where I could barely move while he closed in on me fast. He tackled me, and then there was a blur, and I was suddenly riding the bus on a totally different day, about three miles from where I lived.

Diemus was driving. He fast-forwarded through my memories and now drove while looking up and out, searching for a break in the clouds where he could get a visual—my visual—of the sun that day. I looked past Diemus and saw the date hologram atop the Times Building—June 18, 2999—the darkest day of my life, the day my fiancée was murdered. I panicked and tried to open a window, but none would budge. When I pushed the person next to me, they were like an immovable wall. I was desperate to break away from this timeline, this same bus ride I took before finding her at home. The worst few moments of my entire life were being converted into a torturous dream, making me feel claustrophobic and short of breath.

The bus crept forward and then came to my stop. Diemus pulled over and opened the door. He didn't look at me or say one word. He scanned the cloudy sky while I got off and ran down the street toward my apartment building.

I could run at full speed again, and in my hypnotic state, I forgot the ending and started to think I could race back in time and save her before it was too late. My perception of reality was jumbled to the point that I didn't remember how I got here, and I was overcome with passion to save my love.

As I passed people, they sneered at me and said I couldn't save her. A small boy laughed while yelling, "It's too late, mister!" The nightmare had turned against me, and the closer I got to home, the more intense the attacks became. The trees started to give off a sinister laugh; a large black cat blocked my path in the middle of the sidewalk and grinned as I ran toward it. It was the biggest cat I had ever seen, and it seemed to enjoy seeing me gripped by fear.

The last hundred yards out, all the people out and about stopped what they were doing, to watch me in unison and they laughed non-stop until the roaring sound of their mockery was all I could hear.

I got off the elevator and sprinted down the hall to find the apartment door already open. Audience laughter was replaced by Maura's screams coming from our bedroom. I raced in, and time stopped—I was frozen in the doorway while the murderer was strangling the life out of my love, and I could not move an inch to save her.

"No!"

My body shook with rage. The intense pain of witnessing a murder that I never really saw with my own eyes was now killing me. It was like I was being strangled while knowing that I had to get out of this dream the only way possible. The bedroom window was open, and I forced myself to stare at it while I could hear the gurgle, cough, and struggle of Maura being killed. I heard bones break, moans of pure horror, and then the killer turned around and looked at me. It was Diemus with a smile that cut my spirit right in half. I don't know how, but I broke free, ran to the window, and dove out headfirst. I wanted to hit the ground so hard that there was no way I could stay trapped in his spell.

Diemus grabbed both of my ankles seconds before I hit the pavement. He could float and lowered me down to the ground gently. I got up and scurried backwards with my hands and feet, but he towered over me with his death stare and jagged shadow.

"You cannot escape the mind-bridge until I release you. There is no place to hide, you feeble-minded animal."

"What do you want from me?"

"I already have it."

"Do you like what you see here?"

"Yours is a world of untamed minds. Overflowing with foolish creatures unaware that you are nothing more than a lowly subspecies."

"Then why are you desperate to find it?" As the words rolled off my lips, the clouds started to break, and the sun appeared to our east, big and bright.

"To transform your kind and remove all weakness from the universe until there is only Omim."

He turned away from me and studied the sun, lingering on it while scanning with his head, back and forth like a machine. I felt lighter, less restricted, so I got up and stood close to him. When his head turned back to mine, I head-butted him like an angry ram, smashing his skull into an explosion of darkness that spread like spilled ink—and the spell broke.

I was standing back in the rounded hall with him. He looked startled and confused that I broke free. I pummeled his face with my fists. Each punch crushed my bones and left a dent in his head. Soon there was a wide gash above his right eye, revealing emptiness on the inside. I grabbed the hole, forced my fingers inside, and with all my strength ripped the bastard's body apart with my bare hands.

Omim were hollow. Completely devoid of organs, bones, veins, and blood. A black substance oozed through damaged skin. His old shell turned to black soot, leaving a clump of electrostatic energy, boiling and sizzling on the floor. The hissing mass cried a sad high-pitched scream similar to a kettle of boiling water. It slid toward me and I stomped on it, splattering the slug-like substance that rapidly regrouped and slithered up my leg, all the way to my chest, where it collected and pulsated in a black pool around my heart. It was trying to burn a hole into me. I heard the sound of approaching footsteps and ran back through the portal where I saw the memory loop, to remain hidden. As I stood facing away from the door, watching the replay, I felt someone come in and stand behind me.

"I sense an instability, Diemus. Return to the temple and be replenished."

The voice made the alien substance on my chest vibrate excitedly and sent a chill down my spine. I kept my head low, nodded, turned around, and started to walk out. As I passed the Omim who spoke, I noticed a strange golden robe hanging around cloven feet. I was almost to the door when I felt a giant hand lay on the back center of my shoulder.

"Hold still for your blessing."

A jolt of terror was pumped from my skull through my nervous system. I felt fear.

"Prepare the sacrificial altar when you are renewed. Tonight we will finish the human female. She is of no use to me anymore."

I nodded again and walked through the portal, heart racing and palms dripping. I turned left and took the portal to the ground floor again, but something was changed about me. I didn't feel the same and couldn't identify exactly what it was. It was as if I had an out-of-body experience that was sustained, and I now walked as two beings—the physical me and the energy that was me, separated just enough to feel apart. There was also the third presence, heavy on my chest like a dead weight. I didn't like the feeling of it trying to break through my skin that was already dripping blood. I could feel it trickling down my chest under the cloak, and the pressure was intensifying around my heart. I was certain that time was limited before it would completely overcome me, and I didn't know what to do.

I ran back down the dark corridor toward the torture chamber to look for Uncle, but he was not present. The moment I stepped into that room, the chest pain increased like it was activated by the sounds of wailing Omegans. I leaned against the wall, hidden in the shadows, where I was unseen, and tried to rip the thing off with my bare hands. Touching it was like grabbing a ball of glass shards that cut my fingers. There was nothing sharp in sight either. As I struggled with the chest beast, I fell down into the pit with the wailing Omegans. When I stood up, I was right behind one of the hands growing out of a pedestal. It let go of the Omegan skull and stood tall like it was trying to reach me. I felt the center of my chest pulling me toward the hand, strong like a magnet. I used both hands to brace myself with the pedestal to prevent the hand from touching my chest. Something was happening under the cloak, like the two things wanted to merge. I was too weak to resist any longer, and the hand grabbed the glob and ripped it right through the cloak and held the black rock like a prize. Freed, I fell back to catch my breath. The black rock liquified and oozed down to the wrist area where it attached and began to regenerate.

"No…"

I stood up and grabbed the fingers with both hands and tried to bend and break them, but they were strong like steel. A body was growing back slowly, but right now it was still a clump and a hand that flailed on the ground like a fish out of water, getting bigger and bigger one inch at a time. I was afraid to touch it but knew it had to be killed somehow.

"Savior!" cried Uncle from the entrance, looking down at me fighting with something he could not see.

"Help me. I killed one, but it's trying to regenerate."

Uncle hopped down and ran to me. When he saw the Omim trying to reform, he stopped in his tracks, terrified.

"Nothing will kill it but the fire of eternity."

I picked up the evil hand and its newly grown forearm and slammed it repeatedly against the wall. It deadened its movements and growth for a brief moment.

"Take me to the fire!" I smashed the wall so hard that the knuckles shattered and the hand looked a little flattened. Uncle started to run, and I followed right after him, up and out of the pit of despair and down the dark corridor that Nandee brought me through. I held the evil hand at the wrist and elbow and hammered it into the wall every few steps, its fingers kept trying to bend back and get me. Uncle was terrified and stayed well ahead. He waved me out the door and then ran as fast and as far down the side of the tower all the way to the end and peeked around the corner.

I battled the growing arm the whole way to him, and by the time I reached the end, an entire arm had regenerated. It reached up to grab my head, but there was no way I was letting that happen again. I flung the arm round and round to keep it off balance, but I could feel it getting stronger.

When I stopped running, the arm bent in half and tried to hit me. How could one appendage of a fake body be so strong? I was struggled to keep the arm under control, and by the time I reached Uncle's position, a shoulder had formed, making it heavy and clunkier to carry and overpower.

I passed Uncle, and he ran to the golden tree and hid behind its great wide trunk. The garden was empty except for me and the appendage. The hand became strong and was able to grip my wrist while I ran.

"No, no, no, no!" I cried as I sprinted across rolling hilly land, past a shimmering pond with diamond rocks on the shore, and toward a large hole in the middle of the green field with a blackness around the rim. Heat emanated from it, sending waves into the air that distorted the view. Half of the Omim head was regenerated now, just a shell with eye sockets but no eyes. A mouth line appeared and formed a wicked little grin that filled me with rage. That powerful hand twisted and turned to break free from me. I let go and started bashing the head, swinging it down like a club and mashing it over and over. A second arm started to grow out much faster, and I didn't notice until it had a grip on the back of my neck. The Omim torso was complete. Two slits on the face opened, revealing black eyes. I could feel the Omim trying to connect into my brain and thoughts again as I fell to the ground and wrestled my way out of its octopus grip. It ripped and clawed at me as we fought. I could feel the heat now and tried to avoid fighting backward so I didn't accidentally fall in. I ended up gripping both of its hands in my fists, so I swung up the torso upward and kicked it right in the center with the flat of my foot—the body fell back and rolled into the pit. I lay there exhausted and breathless until I noticed its hands were holding on to the sides.

"Go to hell!" I got up and ran over to push in its hands when the fully formed Omim pulled himself up and out of the pit, with red-hot legs and a torso that looked like heated charcoal. It was disoriented, attempting to stand, fists clenched and ready to fight, so I rushed him, went low and put my head right between its fiery legs, power-lifted the bastard, and fell forward to dump him headfirst into the fire. This time he went all the way in, and there was a hollow sound that roared from the pit, shooting flames miles into the air before falling back in. My face and beard were singed. Burns on my neck and cheeks generated intense heat. I stumbled to the nearby shimmering pond and fell to my knees to splash myself; my body froze the instant my hands touched the water. A sudden coolness overcame me—for a moment I was peaceful and free from all torment, mental and physical. A hideous sound emanated from the pit behind me, but deep in the water I saw the image of a shimmering sword of pure white light, floating there like I could reach down and grab it. There was strange writing on the blade, but those letters morphed into words I understood. It read "Divide that which is not One." I tried to pick it up, but nothing was there. Then the image faded as if falling into deeper water until it was gone.

I was left with a vision implanted in my brain that showed it was locked away behind a wall of skulls and bones somewhere. I snapped out of it and touched my face. I was healed. I looked across the garden; the place was quiet again. There was not a living soul anywhere, so I sprinted back through the grass to where I assumed Uncle was still waiting. When I rounded the corner, he was nowhere to be seen.

THE BOOK OF DRADE

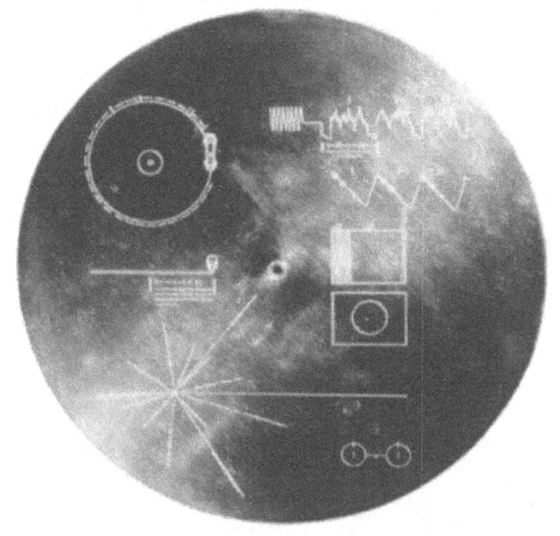

DRADE'S PROPHECY

Drade knew the moment Adam defeated an Omim with his bare hands. He felt the fracture to the Omim hive mind and the shocking victory symbolized a moment of truth. It was time to move again, not to hide, but to fight for freedom one last time. In the spacious, wet, underground cave that the Omegans called home since evacuating the volcano, Drade looked upon his poor refuges camped out, scattered across the pebbly grounds. When the Omegans noticed him standing atop the rock, they knew to be quiet and gather around.

"The One's power has been weakened. Our human savior has breached the Omim mind, but he will need all of our help to overcome them all. The time has come to sharpen your spears, prepare your slings, and load up on rations—the battle for our liberation is truly at hand. You must begin the journey to Omim City at nightfall."

"Lord Drade, what happens if Savior fails to destroy the One?" asked a strong young Omegan in the front of the crowd.

Drade looked somber and serious. The truth was heavy. "If Savior fails, then the whole universe will be lost to darkness. Intelligent life will never again be free. Mankind is our only hope."

"Humanity will not let us down!" shouted a voice from the back. The Omegans pounded their spear handles on the ground, creating a drumming sound that echoed inside the cave and inspired a battle spirit among them. Drade filled them with hope by preaching that the revolt will succeed this time because the true creator, the true and everlasting One has sent them a savior that is a child of His. Everyone believed, despite having attempted to invade Omim City many times over the ages and always suffering brutal consequences in return. This time was different. The Omegans were prepared to lose everything for the sake of saving the universe from the hideous force of evil that they alone had encountered and knew all too well.

"Long live the Savior! Long live mankind!"

The chant erupted and went on while the work of getting ready for the journey and battle began. Eventually, a hushed seriousness fell upon them as families said goodbye to relatives preparing for a suicide run that would result in mass casualties.

Drade's planning was well thought out, and by nightfall, he had his people safely far out in the ocean, where the northward currents pushed thousands of leaf boats up the coastline. Each leaf boat carried four Omegans and their fighting gear, hidden and quietly watching as the remains of their hand-built homes and tunnels were pulverized. Many of the young cried, witnessing the awful power of the Omim for the first time, but most were too hardened to show emotion by a lifetime of living in total fear and oppression. Older Omegans thirsted for one thing—freedom from tyranny—and were desperate to overcome the historic mistake of their ancestors who first encountered the Omim with peace and hence, lost control of their world.

At the same time, Drade had the golden sky disc strapped to his back and hidden under his cloak as he rode south through the night on a beast with a torso like a horse, a head similar to a lion, and with reptilian legs like a dragon. The beast was low to the ground and moved fast but stealthy, leaping and galloping through a misty forest that was alive with sounds of wildlife.

Drade rode through the night under a shroud of darkness. The stars were their guide, and the cool southern winds indicated that they were getting closer to the ice gorge.

The South Pole was as far away from Omim City as possible, and Drade counted on the Omim being distracted by Adam and the hordes of Omegans while he slipped away with the precious golden disc to await victory. The sky showed signs of morning approaching as the beast carried Drade down into an icy stone valley with dozens of small rivers running toward a large one that butted up against the southern ice cliffs—a fortress of skyscraper-sized natural ice deposits that formed squared-off blocks, shaped by time and winds that blew over them. This was the last home the Omegans would have and the most extreme conditions yet.

Light hit the main river, revealing its crystal-clear water that flowed from east to west. A small crude boat was waiting at a lone post down at the water's edge. The beast used its nails to stabilize on the slippery ground. Once they touched the flat surface, it ran toward the boat, racing to beat the sunrise.

Drade got down from the beast and stroked the side of his neck while looking him in the eyes. He was thanking him, and the beast nodded down in mutual respect before backing away. Drade checked the sky. The light was changing, purples shifting rapidly to blue. He got into the small boat, cut himself free, and pushed off, letting the water carry him downstream along the ice cliffs. He stood up and balanced, using a long stick to navigate toward an ice tunnel.

The tunnel was dark. Drade produced the glowing stones that illuminated the underground vault in the volcano and held them in the palms of his hands. He remained silent, floating toward a distant cavern, relieved to have made it this far undetected. Many native Omegan creatures went extinct at the hands of the Omim, but Sheeol reintroduced them into the wild, new and improved, as a way to spy on the Omegan population and keep track of someone important to him. The beasts served as the eyes and ears of Sheeol and had been actively hunting for Drade since the humans arrived. He had to always be on guard.

Sheeol knew Drade well because he gave him life. Drade was his first creation, made in his image, the only Omim Sheeol granted free will. Drade was connected to the Omim hive mind but also had a mind of his own, and it didn't take long for him to defy his orders and go AWOL from the One. Drade was built to last for many millennia without the need to feed off the living energy of others. In a strange and unpredictable side effect, he developed the emotion of empathy—a quality long ago eradicated by Omim science. He didn't want the Omegans to go extinct and made the decision to act in pursuit of that desire. He was Sheeol's flawed masterpiece and the only Omim that turned on its creator and wanted to be free from the One. In return for this betrayal, Sheeol banished Drade to live among the lower life forms and their muck, far from the opulence and power of the Omim mind, to teach him an unforgettable lesson. But Drade had a good reason to revolt. Something strange happened inside him once his free mind started to make opinions that didn't align with the One's. Drade grew a conscience. How could it be? Caring for the well-being of non-Omim was not part of the program, so how did it emerge in Drade?

After millions of years of Omim evolution, wars, famine, and space exploration, Omim scientific discoveries led to the consolidation of power in the Omimian sector of the universe, which led to the systemic cleansing of all impure beings and gave rise to the One, who desired to rule them all. When the Omim worlds were nothing but a hollowed-out lifeless string of planets that had been decimated by their rapid mastery of psychotic powers and quantum technology, the One set about making his way through the cosmos in search of new life energy to feed off. When they arrived on the Omegan world, they hit the jackpot of souls to devour, plentiful enough to maintain their dark order. The Omegans were inherently good, and that made them inherently delicious to Sheeol and his dark apostles.

Drade was different, though—he was formed in the exact image as Sheeol, but younger—a teenager in Earth years. He was the apprentice to the One and acted as his right hand in all affairs. At first, Drade wanted to please his master, so he learned to be the fiercest Omim killer of all. He took great pleasure in torturing the lower life forms before feeding their souls to his creator. Drade himself didn't live off the life force of others, he was essentially human on the inside, with organs that worked and blood that flowed. He had guts and a heart, flesh and bone. Sheeol created Drade as an experiment using superior DNA that enabled him to live for thousands of years. Drade escaped from Omim City in protest, sided with the Omegans, and used his Omim intelligence to stage the first revolt.

Drade reflected on the time when the changes inside him began, the time he ventured outside of Omim City to explore and encountered a peaceful and wise Omegan who was fishing in the high mountain rivers. Drade was curious about the small being who minded his own business and didn't hurt anyone. There was a kindred spirit between them, despite being born of different creators.

Day after day, Drade observed from afar as the Omegan cast a line before pulling it toward himself until he lucked upon some food. Each time a fish was caught, the Omegan would raise his hands in the air and give thanks to an invisible being that was not present. The act of survival and the gratitude to an invisible being fascinated Drade, who didn't have the burden of working hard to keep himself alive, but he felt drawn to that struggle the more he witnessed it. He was intrigued by the way the natural world maintained itself in a cycle of life, death, and renewal. He became obsessed with death itself and one day appeared beside the Omegan, who bowed his head, anticipating being killed. But Drade didn't kill the elder—he pulled back his hood and befriended him. It was the beginning of a secret relationship with the Omegan, who taught Drade the Omegan way of life and told of the mysterious golden sky disc that would one day send saviors to free them all.

The perfection and predictability of Omim life couldn't satisfy the restless living heart of Drade. He longed for a deeper connection to the natural organic world around him and grew more and more aware of the mysterious happiness inside all Omegans, and he wanted that for himself. It was only when the old Omegan was captured and Drade saw him sacrificed that he began to actively work against his own kind to try to preserve and save the Omegans, who he now loved and felt obligated to protect and lead.

Love was a new feeling to Drade and not one that he understood very well. This was right before the last failed attempt to overthrow Omim City by the Omegans. During that insurrection, Drade used Sheeol's galactic broadcaster to send a secret message to the human beings of Earth, who had sent out a calling card in the form of the golden record. After that act of betrayal against Sheeol, Drade chose to vanish from Omim City, never to be seen again. He organized and led the resistance against the Omim while establishing an underground society that awaited its savior to come and liberate them from tyranny. Drade knew the beings who sent the golden sky disc were not made by the One, and because of that fact, everything the One proclaimed about his powers was false. Drade craved the truth and was willing to wait forever in a game of cat-and-mouse to learn it.

Drade reached the entrance to the secret lair, climbed out of the boat, pulled it up, and hid it inside an ice pocket. He began the short trek down into a cavernous ice cathedral.

Sheeol was there, waiting on Drade's ice throne with his head down and covered by the golden cloak. Drade stood still. This was the first time he had seen Sheeol face to face in a thousand years. Sheeol pulled his hood back, revealing an unchanged face that was perfectly flawless after all this time. Drade looked like an extremely old Omegan by comparison. Sheeol looked upon him with disgust.

"You have betrayed me for the very last time." Ice cracked and broke off from the volume of Sheeol's angry voice.

"You betray life itself!"

"Your plan to overthrow my throne will fail. You have aligned yourself with the weakest link in the universe."

"And for that reason, they are stronger than you."

"There is no strength in those vile humans. Only weakness and imperfection. Hand over the golden disc."

"What good will it do you now? The human has already won."

Sheeol stood and pointed his right hand at Drade, his voice thundering louder and louder as he walked toward him. Ice chunks fell from the ceiling and exploded around them, narrowly missing Drade.

"How dare you turn on me! How dare you!"

Sheeol had Drade by the neck and lifted him off the ground with one hand.

"I am the eternal and all powerful One, and you will only be alive long enough to witness the casting of the humans into the fire of no return before you join them."

Sheeol turned Drade around and pulled the golden record from the hiding spot on his back. He dropped Drade and inspected it with both hands, flipping and turning it until he focused on the etched map where the Earth was located in the stars.

"There you are. The new world. The feast I have been searching for. The humans are insects compared to you and I. It's a pity you wish to share in their fate."

"I'd rather die among insects than exist in your cold and empty world."

"Then die among them you shall."

Sheeol held Drade by the collar and dragged him out of the ice cave to his levitating gravity board, hidden behind a tall ice formation. He pulled Drade onto the board and held him flat on his back with one foot, holding the golden record in his right hand. Drade looked up at Sheeol as the board lifted straight up into the air and then started to cut up and speed over the land, heading north. The board created an invisible force field that shielded them from the wind and made it silent.

"You were once like the humans. Omim didn't always have eternal life."

Sheeol ignored Drade, gazing ahead at Omim City in the distance, sparkling and shiny, the crown of Omega.

"I know the truth. I know what happened in the beginning."

"You know nothing."

"I know you are not the One."

Sheeol knelt with his knee on Drade's chest and grabbed him by the throat, squeezing the life away in a cold and unconcerned fashion.

"I should have sent your soul into the fire of no return a long time ago."

Just before Drade's eyes rolled back, Sheeol released his grip, letting him gasp and choke.

"You can't… it would mean you made a mistake…"

"The One never makes mistakes. I am the truth, the way, the One!"

"You are the one who murdered the truth. You are the one who is afraid of death. You are the one who turned on your creator!"

Sheeol shifted his weight so his gravity board made a wide bank around, and he sped over the volcano where Drade once lived. It was now a pile of rubble and rocks. They lowered down into the smashed caldera, down through the rocks and buried walls, past the remnants of Omegans' cave homes in the walls and down to where the Omegan temple still stood, although heavily damaged.

"Do you see that pitiful little temple you had them make for you?"

"They wanted to make it, they want to worship the true One who made all things, including you—"

"Do you understand that I made you to be my right hand, my only son? To enforce the Omim code and that is why I left you alone until this betrayal? You want to be me."

"I never wanted to be anything like you. You're not the real maker!"

Sheeol walked off the board, but Drade could not move and watched as Sheeol entered the temple and disappeared. He came out moments later with the crude record player in hand and set it down on the ground, put the golden disc on it and used his pointy index finger as the needle. Turning the crank started the spin, and soon the sounds of greetings from Earthlings poured out of Sheeol's ears. He watched as Drade's eyes welled up with tears.

"You care about the lowly life forms. That's not how I made you."

"Because you only assembled me. My soul comes from someplace else, and you are not its author."

"It does not come from the human world, the human mind!"

"It comes from the real true One, and that is not you."

Sheeol smashed the golden record with his fist, ending the sounds of Earth and fracturing the disc into shards. He picked up a shard, walked back to the board, and grabbed Drade by the throat.

"I gave you a piece of my eternal soul, and because of your disobedience, you will cease to exist today. You will be thrown into the fire of no return, to spend eternity being tortured by the memory of what it was like to have life through me."

Sheeol stabbed the record's shard down into Drade's side, where it stuck. Drade cried out as Sheeol pushed him back, placed his foot on his chest, and lifted them up and out of the volcano, flying away toward the distant mountaintop where Omim City glistened.

THE BOOK OF OMIM

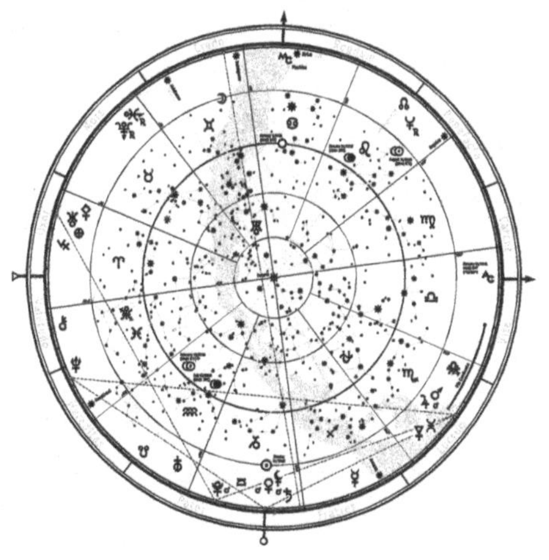

THE SCIENCE

"WHERE ARE YOU taking me?" asked Lilith, following behind Sheeol down the corridor that leads to the species lab. Her stomach was large now, but her face was sallow and sunken, she looked many years older. Her eyes were half-lit compared to when she first arrived on Omega full of hope and optimism. She resembled a drugged-out mental patient whose demeanor was reduced to that of an abused puppy.

"Our baby must be fed what Omim live on."

Sheeol bled the life from her soul like a tap into a fountain of youth, while using her body to breed hybrid beings who could both live organically and feed off another's energy. He made the dark rituals seem like a wondrous step into the future of existence, and she was the fortunate first human to receive the gift. They entered the Omim lab and walked past tall tanks with faceless Omim body shells suspended in pinkish-red liquid. Sheeol led Lilith into a dimly lit room with a large black water pool in the center and a circle of red glowing orbs hovering above it.

"Today is the day when you really come alive."

Sheeol moved her aside as one of the clear orbs floated into the room containing a trembling Omegan youth no more than thirteen human years old, a frightened and confused child. The orb moved to the center and dipped into the pool. It dissolved when it touched the liquid and left the Omegan there curled up in a ball, shivering. The black liquid contorted and pulled the Omegan's body until its arms and legs were splayed apart as if to dismember it. The child cried out for mercy but was ignored by Sheeol. A tear fell from Lilith's eye. She wiped it away.

"You're hurting the poor creature."

"His pain is temporary and his glory forever. When his life force becomes mine, he lives through me for the rest of time."

Sheeol moved around and stood behind the head of the little Omegan. With his long-fingered hand, he split the youth's chest right open down the middle. The Omegan screamed before its body went limp and its eyes rolled into the back of its head. A small wisp of bluish light leaked out and lingered above the body in a loosely held ball.

"Come. Breathe in the life force. Feed our child."

Lilith shook her head, still human enough to know it was wrong.

"I command you to inhale the soul before you. Feed my child what it needs."

"I can't." She broke down into tears. Sheeol wrapped his left hand around her sickly and tired face and forcefully moved her closer to the wisp.

"Inhale this soul!"

She stared at it, frozen and unwilling, but Sheeol reached into her heart with his right hand and pulled her soul halfway out. She gasped, and in doing so, inhaled the divine wisp. He released her soul, and when it snapped back, her skin became flush and her body regained strength and lost years of aging. Her pregnant belly grew twice as large. She covered her mouth, guilty yet replenished from the effects of the youth serum at the same time. She could see her own reflection in the black liquid and noticed how young and beautiful she looked again. She examined her cheeks and lips with her fingers, in shock at the effect.

"What did I just do?"

"You are becoming Omim."

"Why this way… taking the life of others? You are the master of science. Why do you have to eat souls?"

Sheeol used his finger to lift her face up and make her look into his eyes. "It is the order of the cosmos that energy consumes organic life. The soul of every living being contains eternal energy. Omim is pure intelligence sustained by eternal energy. We harvest it from lower forms of life to expand our perfection and those we eat should be grateful."

She was at a loss for words. He held her gaze that way for a long moment. The Omegan body was sucked down into the liquid, dissolving inch by inch, creating a dank, repulsive odor that she had to move away from.

"What will happen to me next?"

"Soon your human body will die, and I will move your Omim soul into a new body made for all time. You will be seated at my right-hand side in the throne room."

"I feel the baby kicking."

In a strangely human moment, Sheeol got down on one knee and held Lilith's stomach with both hands. "My only begotten son will be ready soon. When I find your home world, I will send him there to bring the entire human race in line with my spirit."

"You don't want peace with humanity, do you?"

"Humanity is a flaw in the system that must be corrected."

Sheeol stood tall again, and looked into her eyes with a stare that brought instant self-doubt to her feeble mind.

"You should be more grateful that you will not suffer the same fate as the rest of your kind. The only thing as permanent as death is Omim."

"You kill to live. How is that strength?" she challenged.

"It is strength because we live!"

Sheeol backed Lilith into a corner of the lab, angry that she dared to challenge the Lord of the Universe after he fed her a taste of eternal life and its fountain of youth. She felt something puncture her gut and looked down to see Sheeol digging out the small baby that was growing inside of her.

"Look. My son is ready now."

He pulled the bloody, small human baby boy out, snipped the cord with his finger, and ate the small human like a piece of fruit as he walked away, leaving her to bleed out alone on in the lab. She slid to the floor, gasping, holding her blood-soaked abdomen, reduced to nothing in a horrific instant. Her heartbeat intensified. Delirious, she stood up and stumbled out of the room after Sheeol. Blood dripping from her cloak, she took small steps all the way back to the portals, sobbing the whole way.

She made it back down to the garden and picked fruit from the first tree she came upon. She lay up against it, destroyed, eating the fruit in small bites, bleeding but not really dying, in a setting of splendor with a backdrop of towering evil and doom before her. Her eyes closed, and she fell to her side under the weight of Sheeol's terrible hypnotic spell.

When she opened her eyes again, she was back in the lab, looking at dozens of clones of her small human baby boy that were suspended in the same liquid tank as the Omim bodies. The solution kept them alive and ready for consumption. Sheeol stood in front of the tank with the eleven remaining Omim kneeling around him in the lab. She was kneeling with them but didn't want to be there. She tried to look away when he reached into the tank and pulled out a baby that was alive and kicking. Her eyes were locked onto him as he turned around and held the small human infant in both hands, using his long fingers to trace a line along the back of its head. With his thumbs, he poked through the center and split the child open like fruit, the blood and brains bursting to Sheeol's delight and Lilith's horror. She could not scream or cry out as he plucked out the small, glowing soul and held it in the palm of his hand, waiting. It tried to wiggle away, to fly to its mother, but Sheeol trapped the tiny soul in his clenched fist then stuffed it into his mouth.

He reached in for another one.

Lilith shot bolt upright and came up from under water, awakened from her nightmare. She looked down and was back in her floating waterfall and pool beside her suite, still pregnant, but that dream was too real. She stood under the waterfall and let it pound down on her head, shoulders slumped and looking defeated. First there was only a slight bit of red coming over the waterfall, but soon it pooled together, spreading out until the water everywhere was blood red. Lilith screamed and screamed but nobody came.

Sheeol and the Omim apostles were still in the species lab, standing around a small crying human baby boy, another one of Lilith's offspring that he harvested from her womb in a fog of mental anguish. The baby was on the examination table, cold and naked. The Omim formed a circle around him with Sheeol directly behind the baby's head. Their deep, lyrical chanting came together and created an unbearable sound-wave. Blood trickled from the child's ears and down the sides the baby's neck. Its face looked frozen in absolute confusion.

As chants reverberated the baby's soul floated up, separating from its human body, but retaining its human shape. The baby wailed for its Mother. Sheeol used his index finger to slice a line right down the middle of the baby's chest, which he pulled upon, so the small soul collected like a glowing ball that hovered there. Now each of the Omim pulled open their own chests at the same time, revealing pure blackness inside, which sent thin, black, smoky tendrils out to merge with the glowing ball and begin to darken it.

The chanting intensified. The dark spirit grew and merged until the clean soul was no longer visible. The baby was lifeless, and the blackened soul settled down onto the child and slowly dissolved its body until the only thing remaining on the table was the black, oozing substance that made up an Omim's life force core.

Sheeol summoned one of the Omim shell bodies. It was lifted from the tank by a mechanical arm that brought it to the table with the raw Omim dark soul on it. The body dripped as it was straightened out and lowered onto the ooze, which absorbed into it like a sponge and animated the body. The hands clenched, the mouth moved, and its eyes opened to reveal blackness.

"Rise."

The new Omim rose and sat motionless and expressionless. Sheeol moved to the front, so he was facing him. The other eleven flanked

Sheeol and put their hands on his shoulders and arms before he placed both of his hands on the new Omim's head.

The new Omim's eyes opened and began to flutter. Sheeol was downloading the knowledge and the way into the new being's core. When it was done, its eyes opened, and the face contorted and shifted until it looked like Diemus again.

"Forgive me."

"How did the human being defeat you?"

Diemus was fully reincarnated and back as if nothing had happened.

"He was able to overcome the mind-bridge. The human man possesses a strong free will. He is dangerous to our kind."

Sheeol backed away from Diemus and ordered the rest of the Omim to fall into position around him.

"Spread out and find the human man, and bring him to me alive. His physical state is his weakness. Use violence to defeat him, but do not kill him. His soul is all mine."

Diemus and the eleven other identical Omim nodded at the same time, as if they shared one mind.

"It shall be done, my Lord."

Diemus led the Omim apostles out of the lab, leaving Sheeol alone. He faced the tank that held the empty Omim bodies lined neatly on a floating rack. Beside it were a row of human/Omim hybrid babies that grew fast and were harvested from Lilith without her knowledge. They were attached to a central rod by their umbilical cords. He stared at the closest baby floating directly before him.

"Awaken."

The baby's eyes opened and were normal with whites and pupils, nothing like the Omim.

"Come, my child."

Robotic arms moved swiftly, down into the tank, where they cut the baby free and cauterized its belly button with a laser before lifting it up and out, cradled in robot hands. The infant was lowered down into Sheeol's waiting hands and didn't cry or wail upon seeing him. It just looked into the emerald darkness of Sheeol's bottomless eyes, searching for something it would never find. Sheeol smiled his wicked grin, held the small human/Omim hybrid in his hands, and left the laboratory. He walked down the long corridor back toward the throne room and ascended the stairs with the baby in hand.

"You are the chosen one. You will overtake mankind from within, and they will call you their true savior."

Sheeol sat in his throne with the infant in his hands. The throne sank down into the floor though an opening that led to an underground passageway. It then moved backward down a dark tunnel. Sheeol kept stroking the small baby's head and whispering into his ears as they pulled back into darkness.

"You will teach them the Omim truth. You will lead them to all to me."

The tunnel opened up into a large, dimly lit room deep in the recesses of the central tower. Sheeol's throne rotated around and faced a large black orb hovering above a black hole in the ground with a small wall around its perimeter. It was as if the black pit had coughed up a black sphere and it was suspended above it. The sphere shimmered and vibrated as if alive, and when Sheeol approached, its middle split open, revealing bright white light on the inside. He stood before the open sphere with his right hand clamping down around the baby's head as he transferred knowledge and instructions to him though the mind-bridge. He placed the baby inside, and when the small body was awash in the light, it froze and curled into the fetal position. Sheeol looked upon his new creation as the sphere sealed itself into a perfect closed circle again and it was impossible to see into it. Gravitational waves emanating from the pit below increased when he moved to the side and placed his hand around a fist-sized sphere that was attached to a golden rod. When his hand touched it, the blackness beneath the sphere opened up and started to look like a window into deep space. The stars came into focus, bending and moving, going somewhere at superluminal speed. He used his hand to fine tune the image that was visible inside the pit. The clarity and detail of each passed star system, world, or nebula was picture perfect. He was setting the destination, and soon a familiar planet zoomed into view—Jupiter. The movement slowed as Saturn appeared on the horizon until the scene came to stand still. The image rotated around Saturn and paused under its rings so that a lone bright light could be seen with a glowing green diamond around it.

"Do my bidding."

He pushed the lever down until it locked into position, stepped back from the pit, and sat in his throne. Gravitational waves intensified under the floating sphere and cascaded up in regular intervals around it. The louder and more intense the wave, the more the black sphere wiggled and reacted like water to music. There was a flash of light, then a hole within the hole opened up, and inside it was swirling starlight. The black sphere dropped into the star pool below, and the hole closed with a flash. All that remained was the shimmering black pit.

THE BOOK OF ADAM

BEHOLD THE EVIL

I HAD ELIMINATED ONE Omim with my bare hands, leaving only twelve more of the evil bastards to go. I found their weakness and had a vision of a sword that would help me do the job, but I didn't know if I was hallucinating or not. My whole sense of what is real and unreal was mixed up, so I kept my goals very simple and clear— find and rescue Lilith and locate the place where the signal was sent to Earth. If I could kill all the Omim over time, then their entire ghost city could be handed to the Omegans. If I could find the signal room and send a new message to Earth—Lilith and I could work with the Omegans to rebuild their society until humanity learned what happened here. Maybe we will be able to repair the rebel ship and go home. So many possibilities flashed through my mind as I approached the eerily quiet torture pit and turned into it.

The crying Omegans were dead. Their small heads were crushed by the demon hands. Omegan blood was splattered on the floor and walls, with their limp little bodies everywhere; it made me sick. Evil hands hung loose and lifeless from the pedestals. Uncle's corpse had a hole in the center where his heart used to be. He hung upside down on the wall behind them. By defeating one of them, I pissed someone off and did something to their power.

I sneaked away understanding that Omim were nonhuman on the inside, and their body was just a shell. Their only real power was over the mind, and the ability to read and manipulate thoughts was a major advantage once they trapped you. I decided to be like a spider and find dark places to hide until the opportune moment arrived and I could eliminate another one, like a serial killer in their city of souls. If I could stay out of sight long enough for Nandee to recover BigBoy, I might have a fighting chance.

I rubbed my chest where the thing once was and felt it all bruised and raw. I pulled the front of the robe out so I could inspect the damage and found the bruise was in the shape of jagged star, like a starfish shape but with extra wild tendrils that were short compared to skinny long ones that snaked all the way to my neck. My skin was otherwise healed but left with the dark mark right over my heart that I didn't like. It felt as though I was branded by evil that wasn't truly gone from my system—it was still part of me in some way that I didn't understand.

I took the portal on the right this time, in hopes that it would lead me to where Lilith was being held, since the one on the left went to the ring that is dedicated to science—science so advanced it was indistinguishable from magic to me, and I came from an advanced three-world society. I rode the portal with my head down, fists clenched, ready to fight.

At the top, I stepped into a central grand hall with magnificent archways and windows that let in the sunlight and was misted from clouds rolling by. This floating ring was leisurely, opulent, futuristic, and cold. I wasn't expecting to see people—what appeared to be Omim citizens that seemed to be made for pure indulgence. None of them noticed me standing there in the black hooded cloak.

These "people" hung out at open bars like humans do, wearing flashy and dramatic outfits. Some had hair that looked like glowing metal or fire. Many were bald. They dined on exotic food, eating with their mouths like real humans. Hypnotic music flowed from place to place like this was one giant playground for the perfect. Their physiques were anatomically balanced. Nobody was ugly. No arm was too long, no leg too short. Why hadn't I seen these "Omim people" before? And although their faces were all flawless, they lacked beauty and looked fake. Their emotionless reactions were the most unsettling. I walked by a lone Omim male gazing out at the sky. He appeared to have no purpose whatsoever, and it struck me as ironic that at the height of scientific achievement, the dominant life form had to live off the souls of others in order to create beings with no souls.

As I moved about them, I started to suspect none were real. It looked like someone animated all these human characters and set them about in scenes. I was here to find Lilith, so I walked in a straight line with my head low. The scenes I walked through as I went down the long hall got progressively more disturbing. I saw Omim males beating Lilith with whips straight ahead. I ran to her and tried to intervene, but it was all an illusion, and they vanished when I grabbed one, so I cut right and kept going.

The next encounter was one Omim violently raping and strangling another Omim, but they had no sex organs. This was all a bizarre, disturbing show. I spun around and found myself in the halls of human degeneracy and was sure this was another Omim mind trick. I felt pain in the center of my chest again and started to sweat, but I kept on walking, hoping it would soon end, hoping to locate the real Lilith somewhere up here among these zombie illusions. Maybe they were set in motion for her entertainment. I didn't notice that the people around me started to fade away and the illusion was over until they were all gone. I found myself standing alone in a large open space. This was some kind of systems room with thick, veinlike wires wrapping up the walls and disappearing somewhere out of sight.

When I turned to find the way out, an Omim in a dark cloak like mine, hood up, was stepping toward me. I walked right into his trap, led here by a series of disturbing scenes that made me change course until I was cornered. The Omim moved forward like a laser shot, landing his clenched fists directly in the center of my chest and sent me flying across the room, gasping for breath when my back smashed against the far wall.

This Omim was no mirage, and it kept coming at me, marching with intent to do damage. I heaved and caught my breath, getting up just in time to avoid having my face smashed by his steel fists. This Omim was different from the last; it was like fighting a mindless robot who was programmed to find me as the target. I ducked and moved away, trying to spot something sharp that I could use to pry it open and spill its evil spirit out. The walls were smooth and the equipment embedded, so I didn't see anything useful with my darting eyes. This time it came after me by teleporting into a face-to-face standoff and like a boxer, unloaded brutal blows to my sides, finishing with an uppercut to the chin that knocked me off my feet. I scrambled and fought back in the same way. It wasn't expecting my side-to-side evasive moves. I railed on its chest and sides to push it back, then rounded out and elbowed it across the jaw with all my might, sending it crashing to the floor. I knew this Omim was stronger than me, smarter than me, and hollow on the inside, but it didn't want to kill me, and that was obvious. It wanted to fight me.

Omim moved slowly until they didn't. While it was getting up, I ran behind it, went to heel-kick it in the head, but it spun around, grabbed my ankle, and pulled so hard that I went flying across the room and crashed though one of the portals into another room—some kind of medical lab with hideous hybrid creatures kept in separate spaces behind a clear, shimmering wall. They were Omim creations that were a hodgepodge of different beasts, and all of them had a little red light on their collar like the wraths we fought in Ciria.

Just as I stood, it was on me again, grabbed both of my feet and swung me into one of the walls. The wall gave like water, letting me fall deep into it, but it didn't burst.

Before I could move away, it had both hands around my neck and squeezed so tight that my eye sockets filled with pressure pain. I choked, looking into its black, emotionless eyes—there was no life on the other side of this thing that was about to end mine. Right when I felt like passing out, it let go, stood up, and looked upon me with those empty black eyes.

I crawled away, gasping, trying to breathe normally. My neck felt like it was caved in, not letting air pass. The Omim grabbed me by the back of my hair, held me at arm's length, and began to pull me out of the lab. I grabbed its wrist with both hands, kicking to break free. It threw me into the nearest wall again and watched as I lay there mangled and delirious.

My throat started working, but as I caught my breath, I pretended to be choking and weak. This time when it came for me, I played severely injured until its hand was close, then I grabbed on, pulled it down and flipped it over with a maneuver I learned long ago in SIA training. I drove my knees onto its arms and used both hands to poke its eyes out like a crazed madman, pushing so hard into the blackness that my thumbs felt like they were breaking.

There was a bizarre pop sound before the black substance that animated its shell started to ooze out onto my hands and trickle up my arms. I knew the evil wanted to merge with me, and I knew I could carry its burden until I properly destroy it. There's no way I could defeat an Omim in a standalone fight to the death, since their physical state is not a living thing that can die. But that dark soul can be eliminated, so I pushed and pushed until its head split open at the nose and the black soul came flowing up my arms, around my neck, and gathered over my heart.

My second dose of pure evil created intense pain, like being stabbed in the center of my being, but somehow, I could bear it and stood up, feeling that strange disconnect again, where I felt like three beings in one: myself, the Omim and some mysterious evil consciousness. I fought through the disorientation with my mind focused on my mission to find Lilith before eliminating the Omim spirit that was attached to me.

Running out of the lab, I turned left and kept going down a plain corridor that was silver and dim. Portal doors lined both sides, and I was going to check every single one. The first portal on my left opened into a room that was filled with holding tanks lined with Omim shell bodies. When I walked down an aisle of clones, the mass on my chest moved violently as I passed the shell bodies. I stopped to look at an empty body up close for just a moment, and the evil attached to me must have slithered under my robe and into the tank. I did not see it merge and bring to life the shell body. It all happened so fast, and I didn't have time to react when it grew eyes and an evil grin right as it punched through the clear barrier with both hands and grabbed my head.

My vision blinked in and out. It was trying to mind-bridge with me. Slippery liquid ran out of the smashed tank, and the newly animated Omim slipped and fell. This was my chance to get away, and I took it by running out into the corridor and down the hall. When I looked back, the Omim was right behind me, dripping tank water, marching forward in that relentless artificial way. At an intersection, I took a right because I saw the sky and distant oceans through a large open window down another hall. I wanted out of here. I needed to regroup and find something to arm myself with, but there was never a sharp object to be found anywhere in this godforsaken tower.

The hallway sloped downward, opening into a large solarium-type room that was covered in windows connecting to another hallway on the opposite side. I ran to it and found my way to a platform deck below the rings that looked over the city. I located a spot that I could physically climb down from and hide myself underneath its structure. Like a small bug, I slid over the edge and hung on to smooth beams that held the landing deck up.

As I hung monkey-style, pulling my way down toward the section where the beams meet the central tower, I realized that Omim City was a massive spaceship and not one giant alien skyscraper. I swung on the long bar, almost falling more than once before I kicked my legs up and pulled myself under the chassis where I could climb into the open cavity and regroup. It was at least a mile to the ground. I slid back into the cavity to catch my breath when I saw the cloven feet of the Omim dangling down after me. Soon its whole androgynous body hung there with its face void of facial features, just the shape of a head. I sat perfectly still while it scanned the area by moving its head side to side. Then its head transformed into a mirror image of myself.

Moving like a mechanical android, it swung both feet up and onto the platform and then hung in that awkward unbalanced state for a moment. When its hands let go, I thought it would fall, but instead the feet held the body in place, and the Omim used its midsection to lean into the standing position so its back was to the outside and it faced me hiding in the shadows of the chassis. It stepped forward, and when I moved, it homed in on me and attacked. I rolled to my right to try to get away, but its fast hand grabbed my leg and pulled me up. I was hanging upside down over the ledge.

I flailed, waiting to be dropped, but it didn't let go and pulled me back in just to punch me hard right in the chest. I lay there, severely winded by the impact, certain I had broken ribs, but there was no way I could beat the thing in a boxing match. I stayed still while the Omim moved closer and stood over me with its back to the ledge. I don't remember how I did it, but I grabbed its ankles, stood up fast, and dumped the bastard right over the side before it could react. It didn't let out so much as a peep until the loud impact of its hollow Omim body struck the ground below with a loud pop. I looked over the side at the contorted black mess, and in moments it started to pull back together as one whole being again.

I scurried back and searched for a way out of the trap I put myself in. The space was tight but came to a point where there was a gap. I squeezed through and found myself on the inside walls of this unusual structure material.

Omim City, which I now understood to be a gigantic Omim spaceship or time machine, was built somewhere else before it planted itself here. I studied the beams shooting across great distances that led to other landings with glowing orbs, systems, and nodes arranged on floating islands in this internal cavity. I had found the ship's core, and it was a machine so sophisticated that you couldn't tell unless you were inside it.

I climbed the beams and pulled myself up onto the large, round central platform where its systems interconnected around a dark red light contained inside a translucent sphere. It pulsated like a heartbeat.

Everything connected to this sphere by way of smooth blue veins that extended from the sphere's center and then embedded into the walls, where they spread out like arteries in a heart. Something about the sphere was drawing me to it. It was hypnotizing as I stood awash in the red light.

I reached out and touched it. My hands stuck to the sphere, and my brain flooded with flashing images of Omim history as a rapid download of alien memories rushed from the sphere to my mind's eye. I saw visions of the Omim as a race originating in the Methuselah star system, with powerful scientific capabilities that gave them a super-being edge in their domain of the universe. Their race pursued ways to extend life and live forever. Eternal life became the focus of Omim civilization. I saw Omim unlock the science that allowed the essence of one life to be taken away from a host body and placed into another. I saw the breakdown of Omim society accelerate, images of death as they exhausted their supply of hosts. There was a war. I saw planets erupt like firebombs. Spaceships fighting to fiery death. Their arrival on Omega. It all came flooding into my mind so fast, but I understood clearly that when everyone can live forever, there is no need for new birth, only survival of the ones who have the power. An elite group of Omim grew too powerful, ruled by the selfish desire to overpower one another. Millions of bloody violent years later there remained only thirteen immortals, and of those thirteen, only one last Omim holds all the power.

Spooked by the epiphanies I pulled my hands back and inspected my palms. They were burned red, but I felt no pain. The whole structure started to make noise like some giant system that I couldn't see was starting up. Vibrations rained down from top to bottom. It was time to find my way out. I used my eye to trace one vein that ran across and then down the interior. I had to scale down and find my way back out.

Going hand over hand, I made it across, trying not look down at the nest of blue veins that created a web pattern below me. If my observations were right, I could cross through and find my way back to the interior corridors, so that's what I did, one pull at a time across the vein.

THE BOOK OF NANDEE

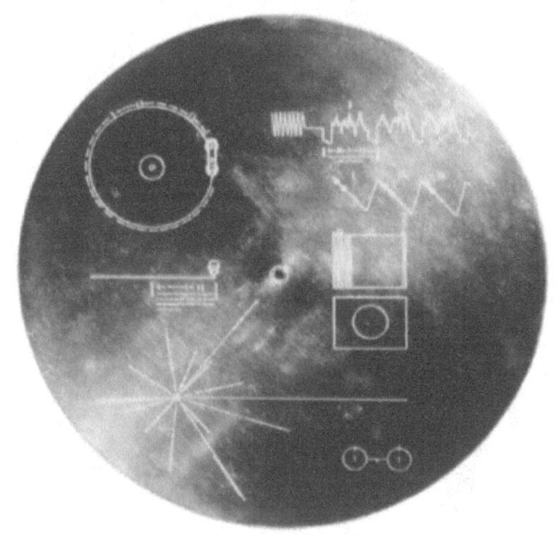

THE HEART

NANDEE PERCHED A safe distance atop a ledge of rocks beside the small pebble beach far away from the Omim trap. She observed a small beeping device and BigBoy beside it. She knew the power of the traps and didn't want to get pulled in, so she looked around for something to use to push the items away so she could retrieve them. Stalactites hung overhead in abundance. She leapt up and hung on to one, swinging and shaking it loose until it came crashing down. The stalactite was longer than her body. She heaved it over the edge and watched it fall and stick into the pebble beach.

She hurried down the side and got behind the stalactite. Using her back, she pushed until it tipped and lay flat on the ground, pointing right at the small beeping device. She was close enough to see red and blue alternating lights that went with the beeping, repetitive and never-ending. BigBoy lay beside it, ominous and threatening. She remained poised to leap away if she felt even a touch of the pull. With her arms stretched out, she rolled the stalactite toward her at one end, and it pushed the beeping, flashing item away from the trap at the other end. When the device was far enough away, she trudged through shallow water and picked it up. It was an arm-shaped metal device with buttons below where the lights flashed. She pressed them, and the lights both turned red and stopped flashing.

She ran back to her safe spot on the pebble beach and set the device down in front of her. It crackled and hissed as if receiving a weak signal from someplace distant, then projected a small SIA badge hologram that spun in the air like a genie. Nandee stood back, unsure of what was happening. The logo spun, and then—

"This is Commander Octavius Lockhart of the United Planetary Space Force. You have activated the fedcom device that was issued to agent Adam McShane on planet Earth. Please identify."

Nandee understood. She grabbed the device and spoke to it like her life depended on it.

"This is Nandee. I Nandee."

There was no reply, just more distant faint static sound that echoed off the cave walls and blended in with the trickling water.

"This is Nandee."

Still no sounds beyond a faint wave noise going in and out at a low pitch. Nandee slid the fedcom over her shoulder and held it there like a piece of armor, using a rope of seaweed that collected on the small pebble beach to tie it there. She pushed the stalactite back then pushed down on her end, so the other side went up and over BigBoy. She then pulled it back again until the huge weapon was cleared from the trap. She plodded into the water and tried to lift BigBoy, but it was heavier than it looked.

She pulled BigBoy ashore and then went around collecting as much seaweed and other plant material as she could find. When there was a large pile of wet and soggy material, she started to wrap it around BigBoy until the whole thing was covered. She applied thick layers of plant material to the shoulder pad fedcom too. With everything covered up thick, she hoisted BigBoy so that it was standing tall and she could pull it toward the Omim trap. Little by little she edged her way there until the pull started. She wrapped her entire body around the wet plant-covered weapon and let the trap pull her right in—this time BigBoy went too. The Omim traps can be fooled with organic material, and Nandee knew this trick from years of traveling the system as a messenger.

She held on to BigBoy with her body wrapped around it as they floated up the long, black void toward the light at the top. The fedcom lit up again, flashing in a fast, repeated pattern. She kicked and swam to keep herself lying back so she would be facing up on the other side. The light expanded and swallowed Nandee, BigBoy, and the fedcom, pushing them straight through to the other side.

She made it through in one piece, looked up, and saw a dark Omim standing right in front of her. The seaweed dripped and slid off BigBoy, and she struggled to hold the large weapon at her side with the barrel pointed backwards and her little Omegan finger barely touching the trigger. With no understanding of how to operate BigBoy and no time to move, Nandee pressed the trigger and shot a red laser into the dome behind her, cutting right through and smashing open a row of domes that held large wild beasts inside them.

Liquid inside the domes exploded and steamed up as the laser kept going. She moved her hand from the trigger, and the laser stopped, but the wild beasts, with claws and beaks and razor-sharp teeth, all descended on the Omim and began to rip its body apart.

Nandee got down and dragged BigBoy into the underground tunnel, escaping as the creatures split the Omim right down the middle. Its black-ooze spirit spilled out onto the claws of a large four-legged beast that resembled a bear but with a head like a bat, talons of an eagle, and wings like a dragon. It started to creep up the beast's leg and then its chest, where it easily broke though the animal's skin and filled its heart.

Nandee pulled BigBoy through the secret tunnels with the fedcom still flashing. She reached over and tapped the buttons again to try to make it stop, but the static, wavy sound was persistent, and the lights kept flashing. When she made it all the way to the tunnel behind the golden willow tree, she stopped to catch her breath and silence the fedcom so she was not discovered.

"This is Commander Octavius Lockhart of the United Planetary

Space Force. You have activated the fedcom device that was issued to agent Adam McShane in the year 2994 on planet Earth. Please identify."

Nandee ripped it from her shoulder and sat on it to muffle the sound. The message kept repeating this time, and Nandee got low and whispered into it. "This is Nandee. I Nandee. Adam here."

A high-pitched whistling sound came from the fedcom before alternating to a low tone and then a high pitch again. Nandee tried to hide it by pushing the speaker side against the dirt when a muffled voice started talking.

"Greetings, Nandee. This is the United Planetary Space Force."

She flipped it over, dusted away the dirt, and got close to it.

"Greetings."

"How did you come into contact with the device you are speaking into?"

"Adam danger. Adam fight Omim."

"Agent Adam McShane is with you?"

"Adam savior. Adam fight Omim."

"Where is Adam?"

"Fight Omim."

"Is Adam alive?"

"Adam lives."

There was a long pause of static again. Nandee looked at the fedcom waiting, but there were no more communications. Then all the sounds went dead. She smacked it to try to wake it up again. Nothing happened, so she made her way into the small dirt bunker at the end of the tunnel. The fedcom was silent except for a low static hiss. She peeled the remaining seaweed from BigBoy and looked directly into the barrel before leaning it against the dirt wall. She poked a small hole in the area where the rock covered the opening and bent her head sideways to peek out and assess the situation.

THE BOOK OF
ADAM

THE CONNECTION

I watched Lilith sitting next to the windows on the floor of her suite, head down, knees under arms, sobbing but with no tears. I stood still, observing to make sure she was alone, before approaching her. I stood next to her, my shadow casting a normal human reflection. She glanced to her right, saw my human feet under the black robe, then looked up with hopeful eyes. I squatted down and hugged her. She was disoriented and frightened.

"Is it… you?"

"It is me, Adam. I've been searching everywhere for you and almost died trying, but I am here now."

"Who are you really?"

"I am Adam from planet Earth, and I arrived on this planet in a spaceship with you."

"I remember… we came in peace…but there is no peace of any kind."

She reached out to touch my face, afraid that I might be just a mirage, and I understood why after dealing with the Omim. I held her arm and touched it to my warm cheek, so she knew it was really me. The smallest smile made her eyes warm up. We were both human, with hearts and minds that connected in a good way.

A confidence filled me as I looked into the eyes of another person who had life—true life—and I burned with a desire to avenge her against the evil one who tried to take it away. Lilith looked like she had no more tears. Like she was defeated and dead on the inside. I had a vision that her body was being used to mine new souls, while she was promised a new body. But that never seemed to come, and she probably didn't want one either. She looked like she wanted to die, but even that was impossible. Sheeol had her under a spell where anguish and anxiety and pain are ever present, but freedom from those forces is nonexistent. There was only serving the One until the final sacrifice, which she must have longed for every day. She was a zombie filled with emotional terror that kept her afraid to take any action other than sit staring off at the Omegan sky from her prison suite high up in the ring. Somewhere, light-years away, was her true home, Mars, and the home of our ancestors, Earth. Her family must all be dead and gone by now, and that compounded her deep sadness I'm sure. Lilith was alone in the universe and being used like a toy by the One who was evil incarnate and only planned to kill her when she was of no use anymore. The opposite of love is use and Omim were using everyone and everything to maintain their pitiful existence.

A long, jagged shadow cast across the floor, wild and uneven. Lilith looked past me, and I could tell by her frightened expression that an Omim had found us. Before I had time to turn my head and look, he lunged. Lilith slid back, screaming. The Omim clamped down on me with his entire body, squeezing me into a cage of immovable steel. Our cloaks made it impossible to know who was dominating as we wrestled on the floor. I grabbed on to something and popped my head up so the hood would fall back. I yanked the Omim's head back by its chin, tugging and twisting with all my might while shimmying my knees onto the center of its back.

"I need something sharp!" I called out.

Lilith got up and disappeared in a side door, while I barely held the Omim in a headlock with my legs wrapped tight around his body. The Omim convulsed and bucked me off by violently rotating its torso around 180 degrees, then grabbing me by the shoulders before smashing my nose with its cold Omim head. Blood splattered everywhere, hitting the Omim, the floor, the ceiling, and making the pristine room look like a murder scene. Lilith returned, holding a long piece of wood that was detailed with Omegan carvings and had a fine, sharp point. With revenge in her eyes, she ran at the Omim, plunged the stake deep into his back and pried it side to side. The Omim's head turned back, and the body let out a deep, wailing sound that was like a tortured animal dying. I saw the black ooze starting to work its way up the spear and moved out from under the Omim just in time.

"Let go! Get away from him!"

I took hold of the spear, using it to push the split-open Omim body across the floor and away from her while constantly jamming and rocking it side to side to widen the hole. The black ooze flowed up toward my hands. I pulled the spear out when it was covered, ran out to a floating island waterfall filled with blood-red water, and chucked the spear with all my might out into the open sky—it soared in a wide arc with the black ooze squirming as it fell out of sight.

I stood on the edge and watched it fall and make a direct hit on one of the beasts that was running loose in the garden. The beast was overtaken by the Omim presence, looked up, and bellowed out a deep guttural warning at me. The black ooze of the Omim was still alive. It rippled across the beast's body until the whole creature was like liquid death. It spit a large glob of the evil substance upward. It hurtled and splatted against the side of the tower, then formed into another faceless, featureless Omim, who scaled toward me with superhuman speed. I ran over to Lilith and pulled her out from the room.

"Don't touch it! We have to get to safety."

"There is no such place here."

"I know the way out of Omim City, and I know a place where we can hide."

"They have been raping my soul," she said.

"I'm so sorry I couldn't keep you safe from being captured. I failed you once and won't let that happen again."

I took her hand in mine, and when they clasped together, there was a renewed strength between us. I pulled her close, and we ran through the portal together.

Without any weapons but my bare hands, I felt a sinking feeling as I escaped with Lilith down the corridor toward the portals. There was a strange knocking sound echoing down the hall, so I pulled her into the first portal we came upon. It was the room with Lilith's own memories playing out on the other side of the large rectangular hole. Lilith hadn't seen it before and was confused.

"It's an illusion. They can reanimate your memories. That's how they learn."

She ran to the rectangle, and without knowing if there was even a floor on the other side, we climbed down into the scene. Lilith was awestruck. She was back in her Mars base. She saw herself walking around and gawked at the innocent and child-like expression on her face. I kept my eyes on the entrance. The faceless Omim entered. I pointed so Lilith could see him and then I ducked out of sight.

Lilith slid behind and mirrored her own body, matching up with the simulacra, which was standing still while having her white Saganite cloak adjusted. I hid on the floor just underneath the ledge and saw her become paralyzed with fear. From my angle, I knew the Omim was looking directly down into the scene. I tilted my head up, and he was standing above me, sniffing like a dog, despite not having any nostrils. She couldn't take her eyes off him and forgot to move when the scene did, leaving the real her standing alone and afraid. The Omim jumped from the ledge to tackle her, but I grabbed his legs and pulled him down to the floor.

"Climb out! Go, go, go!"

Lilith ran around the side and started climbing out of the projection pit, but the walls were too slippery. She lost her footing and fell back. I held the Omim from behind, but he was too strong and flipped me right over and onto my back. Adrenaline pumped, and I went berserk to get away, punching, kicking, and scrambling like a tornado of panic while this faceless, featureless being tried to rip me apart. I was tiring out fast when I saw Lilith circle around him and fearlessly grab his head with both arms. Together we flipped him onto his side and he went flying into the back wall and crashed to the floor behind the rebel ship. I hoisted Lilith up into the main room and climbed after her. We ran out of there and into the portal two doors down.

"He won't find us in here," I said.

"What is this place?"

"A 3-D map room of the universe."

"Adam, they don't want to kill you. They want to bring you before Sheeol so he can empty your soul."

"My soul is not his to take, and neither is yours."

"He already has mine."

"No. It belongs to God and he's not Him."

We ran through space and time like two giants passing through the cosmos and being one with all of creation. It felt so real—the suns were fireballs, the worlds all different shapes and sizes. Nebulae and star clusters reacted to our passing bodies. When it felt like we were many light years away, I pulled Lilith down into a squat and covered her with my cloak so we could hide and catch our breath. We said nothing as the stars and worlds swam around us like petals floating on water. Lilith put her hand out and flicked a small star; it wobbled but stayed in its zone. I looked at her face in the soft starlight glow. In this lighting her innocence resurfaced. I saw a small bit of wonder in her eyes, as she looked at the universe floating before us. There was no sound in here except for our breathing, but eventually that calmed down, and we sat in silence, hidden and safe for the moment. A bright burst of light across space caught our attention. It was as if one of the small stars exploded. We watched as the galaxy animation started to move and contort around us, making it feel like we were flying, even though we were huddled together and sitting still. The movement through the cosmos intensified until it felt like we were both traveling someplace through a wormhole. Then a familiar world appeared, small at first, then bigger and bigger.

We passed the Jupiter system, and it had multiple visible cities on its moons, cities that weren't there when I left. Next came Saturn and its rings shooting by above our heads. Just beyond it, giant space stations orbited and looked like a major hub. We slowed down, flying right past an overcrowded Mars and toward Earth.

Sheeol had found our home. We held each other tight as the pale-blue dot came into focus, alive like a drop of water. It kept getting bigger until it was the only planet left before us and included multiple orbital space platforms with traffic going to and from the moon and into deeper space. It was a live image.

"My God, this is a telescope."

"I miss home." cried Lilith.

"Humanity is doomed."

One lone tear dripped down Lilith's cheek. She looked at the human world like it was a place she never really knew. A place full of potential human relationships that she never had, and now, a place for the Omim to suck the mystery of life out of humanity, like they do to every sentient being they encounter. We couldn't hide as a species forever, and the chances of Lilith and me getting out alive were now hovering around zero.

"Come on. There is a way out of Omim City. We can survive together out in the wild and just try to live. We must try."

"I want to live," she said.

In that moment, I wasn't expecting it, but Lilith kissed me. It was a meek and shy kiss; not romantic, just human love. I hugged her tight.

"We humans, we're survivors. We're going to live."

We stood up together and walked right through the Earth and past our sun, heading in the same straight line we came in, until we were in the hall. It was empty, so we crept over to the portals I knew led down and stepped into the one on the left.

The darkness inside made it impossible to see the faceless Omim who was lying in wait for me. He had his hand wrapped over my mouth so tight that I couldn't murmur any sound. His superhuman strength was too much in this grip with one arm around my chest, pulling me up against him. When we reached the bottom and the portal opened, Lilith stepped out, looked back, and asked, "Which way?"

The Omim forced me out, and only then did she notice that I was subdued and being led somewhere against my will. I flashed my eyes at her and she took off down the corridor toward the light at the end where Nandee first brought me inside. The faceless Omim didn't care that Lilith got away. He didn't want her; he wanted me, and he had me tied up good. He forced me in another direction, down a long, dark corridor that went past the Omegan torture pit and into even lower sections of the tower. I struggled, but he had me immobilized with his powerful arms. I could barely breathe because one of his hands was partially covering my nose except for one tiny slit. I thought I might pass out as he pushed me down into a dark hall made of the same veiny material as the other sections. I resisted but felt lightheaded. My feet and legs collapsed as he forced me through an opening and into a brightly lit room—so bright I had to keep my eyes closed. The Omim dropped me, and I crashed to the ground, gasping for air, heaving and sore in the chest from his crushing grip. Each inhale now felt like someone stabbed me.

As drool and spit came from my mouth, I saw two cloven feet and the golden cloak before me. I looked up, directly into the eyes of Sheeol for the first time. He radiated like an angel with a physical perfection that was captivating. I was in a trance. I could not take my eyes away from such perfect androgynous beauty. It felt like he was looking *through* me, not at me. There was a darkness about him that I could feel.

"What good is a savior who cannot save himself?"

I tried to respond, but no words came out. My mouth hung agape. The faceless Omim hovered behind me while Sheeol unfurled his long-fingered right hand and traced a line from the center of my forehead, over my mouth, and on down to my heart with his index finger. With his finger on the center of my chest, he pushed, and it went right in. I tried to scream as he worked one long finger deep into my heart, grinning at me the whole time. I looked into the face of evil as it smiled while administering intense pain for me that he enjoyed, illuminated by blinding white light behind him that prevented me from seeing anything but him.

"Please... stop..."

The faceless Omim took hold of both my arms and held them apart, so I was on my knees and in the shape of a cross. At the same time, Sheeol formed the fingers of his left hand into a claw and pushed it into the top of my skull, so it felt like my head was on fire, exploding and disconnected from my body. My body went ice cold as Sheeol plucked my own soul from inside me and pulled it back so I could see the white, milky smoke in his evil grip.

My brain couldn't process what was happening. I felt separated in two and could see it all from a third-person perspective. It felt like a hot dagger was twisting in my center, and I was helpless against this forced out-of-body experience that made my whole being shiver. The One yanked my soul halfway out using both hands and clenched it tightly before me like a rope.

His eyes burned like green fire as he examined my soul, picking and weaving through the mystical substance while I was helpless with my jaw wide open, letting out a pathetic sound like a dying beast. I can't really describe the pain; it was unlike physical pain and hurt like hell down in my core being.

Sheeol dragged me by the soul, and my body followed like a dead fish, until there was a break in the bright light as a large portal opened that led directly out into the garden. When he had me out in the middle, he let my soul snap back, and I felt crazed, like I didn't know who I was anymore. An Omim henchman wrangled me like a wild dog on a leash that was desperate to break free. My body struggled by reflex, but my mind was separate, watching it all.

The Omim beast and the rest of Sheeol's hive mind were already assembled around the eternal fire pit waiting for me. Drade was suspended high up on a shiny metallic cross that overlooked it. He was beaten badly, with one side of his head bashed in and his eye dangling out. He looked to be within an inch of death. Sunlight reflected off a fat shard of the golden record that was bloodied and hung around his neck with a heavy golden chain. I saw another cross laying on the ground beside him, and in that split second, I imagined myself falling into the fire, the same nightmare dream I had before. Why was I forsaken? Why was my ultimate fate a freefall into nothing on a world that didn't want my kind to exist?

The faceless Omim hoisted me up and slammed me onto the cross. Sheeol used his long, pointy finger and drilled a hole in my wrist that felt like my arm was split in two. When he pulled his finger away, an energy nail remained that burned me, shooting down the arm and into my heart so I was in perpetual light shock. This crucifixion was doing something strange to my senses. My screams echoed off Omim tower and bounced right back in my face, mocking my pain as laughter. I saw a third cross and knew it was for Lilith, and that's when my heart finally broke.

"Please, God… save us," I cried out.

Sheeol held my other arm down and started pressing the finger through when an Omim beast to his right exploded into thousands of black bits.

Sheeol turned his head in the direction of the golden willow, and there was Lilith, holding BigBoy aimed right at him. Chaos erupted when he stood up and started toward her and she started shooting again. I tried to break away from the cross. Lilith pulled the trigger but Sheeol used his bare hand to deflect the laser beam far outside Omim City. His dark Omim all turned their attention to her and moved behind Sheeol.

"You foolish child!"

Lilith backed up, firing round after round, and he deflected them all. I managed to rip myself free from the electric nail and ran toward Sheeol to take him down. I was stopped cold by an Omim who grabbed me by the neck and yanked me back.

Lilith ran away with BigBoy in her hands like a soldier. She then stopped, turned, and fired indiscriminately at Sheeol, missing each time but blowing holes in the ground around us that created a smoke screen of dirt and chunks of land.

I lost sight of her while trying to free myself from the Omim who held me by the neck, knowing all I had to do was get the bastard into the fire, and he was done. He was strangling the life out of me. I used my hands to peel his fingers away while he just smiled. I started to black out. The sounds of Lilith still firing rounds and screaming became faint. She nailed the Omim on top of me right in the head, and it blasted apart. I scrambled away as her laser sliced wildly through the ground around me.

Blown-apart Omim fragments formed into long centipedes with tiny human hands and swarmed the grounds, crawling up my legs and arms and neck, scratching and clawing with razor-sharp nails. The torture was constant. I heard Lilith screaming as I batted and fought them off, but her cries faded into silence when I saw Drade's dangling eye looking down at me. His other eye peeled open slightly, and somehow through the dying feeling of my body being eaten alive, we made eye contact and had a connection. All sounds around me disappeared. The body assault halted, and it felt like I was drawn into a trance where time stopped and I felt no more pain.

In Drade's voice I heard, "Divide that which is not one," and saw the image again of the shimmering sword of light hidden behind a wall of bones. The image was vivid and clear before it abruptly ended when I remembered I was being held down by a headless dark Omim. Omegan battle cries rang across the garden as a horde of them came pouring out of the hole behind the golden willow and viciously attacked everything in sight. Four strong Omegans ran to Sheeol and tried to take him on. With renewed strength, I broke myself from the Omim's grip, reversing the whole thing so I was strangling it. It was evil and chaotic—an orgy of violence and madness erupted as the little demons climbed on me again. I chomped them as they tried to enter into my mouth and shook them away as they tried to drill into my ears. Something primal took over inside me, and in one move, I flipped the Omim in the fire. A deep screaming explosion followed while I fought off the little buggers, flicking them in as fast as I could. I saw Sheeol standing over Lilith and holding his chest open. Lilith was on her knees, head back, and what remained of her soul was being pulled from the center of her chest into his. The scream that came from her haunted me, with an echo that rang loud in Omim City. It was clear to me he was supercharging himself and was going to let her die. I broke off in a sprint toward them when a huge explosion rocked the central tower way up high, raining large metal fragments down that crashed and shook the ground. Then another blast, and part of the upper ring came down and the whole ground shook.

Sheeol looked up and stopped sucking in Lilith's soul, leaving her lie there half dead. He looked up at the holes in the ring and the central tower, at the falling debris. I made my way to Lilith as another explosion echo boomed, followed by an aftershock that confused Sheeol while more chunks fell to the ground and smashed whatever they hit.

An Omim hybrid beast stood guard over Lilith's limp body as Sheeol left and ran to the main entrance of the central tower, climbing the stairs with superhuman speed. Another explosion high above distracted the Omim beast long enough for me to circle around to the opposite side of the golden willow, where I could see Lilith better. She was barely breathing. A series of violent explosions rocked the tower. Then I saw the telltale markings of a spaceship in orbit high above Omega. Someone powerful was attacking Omim City from space.

Omegan warriors encircled the hybrid beast and it had no choice but to defend itself. I made my way over to Lilith and crouched over her. I had to get her away from the fighting. I picked her up into my arms and started running from the combat, but the Omim beast noticed and charged after us. Omegans riding its back jammed spears into its neck and head, but the monster would not stop. We were running away in a straight line toward the shimmering pond. My foot slipped trying to turn away—Lilith and I slid into the water at high speed and were sucked down into the depths by a pulling force. We broke apart under water and struggled, trying to swim up, but the force below was too powerful. I reached for her at the exact moment an air pocket water womb formed around us as we descended deeper into the pool.

Lilith's eyes opened, and she inhaled deeply, her face showing relief. The air pocket was a miracle. We were being pulled somewhere deep but were safe and able to breathe in here. I looked up and saw the shadows of the beast being slaughtered up above by the Omegans and felt the vibrations from more blasts.

"I love you," she said, looking into my eyes.

"I love you too."

"Don't ever leave me."

"Never."

I looked up again and saw a fading sparkling light, while Lilith looked down and saw our destination. The water womb tightened and squeezed, forcing us closer together as it lowered us down into a large, round room like a slow-motion drip. By the time my feet touched the ground, the liquid was all gone, and we found ourselves inside a dome-shaped room, surrounded by walls composed of bones—all kinds of strange bones of different humanoids. There were no four-legged creatures, just humanoid skeletal builds in different shapes and sizes, from floor to ceiling like a dumping ground. A large number of them were Omegan.

We turned around at the same time and saw the sword of light encased inside a black translucent gem about the same height as Lilith. Glowing and pulsating, like a heartbeat in the center of the Omim world. I was drawn to it; its light grew stronger the closer I stepped. I felt my heart explode with joy. My mind became connected to a source of total clarity as my hand, shaking violently, passed right into the stone. The sword hummed when my grip clasped around it, and the stone shattered. I lifted it up and felt a healing power surge through my arm that I could barely handle. The hole where the laser nail once was had healed. Light from the sword shot out beams of white fire that penetrated the wall of bones, through eye sockets and mouths, slowly reforming Omegan skin, growing back the bodies that once housed the skeletons. One by one, the undead Omegans started to climb off the walls and knelt down before us.

"Savior, lead us to justice."

"How?" I said.

"Follow the light. Divide that which is not one."

From the tip of the white flaming sword danced a pilot light.

Rippling waves of fluid and smoke traced from the tip, pointing to a wall behind the resurrected Omegans. Lilith held on behind me.

"You are the chosen one," she said.

"I didn't want to be."

The resurrected Omegans followed as I walked toward the explosions on the other side of the wall that continued to rock the tower. I was fixated and entranced by this otherworldly weapon that felt so righteous in my hand, so powerful and true.

A loud, very close blast blew a hole in the wall of bones as we approached. Through it we saw Nandee moving side to side with BigBoy in hand and my fully activated fedcom strapped to her shoulder. Sheeol was across the great room, standing in the doorway. His body was twice the size it was before, his arms long, and his expression one of focused anger. He saw me standing with the sword, raised his hand, and pointed. His voice thundered.

"Mortal, you know not what you possess!"

"You possess that which is not yours!" I yelled back as the resurrected Omegans behind me had heard enough and ran past me after Sheeol. Nandee pulled the trigger and hit Sheeol in the middle of his right hand with a laser that pierced right through this time and made him gasp in horror.

"Use BigBoy to protect yourselves from any remaining Omim. You have to break them open like fruit, then throw their soul into the fire." I shouted to Lilith.

"Where are you going?"

"To divide that which is not the true One!"

"What if he kills you?"

"Then I die fighting for humanity."

Lilith grabbed me by the shoulders and kissed me again. This time it felt romantic and gave me such power that I feared nothing.

"You are the real man, Adam. Go end Sheeol's reign of terror!"

I felt a surge that locked my hand to the sword's handle, and it pulled me up into the air. I could fly, and went straight through the doors in time to catch Sheeol escaping on his gravity disc, riding away from the central tower, flying up the side through debris, toward the highest point, his dome of impenetrable solitude.

I chased right after him, adjusting to the pulling force because it felt exactly like an old Mars jump with the SIA jetpacks, but gravity no longer applied. I sped after Sheeol, gaining fast on his fluttering golden cloak. He zoomed around the central tower, tying to evade me. Passing through gaps, in between the small spaces—but the sword kept pulling me toward him until we were almost neck and neck, speeding up to the very top of Omim City.

Sheeol looped back and dove down toward me with his hands out, like he was going to run right into the flaming blade and then flipped backwards at the last moment, nailing me in the side with his gravity board full force. I felt bones crack. The sword's flame engulfed me for a moment, and I was healed.

Full strength. Full power. Clear eyes. I knew I had Sheeol's power in my hands now.

"You are afraid because you're not the One!" I cried to him as he raced upward again.

He banked a wide circle left out into open air and hovered directly across from me. We circled each other at striking distance.

"I am the One!"

"You are the fraud. You are the fake. You are the devil."

"Your kind is an abomination. I found your precious home world."

"How will you get there if I kill you here first?"

"It's already too late. You have failed, Adam from Earth. You who the low creatures call Savior are the reason your kind will now be eliminated for all time."

"You are not the author of time and I am here to end your reign of terror in it!"

I remained floating there, sword in hand, ready to finish Sheeol. In a split second—he lunged toward me, his long-fingered hands stretched out and going for my heart. I swooped out of the way while slicing down and chopped his fingers clean off. I watched them fall slowly, like slivers of glass that crystallized and then ignited into white flames that were pulled directly into my sword.

He cried out as black ooze ran out of his missing fingers, while continuing up and away from me. The sound roared like sad thunder, the cries of millions of consumed souls across the universe sensing liberation. He disappeared into the thick clouds above. With the sword leading the way, I shot up after him like a human rocket, ready to finish the job. I broke through the clouds just in time to catch a glimpse of Sheeol's dome lowering down into the top of Omim City. I flew down to break in with the sword, but Sheeol was gone, swallowed by a dome that sealed and looked like the nose of a space rocket. The whole tower shook, and I could see the gravitational disruptions under the remaining damaged ring. It looked like waves rippling out from the central tower in all directions. The whole tower, from top to bottom, was a heavily damaged flying ship, and Lilith was still on it.

ARRIVAL

I COULDN'T BREAK THROUGH the top of his dome, so I adjusted my position and flew back down the side until I could find a way back in. I had to find Lilith. If Sheeol was going to get away, I couldn't let her be stuck with him. The closer I got to the gravity drives, the louder the deep, body-penetrating hums felt in my bones and head. I came to a section above the ring where I knew the mind-bridge to be and cut my way in through the top. This time the blade went right in. Whatever Sheeol's dome was made of was going to keep him well protected. I had to remind myself that evil never dies; it just finds a new place to flourish and spread its disease. I needed to get to him first.

I landed in the hallway and ran down the corridor, imbued with power from the sword, looking for a way back to the throne room. I heard BigBoy being fired and screaming from Lilith at the same time. I ran toward the sounds, rounded a corner and down a long hall as she screamed and blasted something out of my sight. By the time I reached her, she was on her knees, crying with blood-red liquid draining out of the tanks and onto the floors around her, then spilling across the floor and over my feet. Blasted Omim body parts floated by everywhere. It looked like a massacre. Nandee placed her hand on Lilith's shoulder and lowered her head. I ran up to them.

"We must go now! This tower is a spaceship, and Sheeol is preparing to escape from Omega."

The vibrations intensified. It felt like the central tower was breaking out of the ground and starting to hover. I took BigBoy from Lilith, put it over my shoulder, and picked her up in my arms. She was weak and had no more energy.

"Get us out of here now, Nandee!"

Nandee started down the hall, then the whole place shook violently, accompanied by three huge booms that left a giant hole not far from where we stood. I felt the tower buckle. Explosions and fireworks rocked Omim City outside. The whole place was under attack from above now. I looked out and could not believe the sight—a giant flying saucer hovered high in the sky, hammering Omim City with precision laser blasts and shock bombs that knocked the whole tower off its launch prep.

"Nandee, take Lilith down the portal, and get away from this tower. I have one last thing to do." I helped Lilith stand. She was lightheaded still but coherent. "Go with Nandee. Get as far away as you can and wait for me."

I knew this was my one and only chance to kill Sheeol. I ran to the central portal, passed through, and sped upward, ready to split Sheeol in half the minute I laid eyes on him. I got off, and there he was, the man in the golden cloak, cowering in a corner of his terror ship's womblike cockpit, awaiting the final judgment from a basic man from planet Earth. But I was more than just a man today. I had the power of this white fire sword and knew how to wield it.

"I've been waiting for you." hissed Sheeol.

"I am here to send your rotten soul to the fire of no return, where it belongs."

"No mortal can wield that sword and live."

"I'm no ordinary man. I am Adam of planet Earth!"

I charged forward with the blade before me. He opened his arms wide, and with a wicked grin, he looked at me as I plunged the sword into his center. We both crashed through the other side of his dome and ended up outside the tower walls, falling together, the sword drained Sheeol of millions of years of souls escaping like cries on the wind, screaming and musical at the same time. Horrific and beautiful echoing moans mingled and danced by as we fell to the bottom, past the destroyed rings, past the flying saucer that had subdued the launch—down, down, straight toward the garden and the open fire pit of no return, where Lilith and all the Omegans had gathered and were watching us fall.

It was surreal. Sheeol looked like he was enjoying his own demise when he reached over and grabbed the blade with one hand and my face with his other and began to jostle us around so that I was the one falling backward. My nightmare became real.

"You fool," said Sheeol as we plummeted toward the fire with his hand over my face, pushing my head back so that I was looking straight down into the fire. It was no ordinary fire. It had a mouth made of flames and pitch blackness in the center that looked like a black hole.

I fought and wiggled, but his grip on my face was too strong. I could see a bit of my reflection in his black eyes when his head exploded, hit by a blast that blew it wide open. I was free and in control again. I glimpsed Lilith standing at the base of the Omim tower with BigBoy. She had taken out Sheeol with one precision shot and was just as surprised as I.

We crashed hard on the ground, but I felt no pain as the headless Sheeol stood, stumbled, and flailed with the black ooze running down his neck, trying to reform a head. We were rushed by Omegans with sharp wooden staffs who surrounded us to make sure Sheeol could not escape.

"No return, no return, no return!" chanted the Omegans. Lilith came running down the central stairs with BigBoy in hand, ready to finish him, but she stopped short as I twisted the sword tip right in the center of Sheeol's chest and backed him toward the fire of no return. His head reformed, and his eyes opened when I had him at the edge.

"What will you do now, Savior?" he asked with that rotten, condescending grin.

"Divide that which is not one!" I cried as I pulled the sword away from his chest and decapitated him with one clean slice while kicking his body into the pit. His shocked and surprised head fell in after, followed by a hideous geyser of blood-red fire and noise that shot miles into space, forming hissing vortexes above the hole that screamed in bitter agony right before being sucked back down into the pits of blackness.

The sword was suddenly too hot to hold, and I dropped it into the fire, then fell to my knees and sobbed at the foot of Drade's cross. It was over. True evil had been defeated on Omega.

Omegans moved fast to pull a heavy stone cover marked with Omim writing over the hole. Only then did I notice it was made of the same greenish stone as the throne in the Omim temple. Lilith set BigBoy down, ran to me, and grabbed me with both arms. Hugging tight, we cried together as Omegans climbed Drade's cross and gently lowered his body down onto the grass. After a long embrace we walked me over to Drade's body. He was dead. I knelt, made the sign of the cross and prayed over him. Lilith joined me and then all of the Omegans circled around and we grabbed hands and prayed together. It was powerful to appeal to the true God of life with the Omegans, asking Him to take Drade's soul home. Nandee was beside me wearing the fedcom which flashed and started emitting a soft hissing sound before a human voice spoke from the small speaker.

"Good work Agent McShane. This is Octavius Lockhart with the United Planetary Federation. Please stand clear while we land."

"Your people came to save you, just like you came to save us." said Nandee.

Omegans gathered around and began singing songs of celebration and praise. A palpable sense of relief and a mysterious feeling of joy settled upon us. A young Omegan tapped my shoulder and pointed up to the sky. I turned around, looked up, and saw three small flying saucers break away from the top of the large saucer where they were attached. The trio of saucers descended slowly in a triangle formation until all three ships hovered about two hundred feet above ground. The ships had no markings and were made from a shiny silver material that reflected the settings around it like a mirror, only visible if you stared or when they banked right or left and created a contrast. I grabbed BigBoy and instructed everyone to get behind me. The lead of the three saucers descended all the way, gravity waves bouncing off its bottom layer, which now hummed deeply as it hovered twenty feet off the surface in the open field one hundred yards away. Landing gear came from the sides and back center and touched the ground. The ship's hum died down, then it went silent. A breeze passing through the golden willow was the only sound now. I could see the looks of concern spreading over the faces of the Omegans. Lilith looked back at them.

"Fear not. These ships are from Earth. They come in peace."

"Peace!" the Omegans cried back.

Lilith held my hand tight, and we walked alone to the Earth ship that landed. It was four times the size of our rebel ship and far more advanced than anything I remember seeing back home. I had to remind myself that time was not a fixed thing in intergalactic reality and hundreds of years had passed on Earth during the short time we were stranded on Omega. A wide ramp came down from the belly of the saucer and settled on the ground. Steam blasts shot out from vents, creating a fog that lingered around the edges. We approached the ship and stopped twenty yards away.

Sleek black boots appeared first, stepping down the ramp and flanked by two identical pairs. The man in the center was not tall and had a spacesuit on that looked like a suit of armor but no helmet. He had a young face—too young, like a teenager, but with no hair. A red cape hung across his shoulders and flowed down his backside. This was our first time seeing other humans since arriving on Omega.

"Greetings, Earthlings," I said. The man smiled at me and waved us forward. I sensed something a little off about these humans, and so did Lilith. She held me tight, unsure of what to believe anymore, and I had the same apprehension. When we were standing face to face, I noticed the perfection in the face looking back, and it stopped me in my tracks. The human being before me was not human in the sense that Lilith and I were.

"Special Agent Adam McShane, it is an honor to meet you. You're a legend and an honorary general in the United Planetary Federation. Lilith Sands, you are known as Gaia the great and are an inspiration to billions of humans, and it is an honor to meet you too. We are here to bring you home."

"Who are you?" I asked.

"I am Octavius Lockhart, General of the United Planetary Federation Force. Don't be alarmed. You are speaking to my holographic simulacra. I am in the mothership that is orbiting off world, away from any danger."

The image of Octavius glitched.

"When did humans begin using… simulacra?"

"I am sure you can imagine how a lot has changed since the time you left. Humanity is spread out. We use the simulacra to explore safely, but this is not what I really look like. I'm much older in reality."

I looked at both of the guards. They were unusually still and had helmets on with no face, just a reflective visor. Their bodies were covered in smooth metal as well. Like an advanced SIA suit.

"Who are these two?"

"Security androids."

Lilith pulled me close and whispered, "I don't think I want to go with them, Adam."

I tapped her hands and reassured her. "What are you planning to do with us when we get home? We'll be aliens there now that so much time has passed."

"You cannot stay here. I have orders to bring you back. You are Sol System heroes, and the arms of human civilization are waiting to embrace you both. You're interplanetary celebrities. The biggest story in all of human history. You'll have no problem enjoying your retirement at last."

Hearing that made me smile. After all, I just wanted to retire and live a simple life before this all began, and now I wanted that even more—to pick up where I left off before being shot across the stars—and I wanted to share it with the only one who will understand what happened here—I want to spend it with Lilith.

"What of the Omegans who fought for their own freedom and many died for humanity?"

"We will establish an outpost here and help them rebuild their civilization. A supply ship and a med ship are on the way to be stationed on Omega now. Some level of trade will be established with them too. This planet is a treasure trove of important natural resources."

"Please wait," I said, then turned around and looked for Nandee. She was at the front of the crowd of Omegans, watching us talk to the humans. She was smiling, and when I waved her to me, she looked surprised and a little embarrassed. Nandee came to us and looked up, wide-eyed and at peace. "Thank you, Savior," she said.

"You are one brave Omegan. You make your people proud. We have to leave you now and return to our world."

"Can she come with us?" said Lilith, hugging Nandee like she was her own daughter.

"We have a strict species quarantine in the mothership. You'll have to be separated until the Omegan can be cleared of disease and parasites." Lilith nodded and hugged Nandee even tighter.

"Do you want to come to our home and live with me?"

Nandee teared up, gratitude filled her Omegan heart and soul, making her more human than the humans who came to rescue us.

"I do! I don't have a family here. Uncle was my last close living relative." Nandee hugged Lilith tight, her eyes big and hopeful despite the tears.

"What will happen if the Omim return?" said Lilith.

"They won't. The United Planetary Federation is going to stay here and help them rebuild life above ground.

"Thank you, Saviors."

I embraced Nandee too. Her hug felt very good, and the tight grip from her small, muscular body reassured me that her kind would survive and thrive. Omegans are also survivors. Lilith turned back to face the crowd of Omegans who were gathered and all taking one knee in honor of us—and honor we didn't really deserve because all we tried to do is what humans do best—survive.

"Stay true to your people!" said Lilith to the Omegans, who cheered for us and in that moment and it felt truly good to be honored by those who suffered so much and still had gratitude.

We turned around and the three of us followed Octavius Lockhart and the two android guards up into the belly of the saucer. The Omegans started chanting, "Savior, Savior, Savior!" We reached the top of the ramp, turned around holding Nandee's hands between us, Lilith and I raised them up high. The Omegans cheered, and we waved goodbye for the final time. It was bittersweet. Omega was where I found my purpose, a second chance at love and a family unlike any I could ever dream of.

THE FATE OF TIME

WITH HIS DETAILED recollection finished, Adam lay back, gazed out at the AI-generated holographic scene of his childhood backyard, and exhaled. It was still snowing out, and the scene made him feel at ease the whole time he spoke. The journey to Omega had been quite an unexpected and unbelievable adventure, a surprise final act in a long, strange career serving in the Space Intelligence Agency. The glowing cube that recorded his words remained silent. Adam stood up and stretched his arms, loosening up the cramps in his legs.

"Can I see Lilith now?"

"Lilith is still resting in the infirmary." said the glowing cube.

"What time is it, anyway? I lost track since you rescued us."

"It's the middle of your sleep cycle. You must be tired."

"Actually, I'm really hungry all of a sudden."

"What would you like to eat? I'll send the order to your nurse."

"A double cheeseburger and a strawberry milkshake. But I want to get it myself. You said I could leave here when my story was finished."

"I did. And you may. I will light a path on the floor for you to follow to the galley."

The illusion of being back home on Earth switched off, and Adam was now standing in a small, pale-blue, sterile room. Monitors and sleek medical equipment were embedded in the walls around him. A light-blue path lit up on the floor and flashed like a heartbeat.

"Just follow the line?"

"Follow the line all the way to the galley. When you are finished eating, follow the line back, and do not deviate from the path for your own safety."

"Will do."

Adam looked down at the line and followed it to the door, which slid open automatically and led into a long, warmly lit rounded corridor. The inside of a United Planetary Federation long-range saucer was impressive in its sleek and minimalistic design. The saucer had three decks, starting with an interstellar flight deck at the top, with the galley, infirmary, hibernation chambers, equipment, and other common rooms below that, and on the bottom were individual living quarters and more common areas for flight crew and officers. On the outer rims, sophisticated battle stations armed with powerful energy weapons were located. From the little that he'd seen since being rescued, Adam couldn't wait to get home to discover what else humanity had achieved while he was on the other side of the galaxy, fighting for its survival. Adam could only guess how much faster the journey home will take in real time now.

He ran his finger along the smooth wall while walking and thought about how comforting it was to be riding back home in such advanced technology, compared to the days of the clunky SIA jump ships. All in all, he was grateful for the whole psychotic ordeal. It truly felt like he lived two lives on two separate worlds and now was about to begin his third life. The fate of time meant he and Lilith were returning to a future on Earth. All of their relatives and everyone they ever knew had perished long ago. A time that he himself would never have lived to see. He kept following the line, stunned at the size of the ship and lost in thought about the events that happened on Omega. The line finally reached the cafeteria, and he entered a round, white room with lush hydro-gardens lining one wall and open seating around small, round tables in the center. The lighting felt like a bright summer day. It was familiar and human. Food was a basic need, and humans still lived on food. This made Adam feel at ease. Normal existence was true life. He noticed a nurse sitting alone, gazing off into space, and walked over to her. He cleared his throat but she didn't move an inch. He leaned down and waved his hand in front of her eyes, and she suddenly blinked and looked surprised to see him.

"Oh—hello, Adam McShane. Is everything okay? Can I help you?"

"Are you okay? You looked like a zombie."

"I am fine. I was just in resting mode. I fall into rest with my eyes open sometimes."

"I'm craving a cheeseburger and a strawberry milkshake. Do you know how I…?"

"You could have asked me to bring it to you."

"I know, but I just finished my story and wanted to get out and walk around. Stretch a little."

"Please sit down. Allow me to get it for you. How are you feeling?"

"Fine. I feel pretty normal again besides the whole time-dilation thing. My body doesn't hurt, and I'm just glad to be back with my own kind. Other than that, no complaints, just the hunger for familiar food, which is good."

The nurse went about ordering up the meal from the nearby food printer that was an embedded vending machine with colorful lifelike options on a holographic display. The meal was ready instantly. She slid open a small silver door, grabbed the silver plate, carried it over to him, and set it down. She tilted her head as he made the sign of the cross and then prayed over his meal.

"What is that gesture for?"

"It's called saying Grace. Part of an ancient religion nobody probably practices anymore. It's my way of giving thanks to God for being rescued, for the food, for life."

"I've never seen that or heard of anyone named God before."

"Yeah? Well, that's sad and wait until you hear about our encounter on Omega."

Adam dug into his cheeseburger while the nurse stared at him with a blank look.

"You are so hungry. That's good."

"When's my debriefing with General Lockhart and the rest of the crew? I have a lot of questions, you know?"

"General is in rest mode right now, but your dinner together is scheduled for later today, right before we make the jump to superluminal."

Adam barely heard her. He was overcome with joy from eating the food. "This cheeseburger… so good. What's your favorite thing to eat?"

"Food is not a necessity for me. When I made the leap into this service body, I requested one without the need for organic fuel, as fun as it is."

Adam stopped chewing and looked his nurse in the eyes. Now he could tell what was off about her. The eyes. She had huge pupils that were not normal.

"What do you mean, when you made the leap?"

"You don't have to live in a body that gets hungry anymore if you can afford it. You'll see, there are many different options now for longevity. Medical science will be alien to you. You've been gone for what—over one thousand years?"

She smiled at Adam and he froze. Her smile was off. Something was not right about it.

"How old are you?" he asked.

"I don't know."

"You don't know your age?"

"Age is just a number when you're young. Life truly begins at the leap, and then you stop counting."

"Do a lot of people make the leap?"

"Everyone would if they could. It's not cheap to live forever. You either have to be mega rich or enlist. I enlisted."

"I see."

Adam finished his burger and looked around for the trash receptacle.

"I'll take care of that for you."

"I'm going to go and finish this milkshake in my room, do some thinking."

"Follow the line back, and ring me if you need anything next time. I'll bring it right to you. That's what I'm here for."

"Thanks."

Adam walked back down the hall with his milkshake in hand, taking loud sips every couple of steps, his mind rolling over the bizarre conversation he just had. Instead of returning to his suite, he blew past it until he got a little further down, turned right into the infirmary, and spotted Lilith in bed. The path light turned red as he stepped toward her.

He stood at the foot of the bed, admiring her sleeping beauty. She looked different from the first time he laid eyes on her in the rebel ship after the hibernation chamber opened up so many, many centuries ago. Her face was worn from the experience of real life, and it changed her looks. She was older, wiser, and somehow, more beautiful. He gently wiggled her toes with his fingers.

"Wake up, Lilith. Wake up."

Lilith's eyes peeled open, and she saw Adam standing there. They had been separated until now. It took her a moment to come out of her grogginess.

"Adam…"

"Hi."

"Hi."

"You look like you're healing. How do you feel?"

"I feel nothing right now. I'm just grateful to be alive. Grateful for you being on that ship with me."

Adam moved around closer to her so he could speak softly and still be heard. He took her hand in his. "Speaking of life…something is off about these Earthlings that rescued us and I think I know what it is."

"Please don't scare me. In what way?"

"My nurse. She's not totally human."

"What do you mean?"

"She's not human. She said she has a body that doesn't get hungry, talking about leaping from one body to another as an option. She told me that some humans live forever now."

"What are you doing in here, Adam?" asked his nurse from the entrance as she came walking toward them with two android guards by her side, then turned to a wall-mounted control panel and pressed a few commands into the keyboard.

"I wanted to see Lilith."

"You should have asked me to arrange a visit. Please return to your room now."

"No. I need to talk to her and see the real General Lockhart, not his simulacra. We need some answers."

"General Lockhart gave specific orders that you are both to remain quarantined away from the rest of the crew until he invites you on deck."

"I want to speak to General Lockhart right now."

"You will have a meeting with him soon."

"You can bring them to me now," came a voice from small speakers in the walls. Adam looked at his nurse, who began removing the IV and other strange-looking systems that hooked into Lilith's body. The android guards stood motionless near the entrance.

"See? That wasn't hard," said Adam as he helped Lilith out of bed. She was wearing a fresh, white UPF outfit and stepped into matching white boots that the nurse grabbed from under her bed. Adam held out his hand, and Lilith took it.

"Follow me," said the nurse. She and the android guards led them out of the infirmary and turned right, walking in silence until they reached pair of round elevator doors that opened like a camera aperture and led into a dark space. Adam and Lilith paused at the sight. It resembled the portals in Omim City. The nurse stood inside, waiting for them. The guards stood behind them.

"Step inside please. This is the way to the interstellar deck."

Adam and Lilith shared a knowing look while still holding hands and stepped in together. The nurse turned around as the elevator door closed. "We exit on this side," she said.

The ride was short, and when the door opened, they walked into a large, dimly lit, domed room that was the command center of the saucer. Space was visible through windows that encircled the entire top level circumference. Four separate bays were manned by security androids in the same armor as the ones who escorted them onto the ship. General Octavius Lockhart stood in the middle with his back to them while speaking to a simulacra projection of someone they couldn't see. The projection glitched as they got closer.

"Adam and Lilith are here to see you, General."

Octavius slowly stepped aside and turned around to greet them, revealing a simulacra projection behind him. The image looked exactly like Sheeol, except he was dressed in an all-black United Planetary Federation uniform. He was the supreme leader.

Adam and Lilith froze. Her lower lip quivered. Adam squeezed her hand, and she grabbed on to his arm. The realistic image of Sheeol smiled that sinister, soul-killing grin and glitched again.

"Welcome home, Mother."

THE END

www.ingramcontent.com/pod-product-compliance
Lightning Source LLC
Chambersburg PA
CBHW010757310726
48980CB00012B/972/J

* 9 7 8 0 5 7 8 3 6 2 6 2 5 *